The Earl's Beauty

by

JoMarie DeGioia

PUBLISHED BY:

Bailey Park Publishing

I0549749

The Earl's Beauty

Book Three of the Bridgewater Brides Series

by

JoMarie DeGioia

England 1829

Chapter 1

Daniel Ashworth, the Earl of Ashworth, and his very good friend, the Earl of Harley, sat in a crowded and dimly lit public house. They each had a mug of ale set before them on top of the scarred table, and were already well into their evening of determined debauchery.

The public houses were establishments where gentlemen took themselves when the confines of Society proved too restrictive. The ale flowed there and the serving girls were known to be as free with their sexual favors as they were with their smiles. Daniel and Harley, another man eagerly sought-after by the ladies of Society, much enjoyed the occasional evening of drinking and carousing.

"Capitol idea, Ashworth," Harley said, holding up his tankard in mock-salute. "I too had no desire to fall prey to all of those marriage-minded young ladies this evening."

Daniel eyed the serving girls moving about the room, idly wondering which one would see to his needs tonight.

"I find the pubs less taxing to my sanity than my usual amusements," he said wryly.

Harley laughed, his blue eyes sparkling. "I must know your meaning, Ashworth," he chuckled. "Surely you don't mean to say you have no desire for the company of a certain lovely widow this evening?"

"Not tonight, my friend," Daniel answered. "I imagine she's at the bashes, setting her dark eyes on another gentleman as we speak."

Harley raised a brow at that. "You don't believe she entertains others in your absence, do you?"

Daniel drank down the last of his ale. "It matters not to me." He motioned to one of the servers to refill both their mugs. "We have no arrangement of any kind."

Harley snorted. "I believe the lady might have other notions in her pretty head."

Daniel dismissed Harley's words with a wave of his hand. "No, Harley. Lady Small and I merely enjoy each other's company when the mood strikes."

Harley set down his tankard and cleared his throat.

"Forgive me for broaching such a, um, delicate subject," Harley began. "But do you take the necessary precautions against certain consequences?"

Daniel laughed. "Why Harley, you're blushing like a

schoolgirl. I can hardly believe that anyone as jaded as yourself would have trouble discussing the topic of unwanted progeny."

Harley cuffed him on the shoulder, a slight smile on his lips. "It's a consideration, Ashworth. Gentlemen such as ourselves must give it thought."

Daniel nodded sagely.

"I know it well," he said. "But Monica told me she suffered from female difficulties during her marriage. She lost a babe and is now barren."

"I have trouble imagining the lady as a mother," Harley offered wryly.

"Believe me, she hasn't one maternal bone in her body."

"Which you've explored quite extensively, I'd wager?"

Daniel laughed and drank more of his ale. Harley sighed then, drawing his attention.

"There is no escaping it, Ashworth."

"And what is that, man?"

"The siring of an heir," Harley said in answer. "We won't be able to dodge our obligations for very much longer."

Daniel shook his head. "Pray, don't press that subject on me. My uncle has told me time and again this past year that I must settle down and see to that very matter."

"Your uncle is a man of determination," Harley said. "And how is the marquis?"

Daniel smiled as he thought of the man who had seen to the raising of him and his brother after their parents died. He was an obstinate old gentleman who only seemed to have his nephew's interests at heart, even if his comments and intrusions weren't welcome of late.

"He's well," Daniel said. "It's his assertion, however, that I marry soon. I'm only twenty-five years old, for God's sake, and he is insisting on my producing an heir before another year passes."

"Your father died young, Ashworth. Your brother, younger still."

Harley's words brought on the crushing memory of that fog-shrouded morning so long ago that had changed his life irrevocably. Such recollections wouldn't change his mind on the subject of matrimony. Not when he was perfectly happy to continue as he was. He would certainly never let a woman touch his heart. He'd seen firsthand what that earned a man.

"Perhaps there is wisdom in getting the deed done and over with." Harley sucked in an audible breath. "My God! What the devil is she doing here?"

Daniel's head snapped up at Harley's words. He turned toward the entrance of the pub, and was stunned as he glimpse the most beautiful young woman he'd ever seen. Her presence in the grimy pub was as incongruous an event as he could imagine. She was wrapped in a cloak of deep blue velvet and he could glimpse a gown of silver gray beneath.

Her hair caught the meager light from the candles, showing like molten gold. Her companion was a slight gentleman, and dressed like a fop. Daniel dismissed him from his notice in an instant, settling his eyes again on the girl. Gazing at the vision caused his stomach to give an odd lurch.

He turned to Harley. "Who is she?"

"The Earl of Bridgewater's youngest daughter," Harley said. "Lord, she is gorgeous isn't she?"

For a reason he could not fathom, Daniel was bothered by his friend's comment. He turned his attention back to the lovely girl. He soon saw that the rabble in attendance had taken notice of her. A wave of possessiveness, a very foreign feeling to be sure, coursed through him. He felt an inexplicable hunger as he ran his eyes over her. Surely he'd consumed too much ale this night. He tamped down his confounding feelings and forced his attention to the foam on the bottom of his tankard.

***

Lady Mary Bridgewater looked about the public house. Her stomach churned. When she'd accepted Lord Stokes' offer of a ride from the last party, she hadn't thought to go anywhere but home. But when he suggested that they stop at a "very charming little pub," she'd agreed. Oh, why hadn't she listened to her sister?

When Betsy and her husband Michael had wished to leave the ball earlier than Mary deemed acceptable, she'd convinced them that she would secure a ride home on her own. They'd been reluctant to leave her, but Mary knew full well how to get her way around her family. If they indulged her a bit too much, she wasn't going to naysay them. And now she was in this muddle?

If she'd gone home with her sister she would be tucked into her lovely bedchamber in her parents' townhouse in London, delightfully fatigued. It had been a long and happy evening, filled with much dancing and laughter. She was in the midst of her very first London Season at the age of eighteen, and couldn't imagine anything more wonderful in the world.

The social whirl was all she thought of, pleased to her toes at the number of gentlemen that have been in pursuit of her. She was most certain to make a very excellent match before the Season drew to a close in August. Yet she'd accepted this ridiculous offer from Lord Stokes, the stuttering fop.

"Lord Stokes," she said as he directed her to a small table set in the middle of the crowded room. "I don't wish to stay here."

"N-nonsense, Lady Mary," Lord Stokes replied, his long thin fingers grasping her hand. "S-sit down and I will s-secure us s-some refreshment."

He helped her remove her cloak in deference to the stuffiness in the crowded room. But when he waved his hand in the air to gain a serving girl's attention, he succeeded only in drawing more notice from the other patrons.

"Quite a pretty fancy woman you have there, milord," one of the men said.

Mary kept her eyes downcast, mortified. The unmistakable sound of chairs scraping against the wooden floor told her what a brief glance soon proved true. The men in the pub were approaching their table. Their eyes glittered as they fastened on her glorious gown, which she'd chosen to gain attention. It showed more of her bosom than it concealed. Oh, why hadn't she wore one of her more modest dresses? She sank down in her chair, wishing in that moment that she could simply disappear.

"What'll you take for her?" another said, stepping closer.

"N-now see here," Lord Stokes said, puffing out his narrow chest. "You will not s-speak so of the lady."

"So you're her protector, are you?" the first man asked. "We be reasonable men, right lads?" The other men in the pub laughed and nodded. "Tell you what, sir. We'll play you for her favors."

Mary's unease increased tenfold as the man held out a smudged deck of cards. He returned her gaze, licking his lips. Lord Stokes faced the challenger, visibly quaking in his well-polished boots. He gave a yelp as the man's hands came around his throat. He slipped out of his grasp and ran from the room, leaving Mary staring after him in shock.

"Lord Stokes!" she cried. "Pray, do not leave me here!"

Her insufficient protector was gone. Mary heard the snickers behind her and turned slowly, forcing a smile on her face.

"Now gentlemen." She spread her hands spread before her. "It appears that I am at your mercy."

"Aye," one of the men said, rubbing his hands together. "What a pretty morsel to drop into our laps, eh lads?"

Mary's heart pounded. Her mind worked to find a new tack to remove her from the deplorable situation.

"Perhaps one of you fine gentlemen would be so kind as to secure transportation for me?" she asked with a glimmer of hope.

Her heart sank as they shook their heads in unison. They closed in on her. One man was so bold as to reach out to touch her arm. She heard someone spit out a curse and looked up as a big gentleman pulled the man from her. He landed a punch squarely on the man's jaw, knocking him to the floor. Mary watched as another gentleman joined the fight. The two of them made quick work of the rabble, causing the few that remained standing to retreat in a hurry.

She stood stock-still as the scuffle ended, her eyes on the man with the golden hair who had first come to her aid. He was dressed like a fine gentleman, yet he had fought savagely to keep the villains from her. Even clad so regally she could see that he was well-built. His legs were long and his shoulders impossibly wide. His strong hands were held in fists at his side as he glared in defiance at the patrons in the pub. When he turned his velvety-brown eyes on her she nearly swooned.

His face was the very picture of masculine beauty, spared

from being pretty only by the set of his strong jaw. For a moment she wondered what his smile was like, and suspected she would never learn that particular secret.

"Are you all right, Lady Mary?" his companion asked, breaking through to her.

Mary blinked rapidly as she glanced at the handsome, dark-haired gentleman at her side. "Yes, thank you…"

"Lord Harley," the man said with a bow.

She gave him a small smile and then looked at the blond gentleman again. He stood staring at her, his gaze intense. Why didn't the man approach her? Didn't he see that she was shaken and needed his assistance as well as his friend's?

At last he stepped in front of her. She smiled up at him.

"What were you thinking, coming into a place like this?" he asked sharply.

Mary pulled back in surprise, losing her smile. The anger evident in his eyes caused her own to rise.

"I had no intention of frequenting such an establishment, sir." She raised her chin. "Evidently my escort had a different notion."

The man spat out a curse.

"How dare you speak so in my presence?" she asked.

He laughed at her outrage. "The gentlemen in this establishment would have done far worse to your delicate sensibilities, my lady."

Mary placed her hands on her hips, glaring up at him. "I did not ask for your assistance, sirrah," she said. "I assure you that I would have soon had the situation in hand."

"Had we not come to your aid, my lady, you would have soon found yourself abovestairs with your pretty skirts tossed up over your head."

Her heart raced and her breath caught. "You can't mean…?" she murmured.

He cursed again and grabbed her cloak from the floor. He gave it a quick shake and draped it unceremoniously over her shoulders. Mary watched his fingers as he fumbled with the fasteners, which ran down the front of the garment.

"Stop that," she said, slapping his hands away. He took a step back from her. "I must secure a hack," she said, turning toward the door.

The gentleman then reached out and grasped her arm. Mary whirled about, her eyes on his hand for a beat before raising her gaze to his. He released his hold and ran his fingers through his hair in an obvious show of frustration.

"I'll see you home," he said.

She had no desire to spend any more time in the man's abrasive company. She was also extremely bothered by the way his warm brown eyes made her silly pulse race.

"Oh no," Mary said quickly. "That would not be proper."

"And yet you can travel about town with Stokes, that simpering fool?" he asked.

She could make no reasonable answer to that.

"Do not fret," he went on. "Harley here will play chaperone."

Mary glanced at the dark-haired gentleman again. Why, she'd forgotten his very presence. How could she see anyone else when this golden-haired devil stood before her, so infuriating with his comments? And his scent! Even in the filthy pub the smells of sandalwood and spice wrapped around her.

"That would serve," she agreed.

She permitted the far-more-pleasant Lord Harley to take her elbow. They climbed aboard a fine carriage and settled on the cushioned seats. She couldn't stop staring at the fair-haired gentleman as the carriage rolled on. His delicious scent was stronger in here, as well. The fine carriage must be his, then.

He appeared quite vexed with her. In stark contrast his

friend appeared most affable, smiling whenever she happened a glance in his direction.

"I haven't told you my address, Lord Harley," she began.

"I know well where your father resides," the blond gentleman cut in. "We'll be there shortly."

Mary said nothing to that. Several minutes of silence passed.

"Is your friend usually so churlish, Lord Harley?" she asked finally. "Or is this how he carries himself in a lady's presence?"

Harley chuckled. "Not in general, Lady Mary," he answered. "Lord Ashworth seems to behave so only in one particular lady's presence."

Lord Ashworth shot his friend a dark look, at which Harley hid his grin. Mary puzzled over that odd exchange.

After what seemed an eternity to her, the carriage stopped in front of her father's home. Lord Harley offered his assistance from the carriage. She smiled at his gallantry and accepted his offer, placing her hand in his. She lost her smile when her gaze fell on Lord Ashworth. He glared at them, his attention focused on their joined hands. Once her feet were on the cobbles, she quickly nodded and thanked them, hurrying to her door.

In a huff, she went up to her bedchamber and rang for her lady's maid. Jane came in a thrice.

"Impossible man," Mary muttered as Jane helped her out of her gorgeous silver gown.

"My lady?" Jane asked.

"Oh, nothing."

Jane put aside the gown as Mary sat at her vanity. The maid returned and unpinned Mary's long golden curls.

When Lord Stokes had suggested their little detour to the public house Mary had no notion of the danger lurking there.

"Lord Stokes should have known better, the simpering fool," she said.

Lord Ashworth's description of the man was quite apt. She could have been gravely harmed. If Lords Harley and Ashworth had not come to her aid, she would have been ruined for certain. Lord Ashworth had insisted that the rabble would have tossed her skirts over her head!

"He is so contrary," Mary said.

"Lord Stokes, my lady?"

"Hmm?" Mary caught Jane's gaze in the mirror. "No, no."

Lord Ashworth was frightfully handsome, though. That she could not ignore. But he appeared most unaffected by her coy smiles, choosing to glare in return. And his words and admonitions? How dare he speak to her so?

Well, there were plenty of other gentlemen in pursuit of her. According to her mother she was most certain to make an excellent match before the Season drew to a close in August.

"Perhaps Lord Grimsby," she murmured as she stood and donned her nightgown. "If he were taller."

"Yes, my lady."

Jane held out her wrapper and Mary slipped into it.

"Certainly not Lord Stokes."

"No, my lady."

Mary gave Jane a smile now. "Why are matters so complicated?"

"I don't know, my lady." Jane clasped her hands. "Do you require anything else tonight?"

"Thank you, no. Good night, Jane."

"Good night, my lady."

Mary was alone in her chamber with her thoughts. Once again, Lord Ashworth's behavior came back to her.

"No matter," she said, climbing into her bed. "I will think of him no more."

But the very moment she closed her eyes his image floated

before her. She tingled from head to toe as she recalled the intensity of his warm brown eyes on her. And his body was so…fit.

She sighed and cuddled into her pillow, giving in to her mind's wanderings.

Chapter 2

"Good riddance, I say," Daniel said as the carriage stopped before Lord Harley's townhouse. "Troublesome chit."

"No doubt the lady was quite shaken, Ashworth," Harley said as he stepped out. "She was most assuredly out of her element."

"And that silly fop left her there instead of holding his ground? He's lucky one of us didn't call him out."

Harley turned to him with a grin. "Would you want me to be your second?"

Daniel blinked and then shook his head.

"Good night, Ashworth."

"Harley."

Daniel fumed as the carriage rolled on. He knew full well what calamity could have befallen the beautiful girl if he and Harley hadn't come to her aid. And instead of expressing her gratitude she'd yelled at him like a harridan!

"Ungrateful chit," he muttered.

Lord she was lovely, though. But she was also stubborn and contradictory, traits he found most unattractive in a female. But as for her other traits? Her hair was like golden fire. Her lips were full and red like a rosebud. And her skin? When he'd grasped her arm he'd been struck by the velvety smoothness of her flesh, wondering if the rest of her was as delectable. And she'd smelled like hothouse roses.

Perhaps he needed a wench. No doubt that was the reason he was thinking of the bothersome girl both in her splendid gown and out of it.

He readied for bed, unable to get the image of Lady Mary Bridgewater out of his mind for more than a few moments. Her eyes! When she'd glared up at him in defiance he'd been struck by the intensity of her violet eyes. A man could get lost in them.

"Enough!" he growled.

When he awoke the next morning, he felt anything but refreshed. His sleep had been full of a certain lovely vision, causing emotions he dared not deem possible to threaten their appearance. He knew well what a beautiful girl could do to a man's senses. That horrid morning so long ago was all the proof he need to that end.

He walked into his dressing room and splashed his face with tepid water from the washbasin. He stared at his reflection in the mirror atop the washstand, seeing more of his brother in the face staring back than ever before. Sighing in frustration, he saw to his morning toilette and rang for his valet.

Daniel had been a lad of thirteen when his parents died, bringing the title and fortune to his brother Patrick at merely five years his senior. Their uncle, the Marquis of Darlington, had filled the paternal role in a fashion, helping to oversee the young earl's vast holdings in Newcastle as well as keeping Daniel out of mischief.

Four years after coming into the title, Patrick met a woman. She was the very picture of grace and breeding. Patrick eagerly made an offer for her hand, which had been accepted in a flash by her widowed father. What Patrick hadn't known was that she played him false with several gentlemen of his acquaintance.

Daniel had learned of it, and approached her with the accusation. She'd responded by attempting a seduction on him. Before he could tell Patrick, his brother caught her with a good friend of his. Outraged that the man would compromise her virtue, he challenged the man to a duel.

Daniel had learned of it too late, rushing to the field of honor only moments after the fatal shot was fired.

He wouldn't make the mistake his brother had, believing in a woman's false virtue. And a pretty face would not sway him from his convictions, no matter how uncommonly pretty that face.

He rose from the table and took himself into the study to pore over several correspondence regarding his holdings. He wasn't surprised to find a personal letter among the papers, written in his uncle's precise hand.

The marquis sent his greetings, along with a request for a visit from his nephew. As Daniel had fully expected, his uncle yet again posed the insistent question regarding the subject of matrimony. Rolling his eyes heavenward, Daniel folded the paper and set it aside on the polished surface of his desk.

Inexplicably he pictured Lady Mary Bridgewater standing before him, clad in a gorgeous satin wedding gown and wearing a beautiful smile meant only for him. Shaking his head, he chose to focus on his estate business. He much preferred to fill his mind with facts and figures than with the troublesome vision of Lady Mary Bridgewater.

***

Mary sat at her vanity, staring absently at the reflection before her. Her lady's maid had dressed her hair in a most becoming fashion, the heavy curls piled elegantly atop her head. Several tendrils framed her face, putting focus on her eyes. She had yet to don her evening gown, feeling out-of-sorts. While she looked forward with some anticipation to attending the night's festivities, she couldn't help but wonder if Lord Ashworth would attend. She hadn't paid him any notice in the past. That was surely due to the fact that he'd never passed within her field of vision before last evening. How could he have escaped her notice otherwise?

He was such a big man, easily as tall and broad as both of her handsome brothers-in-law. And so pleasing a countenance she had yet to encounter. But he must truly dislike her. Why else would he have scolded her after her ill-advised visit to the public house? He also appeared utterly unaffected by her attempts at charming civility.

"Impossible man." She rose from the chair at last.

Jane stepped out of the dressing room, a lovely gown of peach satin held in her arms. Mary stepped into the dress and pulled on long gloves of the same rich satin as the girl fastened the tiny hooks in the back. A quick glance in the cheval mirror showed Mary that she looked quite presentable. She smiled at her maid and went downstairs to meet her sister and brother-in-law.

"There you are at last," Betsy said as Mary descended the stairs. "Michael and I have been waiting for you for over a half an hour."

"I admit that I was a bit distracted."

Mary took light steps over the polished marble floor of the entryway. A large floral arrangement caught her eye as she accompanied the couple into the foyer. She heard Michael let out a low whistle and turned to find him shaking his head at the sheer number of cards and gift boxes littering the top of the hall table.

"I believe your suitors grow bolder by the day, Mary." He smirked. "This arrangement fairly dominates the hall."

Mary smiled absently as she crossed to the flowers. "These weren't here when I went upstairs to get ready." *Perhaps they're from Lord Ashworth?*

A tingle of anticipation coursed through her as she plucked the card from where it was nestled within the stems. Surprise mingled with disappointment. "Oh, they're from Lord Harley."

Michael arched a dark brow. "The Earl of Harley?" He glanced at Betsy and winked. "A most eligible gentleman, to be sure."

Mary shrugged as she searched among the other cards for the name of the earl's most captivating friend.

"I didn't realize that you were acquainted with him," Betsy

said. "Mother will be pleased."

"I only made his acquaintance last evening." Mary bowed her head to breathe in the fragrance of the lovely blooms. "Along with Lord Ashworth's."

"Ashworth? I didn't see either gentleman at the party last night," Michael said.

"Oh, I didn't meet them at the bash," she said, fingering a purple blossom. "It was later. At a public house."

"What!?" Michael sputtered.

Mary spun on her heel to find the two of them gaping at her. Michael looked ready to strangle her as Betsy stood with her hands on her hips.

"You were in a public house?" Betsy asked deliberately, her brow furrowed.

Mary waved her hand dismissively. "Lord Stokes made the suggestion when he drove me home."

"Unbelievable!" Michael growled. "You let that ridiculous fop drive you home?"

"Well, it seemed like a good idea at the time."

Michael ran his fingers through his hair. Betsy placed her hand on his arm to calm him and then turned to Mary and clicked her tongue.

"However could you let that man take you to a pub, Mary?" she asked. "Do you realize what might have happened?"

Mary nodded sagely. "The rabble might have tossed my skirts up over my head."

"Who the devil told you that?" Michael asked.

"Lord Ashworth," Mary said. "He was nearly as angry with me last night as you are now."

"You will tell us what happened, sister," he demanded. "Do you understand?"

Mary nodded and held her hands in front of her. "Several of the patrons approached me but Lords Ashworth and Harley thrashed them soundly."

"And where the devil was Stokes?" Michael asked.

Mary swallowed. "He left me there," she said, bracing herself for the inevitable outburst.

"That worthless sod! I'll throttle him with my bare hands, Betsy," he told his wife. "I'll make him see the error of his ways. Bringing an innocent girl into a public house?"

"She's all right, Michael," Betsy said. "Let's be grateful that Lords Harley and Ashworth were there to come to her aid."

Michael nodded at last, turning toward the front door.

"Fine," he said. "I have need to speak with several

gentlemen this evening, it appears."

Mary felt her cheeks burn as she followed the couple to Michael's waiting carriage.

The ride to the ball seemed quite long to Mary, with the silence in the carriage punctuated periodically by her brother-in-law's grumbling comments.

"A pub," he said in a low voice. "Unbelievable."

Mary looked beseechingly at Betsy, irked by the reproach evident on her sister's face. Sighing, she stared out the window at the darkened streets and let her mind work. Michael had scolded her as loudly as Lord Ashworth had! But while she knew that Michael's anger stemmed from his concern over her wellbeing, she had no notion of the cause of Ashworth's. Surely that man's displeasure was piqued by the inconvenience she had caused him.

And didn't that just make her feel like the silly society miss some people perceived her to be.

Chapter 3

Daniel stood with Harley at one end of the ballroom, his gaze roaming absently about the gathered revelers. He was dressed in formals, with black breeches and jacket paired with a waistcoat of gold. He ran his fingers through his thick waves and adjusted his crisp white cravat, letting out a sigh of mild irritation.

"Is something troubling you, man?" Harley asked with a smile.

"I believe these affairs grow more tedious," he said in answer. "The same decorations, the same revelers."

He froze as Lady Mary Bridgewater entered the ballroom with her sister and brother-in-law. He let his eyes roam freely over her, finding her even more lovely than he had last evening. Her peach dress hugged her figure, his practiced male eye noticed, the bodice dipping as low as fashion dictated. He barely noticed Harley's hand on his arm, urging him in the vision's direction. He soon found himself standing before her, staring silently at her as she gazed up at him.

"Lord Ashworth," she said softly, her expression guarded.

Daniel nodded in response. Whyever was his heart pounding? She was merely another lovely young lady of society.

She was certainly no more remarkable than any other silly girl in attendance.

"I thank you for the lovely flowers, Lord Harley," Mary said, surprising Daniel. "And for your thoughtful note. It was most solicitous of you."

Daniel shot a look at his gallant friend. Harley had sent her flowers, had he? And a thoughtful note? *Well, hell.*

"It was nothing, Lady Mary," Harley answered with a bright smile. "I merely wished to thank you for a most interesting evening. And to convey my concern over your well-being."

Lady Mary blushed most becomingly, Daniel noted with irritation. He opened his mouth at last, only to be waylaid by the lady's brother-in-law, Viscount Balsam.

"I believe we are greatly in your debt, gentlemen," Balsam said. "We cannot begin to thank you for coming to Mary's aid last evening."

Daniel nodded and shook Michael's offered hand. "It was most unfortunate that the lady found herself in such a situation, Balsam," he told Michael. "I'm glad that Harley and I were there."

"Yes, I believe I have need to seek out another gentleman

this evening."

Daniel felt anger surge anew at Lord Stokes, wishing in that moment to have his skinny neck between his bare hands. Just then the orchestra began to play a waltz, turning his attention once more to the lovely girl before him.

"Lady Mary," Lord Harley began.

"May I have this dance?" Daniel cut in, reaching out to take Lady Mary's hand in his.

He was stunned when his own words registered in his mind. He chose to focus instead on the incredible violet eyes staring up at him. As she nodded her consent he allowed a small smile to curve his lips. Leading her out onto the dance floor, they began to move together.

The two of them seemed to glide effortlessly across the floor, perfectly matched step for step. After several moments of silence she looked up at him at last.

"You are a wonderful dancer, Lord Ashworth."

"You seem surprised."

She shrugged her slight shoulders. "It's just that you are such a large man." Her smooth cheeks turned pink words. "I had no notion you could move so gracefully."

"I'm certainly no larger than Balsam," he said. "Surely

your brother-in-law hasn't trampled your toes?"

"No, not at all," she said in answer. "Although he and I have never danced quite so close."

He could feel her supple figure even through the many layers of her gown. She moved her hand ever so slightly, brushing her fingers over the nape of his neck. She closed her eyes, permitting him to lead her quite expertly through the dance. When the number ended she still seemed affected. At least as affected as he was.

"Lady Mary," he said softly, causing her eyes to flutter open at last.

"Yes?" she sighed, her violet eyes soft.

He said nothing. She lowered her gaze. Her body was pressed against his most pleasurably, though she made not one move to remedy the situation. He cursed softly and abruptly stepped back from her.

"Oh!" she gasped.

"Thank you for the dance," he said, bowing stiffly.

He brought her back to the safety of her sister and brother-in-law and crossed to the far side of the room. He spared a glance in her direction at last, pleased that she was turned away from him in conversation with her sister.

Lord, she'd felt wonderful in his arms. And when their dance had ended she'd kept that delectable body pressed to his. It was all he could do to keep from pulling her to him. From kissing her breathless. He cursed again.

"Did you enjoy your dance with the child, Ashworth?" Lady Small asked him.

Daniel turned toward Monica, finding the glint in her eye most disturbing. Could she be jealous? No. She had no claim on him.

"It was pleasurable, yes."

"Hmm," Monica whispered, leaning close to him. "I doubt very much that such an innocent could give you the pleasure that I can."

Daniel heard the envy in her tone and was confounded. And more than a bit irritated.

"I will allow that the earl's daughter lacks your, um…"

"Expertise?" Monica provided with a smile.

"No," Daniel said coolly. "Years."

Monica gasped at that and Daniel left her side. He located Harley, along with the stiff brandy reserved for the gentlemen. He nodded and took the offered glass form Harley's grasp.

"Good man," Daniel said, taking a long sip.

"Ashworth, I believe the widow grows quite possessive."

Daniel chose to ignore what he'd seen in Monica's eyes. "You're mistaken."

"You would think differently if you saw the way she looks at you when your attention is focused elsewhere," he said. "Particularly when it's turned in the direction of the Earl of Bridgewater's youngest daughter."

Daniel shot his friend a look of pique. "You're wrong, Harley. Monica and I have an understanding. She expects no permanent attachment. And as for Lady Mary Bridgewater, I haven't given the troublesome girl more than a passing glance all evening, save for our dance. She's pretty enough, I will allow. But that does not signify."

Harley laughed out loud at that. "Pretty enough? Come now, Ashworth. She is incredible, admit it."

Daniel frowned, irritated by the man's observation of a most obvious fact.

"She's quite beautiful, yes," he allowed at last. "But no doubt she's as cold and vain as every other young lady present, pretty or not."

Harley shook his head but said no more on the subject, to Daniel's relief. The two of them went into the supper room to partake of the sumptuous fare awaiting within.

After supper, Daniel reentered the ballroom. As the evening wore on he saw that Mary danced with any number of gentlemen, provoking his ire though he couldn't fathom the reason. He drank more of the fine brandy and watched as Harley led Mary out onto the floor. He could almost feel her in his own arms.

Her laughter reached him, the sound musical to his ears. Lord he was growing daft. The room suddenly seemed stifling to him, the sound of the many partygoers deafening. He took himself out onto the terrace, staring at the stars visible in the night sky as his mind worked. Monica's strange comments plagued him a bit, but not nearly as much as his maddening response to a simple dance with a certain young lady. What the devil was the matter with him?

The sound of voices soon interrupted his thoughts and he retreated into the shadows, loath to be engaged in the inane banter which abounded at such festivities. He was amazed as the pair of revelers proved to be Mary and yet another gentleman, this one stout and quite short of stature. Lord, did the woman never grow fatigued?

As he watched her bat her thick lashes at her panting

escort, his anger grew. The lady certainly seemed quite sure of herself. Couldn't she recognize the dangerous game she was playing?

Daniel fought the urge to come to her aid, their exchange in the pub still quite fresh in his mind. Yet when the man smoothly negotiated her into a far corner of the terrace, her distress became evident.

"Do permit me one kiss, Lady Mary," her boorish partner cajoled. "I must taste that lovely mouth of yours."

Mary shook her head, her eyes round in alarm. As the man pinned her against the stone wall, Daniel gave up his struggle. Before Mary could so much as utter a scream of protest Daniel pulled the little man from her, tossing him roughly onto his backside. He glared at Mary's tormentor, sorely wishing he would put up the smallest struggle, if only to give Daniel an excuse to pound his fat face with his fist. The gentleman recovered himself and quickly escaped into the ballroom, causing Daniel's hands to clench into tight fists.

He cursed and turned back to Mary, noting her high color and rapid respiration. His gaze fell to her bosom, rising and falling as she sought to catch her breath. His anger grew as he thought of what had nearly happened there on the terrace, and of

Mary's folly to allow a man to lure her out onto the terrace alone.

"Can you not look after yourself?" he growled.

***

Mary took a breath and stepped away from the wall, still quite shaken.

"I…," she began.

"Dancing with every man who asks, flirting outrageously," he went on. "And look at that shameful dress!"

Mary gasped, her fear gone in an instant.

"I will have you know, Lord Ashworth, that this dress is a shining example of high fashion!"

His gaze fall to her bosom once more. "Seems quite low to me."

"Perhaps your mind works in such a manner," she said with a tilt of her chin. "But I assure you that the other gentlemen here—"

"The other gentlemen here no doubt think you're generous with your favors, dressed as you are like a common trollop."

Mary raised her hand and delivered a stinging slap to his cheek. Daniel grunted and then grabbed her by her arms.

She shook to free herself from his hold. "Unhand me this

instant!" she demanded. "I didn't ask for your assistance, Lord Ashworth."

"Take your hands off of her, Ashworth," Michael ordered. "What the devil ails you, man?"

Ashworth glared at her and ran his fingers through his hair. He took a breath and turned toward Betsy and Michael.

"Forgive me, Balsam," he said. "Lady Balsam," he added as he bowed to Betsy. "I suggest that you keep your sister under tight rein."

He stalked back into the ballroom. Mary's mouth hung open as she watched him go, stunned by his actions and his words.

"What was that about, Mary?" Betsy asked her.

"Impossible man." Mary turned to grip the iron railing surrounding the terrace.

She made no further comment, willing her sister and brother-in-law to leave her alone. A rustle of Betsy's skirts told her of their departure. No doubt Michael would blister her ears on the ride home, however. Closing her eyes, she recalled the raw fear she'd felt when Lord Grimsby had pressed her against the wall.

How could he think to attempt such a deed? And what of

Lord Ashworth's comments? Surely her dress and demeanor were not improper in the least! He was merely being as contrary as she'd come to expect in the short time she'd known him. Yet why did his opinion matter so much to her?

She let out a sigh and returned reluctantly to the ballroom. Her eyes immediately settled on Lord Ashworth where he stood in conversation with a very lovely dark-haired woman. The lady was standing quite close to him, and Mary noticed that her dress showed much more of her décolletage than Mary's had. And he had accused her of appearing like a trollop?

He bestowed a dazzling smile on the women and Mary felt her heart lurch. Lord, she had never seen him smile so in her direction. Ashworth raised his head then, pinning Mary to the spot with his gaze. His brow furrowed and he lost his beautiful smile. Disheartened, Mary watched as he took the widow's elbow and left the ballroom.

She took herself back out onto the terrace to await the time when Michael and Betsy would come to escort her home.

Chapter 4

Two weeks passed, and Mary was utterly confounded by
Lord Ashworth's lack of attentions toward her. Lord Harley,
however, had paid several calls on her over the past fortnight.
Why did his friend not pay her the same courtesy?

She hadn't seen him at the many parties she'd attended
most recently, either. She tried not to think about their marvelous
dance that night at the ball. Or the harsh words they'd exchanged
on the terrace.

She donned her chemise and petticoat, readying herself for
a hunt to be held at an estate not far from London. Betsy and
Michael would be attending. Her sister and brother-in-law
enjoyed any opportunity to be around horses. Mary, too, loved to
ride and care for the magnificent animals. Whenever she was in
Somersetshire she spent hours riding about her father's estate.
Michael and her other sister Maggie's husband Philip raised
champion stock there as well as at Betsy and Michael's home in
Cornwall. In Mary's opinion, riding the horses and testing their
meddle was far superior to the sedate riding that Hyde Park
afforded. She was sure to have a pleasant time at the hunt. At the
very least she could ride her borrowed mount as fast and as far
as she wished.

When last she had ridden in Hyde Park, she'd been hard-pressed to restrain her horse. She'd yearned to ride over the silly girls and proper ladies populating Ladies Mile. Even the traffic on Rotten Row, the most preferred track in the park, was clogged with fops and elderly gentlemen taking the air. Lord, she was weary of the niceties exchanged among the *ton*: the false modesty the young ladies of her acquaintance showed, the incessant preening the young gentlemen exhibited to all.

"And I have yet to find Lord Ashworth riding about the park." She rang for her lady's maid to see to her hair. "Perhaps he is busy, seeing to the matters of estate."

"Yes, my lady."

Mary had learned since they last met that his holdings were quite vast and impressive.

"But Father's holdings are impressive, too."

"That is true, my lady." Jane fashioned Mary's hair into a thick coil at the back of her head.

"Still, when Father is in town he seems quite able to take advantage of the opportunities to socialize among the gentry."

"Yes indeed, my lady."

She nodded to Jane and finished dressing for the hunt. She wore a very becoming riding habit of pale blue velvet, one of her favorites.

"Thank you, Jane."

The lady's maid bobbed a curtsey and left Mary still pouting over Lord Ashworth's absence.

"He will do as he wishes, I suppose," Mary grumbled as she went downstairs to join Betsy and Michael. She was determined not to think of him for the rest of the day.

"Oh, curse his handsome hide," she breathed.

"What is that, sister?" Betsy asked.

"Nothing."

Mary fumed as the riders assembled before the stables at the estate in Greenwich, where the hunt was being held. Lord Ashworth was indeed in attendance. And he surpassed the image she'd carried in her mind's eye. What a remarkable specimen he made in his riding clothes. A more dashing gentleman she had yet to encounter. And he sat his mount most regally, as well.

He turned from the conversation he was having with several other gentleman to lock his gaze with hers. He appeared as surprised to see her as she was to see him. Before she could school her expression, she smiled brightly at him. A smile teased his lips and her heart beat faster.

She had the fleeting thought to ride over to him, but

quickly checked that action as Lady Small appeared at his side. The widow spared her the slightest glance before turning her attention to Lord Ashworth. Mary cursed herself for a silly fool. Whyever would Lord Ashworth wish to ride with her when he had such a lovely companion at his disposal? Feeling slighted without cause, she rode off on her own soon after the hunt commenced, leaving the others to chase the fox in her absence.

After passing some time riding and pouting, Mary rode into an isolated part of the estate. Amazingly she could hear voices through the thick trees, a man's deep, rumbling voice and a lady's throaty whispers. Unable to restrain her curiosity, she dismounted and quietly walked toward the source of the sounds. What she soon saw astounded her.

Lord Ashworth and Lady Small were in a tight embrace, and as Mary watched the woman ran her hands over the man's broad back.

"Not here, Monica," Lord Ashworth said.

Mary's breath caught. He looked so powerful. Her body tingled for a reason she could not fathom. Her cheeks flamed as she hurried from the spot and mounted her horse, set on returning to the stables.

***

Daniel set Monica away from him, ignoring her pouting lips. She wasn't the woman on his mind at the moment, despite the fact that she'd had her hand nearly down his breeches not two minutes past. No. He was thinking of Lady Mary Bridgewater.

He'd watched Mary as she'd ridden away from the party, relief flooding through him. He'd been surprised to see her there at the hunt. When she'd smiled so sweetly at him, his pulse had begun to pound. The enchanting picture she made in her gorgeous riding habit, sitting so marvelously on her mount, had surprised him as well. She appeared to ride quite adequately, which shouldn't be a surprise. Her brother-in-law was the premier breeder and trainer of some of the best horseflesh in the country, and Mary seemed to handle the spirited mount Balsam had chosen for her quite easily. *If only she could keep as tight a rein on herself.*

The graceful way she moved, the compelling looks she bestowed in his direction—and undoubtedly in every other gentleman's, was a plague on his sanity. Thus he'd accepted Monica's suggestion for a ride through the less traversed sections of the estate, something he regretted at this moment.

He'd never denied himself what a lady offered in the past.

But even he could not deny the possessive glint visible in Monica's dark eyes as she adjusting her riding habit. Did the lady wish a more permanent attachment? He wouldn't offer her one.

"Another time, Monica," he said to placate her.

"But Ashworth."

Without another word, he assisted her onto her horse and the two of them returned to the stables.

Mary was there when they arrived, and Daniel sensed a strangeness about her. She wouldn't meet his gaze, her cheeks reddening. He forced his eyes away from her and dismounted. Monica smiled down at him, obviously waiting for his assistance. He helped her, chagrined as the woman pressed herself against him. When he set her from him and looked again at Mary, he was confounded by her expression. She appeared hurt and angry both, and accusation was clear in her eyes.

What precisely was provoking her ire? Cursing the ridiculous situation he found himself in, he strode into the stables.

Late that night Daniel moaned in his sleep, his unconscious mind filled with the most provocative image he had ever imagined. He was once more among the trees at the hunt, only it wasn't Monica's body pressed tightly to his. It was Mary Bridgewater's. He kissed her rosy lips and she sweetly begged him to end her torment. To make her his. He most happily obliged her, catching her cries of pleasure in his mouth. She called out his name—his Christian name—and he was consumed by pleasure as he had never before imagined.

He awoke, drenched with sweat. "My God." He ran a hand over his fevered brow. "Lady Mary Bridgewater?" How the devil had she manage to steal into his dreams? He took a deep breath and fell onto his back. He quickly realized that he was fairly throbbing with need, the powerful images from his dream still filling him with wanting. But his weary mind also acknowledged that it was more than his sex that wanted Mary: his eyes wished to see her, his lips longed to taste her, his arms ached to hold her. He raked his fingers through his hair and sighed out loud.

Whyever would he want a spoiled, vain and silly girl like Mary Bridgewater? He rose to see to his morning toilette. A splash of cold water on his face cleared away the clinging mist from his dream. He would banish the lady herself from his mind as easily. That was certain. He would simply focus on his estate work and keep the troublesome chit out of his mind.

After a few hours of being closed up in his study, he was itching to leave his townhouse. He decided to ride through Hyde Park. While the location wouldn't allow the vigorous riding the previous day in the country had, he was comforted by the fact that he wouldn't find himself alone in the woods with a woman who wanted more from him that he was willing to give. Surely his misplaced guilt over his close encounter with Monica had fueled his dreams. And clearing his mind in the relatively fresh air of the park would further banish the images of the other young lady.

He shouldn't have been surprised when his assumptions proved quite false. Riding along Rotten Row he spied Lady Mary almost immediately. The horse drew his attention as surely as its rider. It possessed the long legs and strong graceful build of a horse bred by Lords Balsam and Wilton's stables.

Mary sat the fawn horse beautifully. This day she wore a most becoming riding habit of violet, and her glorious golden curls were unadorned and dressed in a simple braid. The early afternoon sun glinted off of her hair, giving her an almost ethereal glow. Lord, the girl drove him to madness.

Mary didn't see him, he was happy to note. Her eyes were downcast, and she appeared most distracted as she rode sedately about the track. She smiled absently at the other riders, acknowledging the many gentlemen who addressed her with only the smallest nod.

Daniel saw her back suddenly stiffen and wondered at the cause. Mary veered off of the track and urged her mount toward the less populated section of the park, determination clear on her face. Unable to help himself, he followed into the secluded spot, trailing her for several minutes. He reined in his horse as he watched her dismount and walk slowly away from hers. She strolled through the dappled shade afforded by the trees and unfastened a few buttons of her spencer in deference to the heat of the afternoon. She let out a sigh and leaned against a tree.

Lord, she was lovely. His dream came back to him fully, causing him to ache to go to her. He turned his mount, determined to put as much distance as possible between himself and the unspoiled beauty before him. Just then, a reckless young man driving a curricle sped past the trees, spooking his horse as well as Mary's. He managed to restrain his mount, but Mary's bolted from the clearing. He watched as her eyes grew round in dismay. She stamped her dainty foot and clenched her hands into fists.

"Bloody hell," Mary muttered.

Daniel burst into laughter at her unladylike utterance.

Mary spun on her heel to face him.

He dismounted in one smooth motion to stand before her. "I believe I must come to your aid yet again."

Her dainty brow furrowed and, unless he missed his guess, she was vexed. "I did not ask for your assistance, Lord Ashworth," she countered, her chin tilted.

"And yet again you deny the obvious."

The girl blinked in apparent confusion.

"You are in dire need of my assistance, Lady Mary," he went on in explanation.

Mary stared up at him as he stepped closer. His gaze ran over her, pausing at the deep V of her open spencer. She looked down and quickly buttoned her jacket.

"Do not think to use me as you did Lady Small," she said, backing away from him.

He drew back. "What did you say?"

Mary lowered her gaze, twisting her violet riding skirt in her hands. "I saw you at the hunt."

"How dare you observe me without my knowledge?"

Mary took an audible breath. "You were not well-hidden, my lord."

He bit back a curse. "Did you much enjoy the scene?"

"Oh, no."

"I can only imagine what you believe you saw, but nothing happened at the hunt."

She appeared thoughtful for a moment. "But you and she were…very close."

"I won't deny that the lady wanted more than an embrace."

"More?"

"You little innocent. She wanted more, and precisely what your eager suitors wish to bestow upon your fair person."

"No," Mary whispered. "That cannot be."

She stared up into his eyes.

"Oh yes," He assured her, his voice low. "No doubt they find you quite desirable." He stepped closer still, catching the scent of hothouse roses he suspected he would always associate with her. "I heartily agree."

He gave her but a moment to puzzle over his words before he lowered his head and kissed her. She gasped, pulling back to stare up at him again.

"Damn, you're so sweet."

She trembled against him. Her body was so soft. Her lips were so warm. When his tongue entered her mouth, she whimpered low in her throat.

He withdrew and quickly stepped back from her. Mary slowly opened her eyes and stared up at him.

"Forgive me, Lady Mary," he bit out. "I had no right."

Mary said nothing, still staring up at him.

"Please allow me to take you home."

As he watched, she seemed to recover herself. "I think not, Lord Ashworth."

He shook his head and mounted his horse. "You, my lady, would do well to heed me."

She gasped as he grabbed her around her waist and settled her in front of him. As they rode through the park, he was absently mindful of the stares they received. She sought to maintain some distance for a few moments but finally leaned back ever so slightly and relaxed a bit in his arms.

He spied her horse standing at the front gates of her parents' townhouse.

"Your filly beat you home."

She whispered a curse, holding her hand in front of her mouth. He reined in his horse and dismounted, holding his hand up to her. With obvious reluctance, she placed her hand in his. He helped her down from the horse, keeping his hands on her waist for a few moments. Mary stared up at his lips, and he vividly recalled how wonderful her mouth had felt against his.

"Thank you, Lord Ashworth," she said coolly.

He stared at her for a beat. When he made a motion to accompany her up the stairs she waved one graceful hand through the air.

"I have no need for further escort," she said. "Thank you."

He bristled but said nothing in return.

"Good day." She turned and stomped up the stairs, slamming the door with a loud thud.

Chapter 5

How dare she be angry with him? Daniel fumed as he mounted his horse once more. He'd come to her assistance, and yet again she'd berated him for his attentions. He urged his horse through the traffic on Park Lane.

"Contrary chit."

Ah, but the way her mouth had felt against his? He hadn't meant to kiss her. He'd simply wished to quiet that contradictory mouth of hers. But her lips were so soft and so sweet he'd nearly lost himself. My God, the desire was so sharp it left him shaking. And when she'd opened her mouth, welcoming his tongue? How he'd managed to step away from her he could scarcely fathom. The answering heat in her violet eyes had stunned him.

By the time he arrived at his own home, his blood had cooled and he was once more able to objectively consider the girl. She was far more beautiful than even the devil Beatrice had been. Perhaps her beauty masked a heart even darker than that witch's?

He stepped into his entryway and his butler hurried to assist him.

"Good afternoon, my lord."

"Good afternoon, Trimm."

The servant was slight and several years younger than Daniel. He was wringing his hands. Daniel raised a brow at the man's apparent nervousness.

"What the devil ails you, man?"

To his amazement, Trimm reddened all the way up to his shock of black hair.

"You have a visitor, my lord."

Daniel removed his riding gloves and set them on the hall table. "Is it the marquis?"

Trimm shook his head and swallowed audibly. "It is Lady Small," he squeaked.

"What?" He raked his fingers through his hair. "Where is she?"

"In the parlor," Trimm answered.

Daniel swore under his breath. What the devil was the woman about? She'd never paid him a call before. Why would she do so now?

He found Trimm staring at him expectantly.

"I'm going into my study, Trimm," he said. "Please ask Lady Small to join me there."

Trimm nodded and hurried toward the parlor. Daniel walked into his study and sat behind the desk, puzzling over the woman's intrusion.

"Hello, Ashworth," Monica said from the doorway.

Daniel looked up to regard her closely. Her lips were curved in a slight smile, as if she held some sort of secret.

"Good afternoon, Lady Small," he said stiffly. "What can I do for you?"

Monica closed the door and widened her smile. "I have need to speak with you, Ashworth," she said, stepping further into the room.

Daniel folded his hands and placed them on the desk. "What is this, Monica?" He arched a brow. "Whatever can be so urgent that you would risk coming here?"

Monica laughed shrilly, causing him to draw back in surprise.

"Now Ashworth," she began, coming to stand before him. "You cannot send me away."

Daniel saw it clearly then, the possessive glint in her dark eyes. When she placed one slender hand on his shoulder he shook it off with a shrug. There was no use for it. He wouldn't let her intrude upon his life as if she deserved some place in it.

"I'm glad that you are here, Monica," he began, leaning away from her. "I believe that we should reconsider our arrangement."

Monica's eyes lit up with anticipation, causing Daniel to wince at his blunder.

"Oh, Ashworth!" she exclaimed. "I hadn't imagine! That is, you cannot mean that we will make our arrangement more permanent?"

Daniel shook his head. "I believe you misunderstand me. What I mean to say is that I believe that we can no longer enjoy each other's company."

Monica blinked at him. Her brows snapped together in obvious irritation. "What is this?" she countered. "What has happened to change matters?"

Daniel said nothing to that. How could he tell her that he wouldn't be controlled by any woman? Or worse, that she meant nothing to him besides a suitable bed partner? And how could he tell her that his feelings regarding a certain argumentative golden-haired girl had his mind in confusion?

"This is because of that Bridgewater girl, isn't it?" Monica asked pointedly. "I heard of your ride through the park with that child, but I had convinced myself that you were merely seeing the silly girl home."

Daniel blinked at the jealousy twisting her face.

"Mary Bridgewater is of no consequence to me," Daniel said, piqued at the woman's words. "But you are in no position to say a word about any woman I choose to escort, Monica."

Lady Small smiled then, a wicked smile he recognized in an instant. It was sensual and provocative, and so false it nearly shattered in its brittleness.

She leaned closer to him. "I have no claim on you, Ashworth, that is true." She ran her hands over his chest, his shoulders. "But I know what you like. And I know how to make you want me."

She fell to her knees before him and began to unbutton his breeches. Daniel watched with disinterest as she licked her lips and lowered her head.

"Stop that, Monica," he said, grasping her shoulders.

"But you want me to do it, Ashworth," she said, raking her fingers over him.

"No. That's a whore's trick, Monica. It means nothing."

Monica stood then, her hands in fists. "How dare you speak so to me!" she cried. "You enjoy what we do together, Ashworth. Don't deny it!"

"Keep your voice down," Daniel ground out. "I won't have this behavior in my home. My God, you're carrying yourself like a common harlot."

Monica slapped him. Daniel brought his hand to his cheek, shaking his head at her.

"You have made this far less taxing on my conscience that I had anticipated," he said evenly. "I bid you farewell, Lady Small."

Monica clutched at his shoulders. "Oh, I'm sorry," she rushed out. "Please don't be angry with me."

"I'm not angry, Monica," he said coolly. "I wish you well. Please shut the door on your way out."

Monica's eyes held a dangerous glint for a brief moment. That false smile soon curved her lips. "As you wish it, Ashworth." She lifted her nose into the air. "Good day. Perhaps I will see you at the bashes sometime."

Daniel gave a curt nod. Monica breezed from the room and shut the door. He blew out a breath and sat once more behind the desk.

"Well, that was pleasant," he muttered. But what was done was done, and the relief he felt at severing ties with the lovely widow was well worth the inconvenience of their encounter.

***

Mary was in her chamber readying for tea when a servant

rapped on her door. As her lady's maid went to answer it, Mary tugged at the curls framing her face. Jane returned in excitement.

"A gentleman has called, my lady," the girl said.

Mary's eyes grew round. "A gentleman?"

Jane bobbed her head.

Mary's heart raced. Could it be Lord Ashworth, here to apologize for his boorish behavior in the park?

"Thank you, Jane," Mary said, coming to her feet.

Jane hurried from the room. Mary stood and checked her appearance in the cheval mirror. She wore a tea dress of soft green, the color well suited to her fair complexion. Her hair was a riot of curls, held back from her face and caught up at her crown. She pinched her cheeks and smiled at her reflection.

"Perhaps Lord Ashworth will at last find me to his liking."

Let the impossible man fall to his knees before her in apology, she thought with a grin. It would be most fitting. Humming to herself, she fairly skipped down the stairs and into the parlor. The handsome man within turned, a bright smile on his face.

"Good afternoon, Lady Mary," Lord Harley said with a bow.

Her racing heart skittered to a stop and sank. "Lord

Harley."

Lord Harley crossed to her, taking her hand in his. "And may I say you look absolutely lovely this day," he said, bringing her hand to his lips.

Mary accepted his compliment with a small smile. His presence was not a complete surprise. He'd made several calls on her in the last few weeks, always with a ready smile and gallant gesture. She accompanied him to a settee placed near the fireplace.

"What brings you here this afternoon, Lord Harley?" she asked as she rang for tea.

"I'd thought to request a dance with you for this evening," he teased, his eyes sparkling. "For I find the crush of suitors which surround you at the bashes quite daunting."

Mary laughed lightly. "You flatter me, I daresay."

He smiled once more at her. They shared a pot of tea and Mary relished the warmth in the man's gaze. He never scolded her. He always smiled at her and paid her compliments.

"Did you enjoy your ride this afternoon, Lady Mary?"

"What?" she returned in surprise. "Oh, I believe you refer to my unfortunate incident in the park."

"But yet again Lord Ashworth came to your rescue?"

"Yes, impossible man," Mary said before she could stop herself. She started, her cheeks hot. A quick glance at Harley showed her the man was a bit confounded by her words. "That is to say, Lord Ashworth insisted upon escorting me home."

"As I myself would have, I assure you," Harley said with a nod. "Despite its serene appearance, the park can be a dangerous place for a young woman alone."

Mary thought immediately of her encounter with Daniel among the trees, of the incredible kiss they had shared, and her cheeks flushed hotter still.

"Yes. Quite dangerous, indeed."

Lord Harley regarded her closely for a moment, causing Mary's embarrassment to heighten. But to her relief he soon broached the subject of the coming evening's festivities, once more making his requests for at least two dances with her.

Lord Harley took his leave at the conclusion of tea, but Mary was not to spend the remainder of the afternoon in solitude. Her mother entered the room soon after the gentleman departed it, her eyes bright and her hands fluttering with excitement.

"Oh Mary, my dear child," she gushed. "Lord Harley has paid you yet another call. What a tremendous feather in your cap should you extract a marriage proposal from such a man."

Mary blinked at her mother's words. "A marriage proposal?" she asked in astonishment. "Whatever leads you to believe that Lord Harley has such intentions, Mother?"

The older woman smiled slyly. "He is quite eligible, my dear," she said with a nod. "And I do not believe that even your sisters would find fault with your acceptance of such a man."

Mary thought for a moment of her mother's words. The lady's insistence upon the most unsuitable of gentlemen was now woven into the family lore. Mary had been but a small child when her half-sister Maggie had come to live with them, and her recollections of Philip's pursuit of her were cloudy at best. But Mary had been a precocious thirteen-year-old when Betsy found herself engaged to a most unsuitable older gentleman. The match was encouraged by their mother, of course, as the man was purported to be quite wealthy. But even Mary had seen that Michael was the one Betsy should marry.

Her mother had put up a fuss at first, at last coming to love and respect her son-in-law as she saw just how happy he made her daughter. And now she found Lord Harley most acceptable, did she? Interesting. Surely the gentleman must be lacking somewhere.

"Do you truly believe that Lord Harley will ask for my hand?" she asked her mother.

Lady Bridgewater nodded with enthusiasm. Mary wondered at the lady's insistence. Lord Harley was most attentive, she recognized, recalling the many cards and flowers he'd sent in the last few weeks. But marriage? Surely the handsome man found her a delightful dance partner, but that was all. And what of his friend? Lord Ashworth couldn't bear the sight of her. The anger on his face after their encounter in the park assured her of the truth of that. What would he have to say to Lord Harley regarding a betrothal, if such an occurrence were to take place?

"I won't think of him," Mary said aloud.

"What is this, child?" Lady Bridgewater asked. "Whyever not? Lord Harley is most eligible."

Oh, her mother believes she spoke of Harley?

"Yes, yes," Mary said with an impatient wave of her hand. "I know that. Oh, I believe I will go to my chambers and ready for the evening."

"You do that, dear," her mother said with a smile. "And dress with care. No doubt Lord Harley will be in attendance."

Mary nodded and climbed the stairs, her mind in a muddle.

To her own astonishment she was ready and waiting in the foyer when Betsy and Michael arrived to take her to the parties, gowned in a glorious new dress of blue silk. To add to her enjoyment of the evening, Maggie and Philip were also in attendance. Mary let out a gasp of delight as she spied her oldest sister.

Although Maggie was not her full sister as Betsy was, the two younger girls were as close to her as if they shared the blood of both parents instead of solely their father.

"Oh, Maggie!" Mary cried as she hugged her sister. "How wonderful it is to see you."

The sisters' embrace was warm and genuine. Mary greatly resembled both of her sisters, possessing both Betsy's big blue eyes and Maggie's thick golden curls. Maggie looked as beautiful as she ever did, Mary noted with a smile. But the reason for Maggie's own smile was evident in the handsome gentleman at her elbow. Baron Philip Wilton gazed down at Mary, a crooked smile on his face.

"Hello, Mary," he said with a bow. "Although I daresay I'm amazed that you are here and ready to accompany us to the parties."

Mary clicked her tongue at him. "What have you been

telling him, Betsy?" she asked her sister.

Betsy laughed. "Don't lay the blame at my feet, sister," Betsy returned. "I believe Michael has filled his ears with stories of your keeping us waiting for hours on end in this drafty entryway."

Michael shrugged his broad shoulders and grinned. Mary hid her smile at the two rakish gentlemen obviously having fun at her expense. The five of them made a merry party on their ride to the ball, leaving Mary to think that the only possible improvement to the situation might have been if Michael's large carriage had been larger still. All three ladies clicked their tongues and sought to keep their skirts from being crushed by the big men filling the space.

Chapter 6

Daniel stood with Harley as usual. At least this townhouse boasted a cavernous ballroom. He shouldn't be surprised. This was surely one of the most important parties of the Season. The Winstons held the best and most widely-attended bashes. Countless chairs of blue velvet lined the space for the comfort of the older guests and those who needed a respite from dancing. An orchestra perfectly suited to the size of the gathering was playing tunefully, not that he was of a mind to turn about the large dance floor.

"There she is," Harley said.

Daniel knew the identity of the girl Harley indicated. He'd watched as Mary entered the place with her family. Wilton and Balsam had taken her sisters out onto the dance floor, which he allowed was an opportune time to approach her if one wished to. It turned out such effort proved unnecessary, as she was all but dancing in their direction at the moment.

A smile still teased her full lips as she watched her sisters dance. As she made her way around the dance floor, she swayed in time to the music. Her attention occupied, she bumped headlong into Harley.

"Good evening, Lady Mary," Harley said with a bow.

Mary dropped a curtsy, giving Daniel an eyeful of the lush curves he'd felt pressed against him in the park. He let his gaze caress her as his fingers itched to, seeing the answering heat in her violet eyes.

"Lord Ashworth," she breathed.

Daniel opened his mouth to make a greeting, soon closing it with a snap. He nodded curtly at her and turned, shouldering his way through the partygoers in his hurry to be far from her presence.

The evening progressed and after watching her share many dances with many suitors, Lady Mary allowed Harley to escort her into the crowded supper room. Daniel could scarcely believe it when Harley located a chair for her right beside him before taking one across the table from her. She sat, still unaware of his presence although his body fairly hummed with awareness of hers. When at last she glanced over at him, her lovely eyes went round.

"Lady Mary," he said curtly, shifting in his seat to give her his back.

She muttered something under her breath he didn't quite catch. Letting out a sigh of irritation, she dropped her hands to her lap. Harley soon faced her, and his pleasant conversation seemed to hold her attention. It didn't hold his, however. Her arm brushed his repeatedly despite his attempts at maintaining a modicum of distance. Her leg pressed against his whenever she shifted in her seat, burning him through her many skirts.

As a large woman seated on the other side of her rose, Lady Mary began to edge away from him. He couldn't begin to guess what she was about as her fingers brushed the side of his hip. What was she about? She trailed her fingers over him, causing his muscles to tense beneath her touch.

"So hard," she whispered.

When she pinched him he nearly swallowed his tongue. My God, he couldn't have been more aroused if the girl had unbuttoned his breeches and reached inside! He felt her delicate fingers trailing over his leg and bit back a groan. He took a long drink of his wine and spared her a glance out of the corner of his eye. She wore a look of thoughtful interest on her beautiful face. Her eyes were fastened on the fine linen tablecloth as her fingers kept up their sweet torture.

He had been well aware of her from the moment she had entered the party, not needing Harley's announcement in the lease. She was incredibly desirable in her daring gown of deep blue. She'd stood before him and he had looked his fill.

Yes, he'd watched her dance with any number of gentlemen, twirling gracefully about the room and laughing gaily. He'd finally gone into the supper room, thinking to lose himself in the throng within. Of course he was not so fortunate, he now thought.

While he was certain that Mary had been unaware of his close scrutiny during the meal, he couldn't banish her so easily from his senses. He'd watched her lovely mouth as she ate, marveled at her rosy lips as she sipped delicately from her glass of wine. The memory of their kiss in the park still lingered, the thought of the way her mouth had welcomed him caused desire to stir anew. And every time her arm touched his, every time her leg brushed against him, he was confounded. But this? Her feather-light touch on his leg was enough to have him throbbing with acute need.

Daniel took a deep breath and leaned toward her, thinking to keep his voice low to avoid any attention from the others seated at the long table.

"What the devil are you doing?" he asked deliberately.

Mary started and gazed up at him, her eyes round. A most becoming flush spread from her bosom to the golden curls piled atop her head.

"My dress is under your, um..."

He was very aware that her hand hadn't ceased its movement over his tensed muscles despite her obvious embarrassment. He arched a brow at her in question, struggling to maintain his own composure.

"You are sitting on my dress," Mary whispered at last.

Cursing softly, he reached beneath the table to grasp her hand in his. He was sorely tempted to place her hand fully upon him to make her aware of the discomfort she was causing him. But the feel of her small hand in his large one filled him with a strange wanting, one that went beyond the sexual. Her fingers were delicate, her skin as soft as he had remembered. He dropped her hand in her own lap as if it burned him.

One deft tug on her skirt freed her and he told himself as she quickly moved away from him that he didn't miss their close contact in the least. He shifted uncomfortably in his seat, forcing his attention from her. A rustle of skirts told him that she left the table, no doubt to dance with the few gentlemen that had escaped her notice earlier in the evening. He signaled a server for more wine and waited for his desire to ebb, loath to rise from the table with his condition so obvious.

After his desire had abated somewhat, Daniel reentered the

ballroom. His eyes unconsciously searched out Mary, finding her in a thrice. She stood with her sisters, to his relief. He'd grown used to her being surrounded by all of her silly suitors, fops like Stokes and Grimsby who had much more than dancing on their minds. But there she was with her family, and he immediately saw that she shared more than her bloodline with the two women. But despite the sisters' undeniable beauty, neither woman could match Mary in her loveliness in Daniel's opinion.

Wilton and Balsam joined the ladies and Daniel felt envy at the group's easy exchange. He and Patrick had been as close. He had no sisters, however. The way they interacted was something almost foreign.

Mary's musical laughter drifted over to him, filling him with a strange urge to bring out such gaiety in her himself. And her dazzling smile. The Lord knew that she'd never bestowed such upon him. She argued with him and vexed him and made him want her like he'd never wanted another. But such lightness, such lovely sweetness? At that moment he suspected that he would move heaven and earth for her if she were to share such delight with him.

Cursing himself for a daft fool, he left the ballroom and stalked out onto the terrace before he would fall prey to her charms. No woman would truly touch him. He would die before making the mistake his brother had.

No longer would he search for sexual partners among the predatory widows and unhappily-married women that seemed to somehow find their way beneath him, either. He hadn't missed the speculation in the eyes of those experienced women when they noted that Monica was absent from his side. In truth, he'd only just noticed she wasn't at the party. Perhaps she was keeping herself from the bashes to balm her wounded feminine ego. As for him? He would keep himself to the pubs.

Then perhaps he could satisfy his body and empty his mind of the beguiling Lady Mary Bridgewater.

***

Mary stood in the ballroom, surrounding by several attentive gentlemen. Relief had flooded through her when Lord Ashworth had released her from his unconscious confinement, albeit touched with regret. As strange as it seemed to her, she'd been reluctant to remove her hand from him. The strength of his muscles beneath her fingers had surprised her and filled her with a compulsion to explore him more thoroughly.

She knew that his arms were strong, for she'd felt them the first time they'd danced together. And his strength had been quite evident when he'd thrashed the villains at the public house. But when he'd taken her hand in his tonight? Oh, she'd been seized with the delicious notion of his never letting her go! But he had, and quite happily.

He had no need to keep her close to her and she had no right to expect that he would. They were nothing to each other. Perhaps more than acquaintances but certainly less than friends. And by the acute dislike on his handsome face whenever she caught his eye, he would no doubt be content to let matters stay precisely as they are.

Mary couldn't bear the crush of suitors any longer. Her maddening feelings toward the puzzling Lord Ashworth had her most disturbed. How could she think of dancing with one of these undoubtedly suitable gentlemen when she wished to lose herself in his arms?

She gracefully declined the offer of a dance from one of the fawning gentleman and made her way over to where her sisters stood beside the refreshment table.

"Are you having a pleasant time, Mary?" Maggie asked her, handing her a glass of punch.

Mary took the glass and shrugged. "It's enjoyable, yes."

Betsy laughed gaily. "You've scarcely had time to breathe,

sister," she said. "I've seen the throng of admirers that have barely given you a moment to yourself."

Mary thought for a moment and nodded. "I suppose so, although I found them a bit daunting after a while."

Maggie and Betsy exchanged a look of apparent surprise at Mary's words. Mary didn't miss their speculation and sought to divert attention from herself. How could she explain her sudden disinterest in the social whirl when it was all she'd spoken of for so very long?

She waved her hand and asked after Betsy and Michael's little girl, happy to divert the attention from herself and the number of gentlemen vying for her attentions. Betsy cocked her head to one side, obviously suspicious of Mary's actions. But to Mary's relief, Betsy warmed easily to the subject of her darling girl and began to regale her sisters with stories of the stubborn little miss's recent antics.

Mary saw nothing of Lord Ashworth himself as the hour grew later. But she'd seen a group of giggling young ladies out on the terrace and knew instinctively that the handsome golden-haired man was their prey. She would never lower herself to such behavior. If the man wished to dance with her—oh, why didn't he wish to dance with her?—he could bring his magnificent self to her and beg for her attention.

Her sisters' voices seemed faint to her as she recalled the sweet tingle that had filled her when Daniel had gazed at her most thoroughly when she entered the ball. And later, when she'd brazenly explored the very interesting obstacle entrapping her gown. Oh, her fingers had fairly burned at the contact. He seemed most angry with her and her actions. Why wouldn't he be so?

Enough! She would spare no more tender thoughts on the man. Let him entertain himself with those silly girls and leave her alone.

Thankfully her sisters soon deemed it time to depart for home. For once in this long Season Mary was happy to bend to the other ladies' wishes. Her ready acceptance earned her more looks of speculation from Betsy and Maggie. She simply followed them to where their host and hostess were accepting thanks and good wishes. Standing before the older couple was none other than Lord Ashworth.

"Leaving so soon, Ashworth?" Michael asked jovially.

The man turned toward them and smiled, losing that smile when he saw that Mary accompanied her brother-in-law. She stared up at him, searching for some blemish, something to make her find him less attractive. Less intoxicating. It was to no avail. The maddening man was perfect!

He met her gaze then, pinning her to the spot. Mary suddenly felt naked, as if he could see through her lovely gown, through her skin and to her very soul. She slowly lowered her lashes, effectively shielding herself from his beautiful eyes.

"Good evening, Lady Mary," she heard him say.

She murmured something in return, she had no notion of what, and turned from him. She waited for what seemed like forever for her family to cease their discourse with the handsome man, hearing nothing but the thrum of her heartbeat in her ears.

Not long after her final encounter that evening with Lord Ashworth, she bid her sisters and their husbands farewell outside her parents' home and resolutely climbed the stairs to her chamber. She managed to unfasten the hooks at the back of her gown and let it fall down around her feet. Her petticoat followed it to the floor and she stepped out of the high pile of satin and lace to pad over to the cheval mirror. Unpinning her hair, she studied her reflection absently.

An evening at the bashes had always filled her with a blessed exhaustion. She'd always enjoyed reliving the dances and conversations, weighing one eligible gentleman against the other in her mind. But the thought of Lord Ashworth dispelled any of the happiness she might otherwise feel over her successful evening. He was certainly not smitten with her. He could barely stand the sight of her.

"It's of no consequence," she sniffed.

Chapter 7

After nearly two weeks had passed since her frustrating encounter with Lord Ashworth at the Winston ball, Mary was at last able to block the sting of his rejection from her mind. She hadn't seen him at the most recent bashes, a fact that filled her with relief. She couldn't bear to see him turn those dark velvet eyes on her and watch as they inevitably filled with contempt. She couldn't gaze upon his face without imagining his lips pressed to hers, either.

When her lady's maid announced a caller on this particular afternoon she welcomed the diversion, not caring who it was in particular. Nonetheless, she instructed Jane to tweak and tuck her hair into a fetching style. She stood before the mirror and ran her hands over the skirt of her pretty blue tea dress and deemed herself most acceptable for whatever gentleman awaited belowstairs.

She breezed into the parlor and was mildly surprised to see Lord Harley within. He'd kept himself from the bashes as his friend had, and she'd idly wondered if he too now found her lacking. His bright smile and sparkling eyes soon dispelled any such notion.

"Lady Mary." He took her hand in his. "You look

breathtaking this afternoon."

Mary accepted his compliment with an incline of her head. "I haven't seen you in nearly a fortnight, Lord Harley," she said. "I'd come to believe that you and your friend had found other pleasures to tempt you far from town."

Harley laughed and shook his head. "I'm flattered that you took note of my absence."

His words caused a twinge of guilt. She hadn't truly given him much thought at all. No. Her mind had been fully occupied with his intoxicating, infuriating friend.

She recovered herself and sat on one of the settees that flanked the fireplace. "The parties have been crowded of late."

Harley chuckled at her jest and sat beside her. She stiffened at the close contact, unused to his boldness. When he took her hand in his, his expression tender, warning bells trilled in her mind.

"Lady Mary." He dropped a kiss on her palm. "I have tried to distance myself from your charms."

She stared at his bowed head. "Distance yourself?"

Harley kissed the inside of her wrist. Mary found no answering tingle that she believed should accompany such a caress. She gently tugged her hand from his grasp. To her dismay Lord Harley grasped her waist and smiled at her, his face close to hers.

"I have given up the struggle, love," he said.

"Love?" Her lungs seized. "Lord Harley—"

Her words ceased as Harley pressed a kiss on her lips. He quickly withdrew and grinned sheepishly.

"I'm sorry, sweet," he said. "I couldn't help myself."

"Lord Harley," she said again, coming swiftly to her feet. "I don't know quite what to say."

She took several steps away from him, her mind racing. Surely the man didn't wish an assignation? Why would he think she would be open to such an arrangement?

"Do not fret over my intentions, Lady Mary," he said. "They are most honorable."

Mary turned sharply at his words, her eyes opened wide. "You cannot mean, Lord Harley," she began. "You cannot mean that you wish…?" She couldn't finish the thought.

Harley stood and walked over to where she stood, taking her hand in his again. "I have come here to ask you to do me the great honor of becoming my wife."

Mary could only stare up at him, dumbfounded. His wife? She knew she must say something to him. Something to at least acknowledge his offer of marriage. But for the life of her she could not get her mouth to open.

Harley brought his fingers to her cheek, caressing her gently. "This mustn't be a complete surprise, love."

Mary blinked rapidly and shook her head. She straightened her spine and faced him fully. "Lord Harley, marriage between us is something that I must consider carefully."

Harley nodded and bade her to sit once more. She did, keeping her trembling hands folded in her lap.

"Lady Mary, I have given this much thought. It is high time I take a wife and see to the siring of an heir." He smiled crookedly at her. "Or two."

"But why do you wish to marry me in particular?" she had to know.

Harley's smile widened. "You are the most beautiful woman I've ever met, love. You are nearly as wealthy, as I. We enjoy each other's company. I believe the two of us will make a splendid match."

Mary was thoughtful for a long moment. He wanted to marry her because she was beautiful? He wished to sire an heir? What sorts of reasons were those to spend one's life together? Wealth was a consideration, but she didn't find it of much importance when choosing a mate.

She looked at him again, at the very handsome face staring down at her, and was confounded. "Lord Harley, I must think on this."

Harley placed his hand on hers, patting her reassuringly. "That is all I ask at this time, sweet."

"You won't speak to my father, will you?"

"I won't approach your father until I have your consent, Lady Mary."

She sat there, nodding her head in the man's direction as he bowed and took his leave.

"What am I to do?" She nibbled her lip. "Mother cannot know of this offer. The invitations would be penned before day had turned to night."

Perhaps she could speak to Betsy. Lord Harley was a very handsome, very eligible gentleman. But should she take her mother's view and accept his offer based simply on his eligibility? What of love?

Perhaps she had no right to expect to find such warmth of affection, such loving passion, as her sisters had. She couldn't help but wonder if she should settle for less. When Harley had kissed her she'd felt nothing. His caress didn't elicit the searing hunger that Lord Ashworth's had inspired. But that man detested her. She was certain of that fact. His continued avoidance was all the evidence she needed to that end. And yet why did she so wish that it had been him to come to her and make her an offer?

"Foolish girl," she chided herself, leaving the parlor for her chamber.

She would take however long Lord Harley afforded her to consider his surprising offer.

"And I'll keep the particulars to myself."

***

"You what!?" Daniel asked Harley, certain he had heard him wrong. The pub was noisy tonight, after all.

Harley laughed at his friend's surprise. "I've asked the lovely Lady Mary Bridgewater for her hand in marriage, Ashworth. This very afternoon. And the moment I have her consent, I will approach the earl and make our betrothal official."

Daniel grasped onto Harley's words, a confounding hope filling his breast. "Then she hasn't given you her answer?" he asked, keeping his voice even.

Harley shrugged his shoulders and raised his tankard. "She will."

Daniel's heart pounded at the prospect of Mary joining his friend in matrimony. She wouldn't consent. She mustn't.

He fumed as his friend waved to the server to bring them more ale. A serving wench brought a pitcher of ale, her eyes running slowly over the two gentlemen. To Daniel's astonishment Harley grabbed the girl about the waist and fondled her breast. The girl giggled and stepped out of his grasp. Harley slapped her bottom playfully and laughed, picking up his tankard once more. Did Harley truly favor Lady Mary? Then why would he think to dally with a trollop?

"Tell me why, Harley," he said, leaning forward. "Tell me why you asked for the lady's hand."

Harley snorted. "She's wealthy, Ashworth. Graceful and beautiful. I must have an heir, and it would be most enjoyable to see about that task with her."

Daniel's stomach clenched at the thought of Mary carrying Harley's child. Hell, of Mary carrying any other man's save for his own. Where had that thought come from?

Harley's voice drew him again. "You should have seen her today. Those golden curls framing her face? She was an angel."

First his friend speaks of money and heirs, and now he speaks of her angelic appearance?

"You sound like a besotted schoolboy, Harley. Clearly you haven't given this much thought."

"What do you mean?"

Daniel searched his mind for every objection to the lady that he'd used to cool his own ardor. It was passing strange, but those objections now seemed quite inconsequential.

"She's a troublesome chit, that's all," Daniel said at last. "She's silly and vain. She's forever getting herself into one perilous situation after another, or have you forgotten the circumstances that precipitating our making her acquaintance for the first time?"

"I haven't."

"And what of her beauty, Harley?" Daniel went on. "No doubt she will continue to attract every gentleman in town, even after your nuptials. Her vanity will surely increase, along with the nuisance of fending off gentlemen looking for a dalliance despite her married state."

Harley waved his hand dismissively. "I want her for my bride, Ashworth. I would be proud to be the envy of the *ton* and have such beauty on my arm. And in my bed."

Daniel saw red at Harley's words. He clenched his hands in fists in an effort to keep from throttling his very good friend.

He finished his ale as the serving girl returned to their table. Ignorant of his friend's anger Harley bid him farewell and followed the girl upstairs, leaving Daniel to stew in solitude. He refused an offer of female companionship from another of the serving girls and took himself home.

He went into his study, reviewing the past weeks in his slightly-inebriated mind. He'd avoided the bashes of late, keeping to the pubs as he'd vowed after his last encounter with Lady Mary. But he hadn't indulged his man's lust, to his growing dismay. He couldn't get the image of Mary out of his mind for more than a moment at a time.

What was she about? Who was calling upon her? And as Harley had accompanied him to the pubs each night, taking advantage of the eager wenches who wished to share their evenings with handsome titled gentlemen, the man's disclosure held all the more surprise. Harley wanted Mary for his wife, did he? *Well, hell.*

He closed the study door and picked up a bottle of brandy from the table beside his desk. He couldn't banish the thought of his good friend sampling Mary's considerable charms, and the picture causing his heart to clench. She was so sweet. So incredibly desirable. He could nearly taste her on his tongue as he had that afternoon in the park. God, how could he ever allow the wedding to take place? Sleep would no doubt prove elusive tonight, so he set about numbing his mind until he could think of her no more.

The next morning he woke, his head pounding. He'd fallen asleep at his desk, and the empty bottle at his elbow was all the evidence he needed as to why. He sat up, groaning softly. Placing his elbows on top of the desk, he rested his aching head in his hands. A knock came at the door, causing pain to surge anew.

"Who is it?" he growled.

"Trimm, my lord."

Daniel took a breath and ran his fingers through his hair. "Come in."

The butler entered the room, clicking his tongue over his master's appearance. Daniel heard it and scowled at him. Trimm set a tray on the desk and the rich aroma of tea and sweet rolls filled Daniel's nose.

"Good man." Daniel waved Trimm from the room.

Trimm shook his head but wisely said no more. He left his master to his meager breakfast, closing the door as quietly as he could manage. Daniel poured himself a cup of tea and drank deeply. After the second cup his head began to clear and the events of the previous evening came back to him.

Harley had asked for Mary's hand! Harley couldn't marry her. She wouldn't suit him. He wouldn't let their betrothal take place. He wouldn't let Harley have her.

"She is mine."

He blinked in surprise and ran his hands over his face, feeling stubble on his jaw. He drained the tea and slowly came to his feet. Taking up a sweet roll he left the study, bound for his chambers. He splashed cold water from the washstand on his face. Regarding his reflection in the mirror atop, he saw none of his brother in his visage this morning.

Not bothering to ring for his valet, he pulled on a jacket.

"Mary would not suit Harley," he muttered, straightening his clothes. "She is silly and vain."

His arguments rang false to him even before he could fully give them voice. "She won't accept him," he said at last, running his fingers through his hair. "She won't."

He left his chamber with long strides, determination burning in his breast.

Chapter 8

Mary stood in the parlor that morning, her head aching from her maddening thoughts. Should she accept Lord Harley's offer? He'd seemed most earnest in his proposal. But the man had said nothing save that she was beautiful and that he needed a wife. He was charming. And most handsome, although he seemed nothing to her when compared to his friend.

"I won't think of Lord Ashworth," she muttered.

That man wanted nothing of her, not even one simple dance at a ball. Lord Harley had been most solicitous in his calls, and quite generous with his lovely flowers and gifts. He would make a suitable husband. Yet she couldn't see herself linked forever to a man who found her beauty and wealth all the inducement he needed to choose her as a mate.

She'd remained firm in her decision to keep the news of the recent developments from her mother. But there had been no one else available for her to speak to about this. Betsy was otherwise engaged today, and would be with her husband in the country until the morrow. No doubt Maggie and Philip would accompany them, seeing to the horses that they were all considering for purchase. Surely Lord Harley wouldn't be put off for long.

"Oh, what am I to do?"

She paced about the fine oriental carpet. Her head snapped up as she heard the unmistakable sound of footsteps from the front of the townhouse. The light even steps of their butler were followed by heavy, undoubtedly masculine ones. Surely Lord Harley hasn't called for his answer so soon?

She brushed her hands over the skirt of her green day dress and turned toward the doorway, an uneasy smile fixed on her face. She was utterly stunned as Lord Ashworth strode into the room.

"Lord Ashworth!"

The man came to a stop, running his eyes over her in a way that made her heart race. He gave her a curt nod and looked pointedly at the butler. The servant bowed and left the room, closing the doors behind him. Mary watched as Lord Ashworth paced the floor as she herself had done, her curiosity increasing as she took in his appearance.

His clothes were slightly rumpled, his hair tousled. A light golden stubble covered his cheeks. She'd never seen him in such a state, nor had she ever found him so devastatingly attractive.

He came to a stop and turned to face her at last, his gaze intense. "You cannot marry Harley."

Mary blinked at his insistence, more than irritated by his words. Of all of the words she imagined might come forth from his lips, these were most unexpected.

"Who are you to say anything about it?" she countered with a tilt of her chin.

He faltered, and then resumed his pacing. Mary watched him warily, utterly perplexed. What was the man about?

He turned and faced her again, his hands in fists at his sides. "Mary, you must not wed Harley."

Mary started at his familiar use of her name. He hadn't lost his rigidity. His dark eyes stared into hers. She shook her head to clear it of the effects his close scrutiny was having upon her and placed her hands on her hips.

"You cannot tell me what to do." she said. "Any offer Lord Harley has made to me is surely no concern of yours."

Lord Ashworth stepped closer to her, reaching out as if to grab her. He stopped himself and ran his fingers through his hair, leaving it standing on end. He opened his mouth to say something, she couldn't imagine what, and closed it with a snap. How could he presume to come to her home and speak to her so?

"Lord Harley is a very eligible gentleman, Lord Ashworth," she said. "And if I give him my consent it will be my decision, not yours."

He shook his head and approached her once more. "You cannot marry him. He's not the man for you."

Mary snorted at his words. "And may I ask whom it is that you believe I should marry?"

They stared at each other for a long moment.

"Me," he said.

Mary gaped at him. She found the look of surprise on his face confusing in light of the conviction with which he'd stated his intentions.

"What did you say?" she asked deliberately.

Lord Ashworth grasped her arms gently, an expression of determination replacing that of surprise. "Marry me," he commanded, his eyes dark.

Mary ignored the pounding of her heart and shook off his hold, struggling to keep some grasp on reality.

"Marry you?" She scoffed. "Why on earth would I ever marry you? You can't bear to be in the same room with me."

He laughed at that, further confounding her. He stepped closer, holding her once more. "I can't bear to be in the same room with you, that's true," he said. "But that is because when I'm near you I'm seized with the desire to hold you. To kiss you.

To make you mine."

Mary could only watch as he lowered his head to hers. His kiss was deep, and as intoxicating as she had remembered. She felt his tongue enter her mouth and welcomed the intimacy. Wrapping her arms around his neck, she pressed herself fully against him. He moaned softly, setting her heart pounding.

"Ah, Mary." He brought his lips to her ear. "I want you to be my wife."

His words reached her. She shook her head again and stepped out of his embrace, her legs unsteady. "Why do you want to marry me?"

Lord Ashworth took a breath and ran his fingers through his hair again. "I want you, Mary. More than I have ever wanted another woman. I can't bear the thought of another man possessing you, even if that man is my good friend."

His words were far more compelling than anything Lord Harley had said,. They affected her in ways she hadn't imagined. But what of his infamous conquests upon the ladies of society?

"You're far too handsome for my sanity, Lord Ashworth. Women are forever throwing themselves at your feet, making you offers too tempting to refuse."

He visibly winced at her words. He placed his hand on his

chest with fingers splayed, contrition clear in his demeanor. "I know what you saw at the hunt, Mary. I can't turn back time and erase that image from your mind, even if it had been nothing more than a heated embrace. But I can promise you this: I will be ever faithful to you."

Mary heard the sincerity in his tone, saw the tenderness in his eyes, and sorely wished to believe him.

She nibbled her lip. "I don't know."

Lord Ashworth drew her into his embrace again and Mary let herself be lost in his arms.

"I care for you, Mary," he said, running his fingers over her cheek. "I will never hurt you or shame you. You have my word."

She closed her eyes and tilted her head to the side as he brushed his lips over her neck. She couldn't ignore the incredible feelings such a simple caress aroused.

"Lord Ashworth," she breathed.

"Daniel," he softly instructed, nibbling her ear.

Mary smiled at his gentle reprimand. "Daniel" She ran her hands over his broad back. "But you always seem so angry with me."

Daniel lifted his head and chuckled. "You do vex me.

That's certain. But if you promise to curtail your visits to the public houses I believe I'll be well-satisfied."

Mary laughed lightly, amazed as Daniel's velvet-brown eyes softened in response.

"You had seemed ready to throttle me the night of the Winston ball," she pointed out, trailing her fingers over his waistcoat.

He took her hand in his. "My God, woman," he said, brushing his lips over her fingers. "Do you have any notion of the discomfort you inflicted upon me when you touched me beneath that table?"

She could only shake her head, her cheeks warm. Discomfort? Whatever could he mean by that?

"Mary," he said, drawing her attention away from the buttons of his waistcoat.

"Yes?"

"Say that you'll marry me," he said. "Please say that you'll be my wife?"

Mary's heart raced at the passion and affection she could read in his countenance.

"Yes," she whispered. "Yes, Daniel. I'll marry you."

A smile spread across his face, a smile brighter and more

beautiful than any she had ever seen.

"Ah, Mary," he rasped, capturing her lips once more. "We will be happy, love."

His kisses made her nearly swoon, and his sweet words banished any lingering doubts she had over accepting his offer of marriage. He lifted his head at last, still holding her in his arms. She gazed up at him, reveling in the warmth of his embrace.

"I'll speak to your father directly, love," he said, dropping another kiss on her lips. "I cannot wait another moment to make our betrothal official."

Daniel left the parlor, bound for her father's study. Mary watched him go, holding her fingers over her lips. My, he could melt her with those lips of his. And while he hadn't made any mention of love, she was certain that he did indeed care for her. And that would have to be enough for the present time.

She let loose with a giggle and hugged herself. Oh my, she would so love being his wife. He was so strong, so handsome. And the warmth she'd glimpse in his eyes told her that he possessed a tender heart beneath his gruff exterior. Surely he would come to love her. How could he not? She already held him in such high regard and only after one or two searing kisses.

The sound of a masculine voice was heard from outside the

double doors and, with a smile, Mary turned in anticipation. "Did you forget something?"

To her amazement, Lord Harley entered the room wearing a grin on his face. He closed the doors and turned back to her expectantly.

"Lady Mary," Harley said with a jaunty bow.

"L-lord Harley."

Harley laughed and took her hands in his. "I know I gave you my word that I would await your answer with a modicum of patience, but I cannot."

Mary's mind was spinning as she nervously looked toward the doorway.

***

Daniel took a moment to collect himself before facing Mary's father. The taste of Mary's kisses were still on his tongue. *My God, just to press her to him was enough to send desire running through him unchecked!* When she'd laughed sweetly he'd felt that joy he'd envied the night of the Winston bash. *That her laughter and engaging smile had been meant only for him? That was indeed a pleasant surprise.*

The arguments he'd made to Harley were not far from his mind though. *Her beauty would no doubt increase. But would* her vanity? She seemed comfortable in her beauty, and seemed to take for granted the fact that she held every gentleman of her acquaintance in thrall. She wasn't a determined flirt, however. But would the fact that she was betrothed bring a halt to her eager suitors?

She was his. And if another tried to approach her he would live to regret it. She would have to accustom herself to charming but one gentleman.

Pushing aside such absorbing thoughts, Daniel checked his appearance in a gilded mirror just outside Lord Bridgewater's study. He ran his fingers through his hair, giving it some semblance of order, and straightened his wilted cravat. There was no use for it. At the earl's spoken permission he entered the study.

"Lord Bridgewater, sir," he said with a bow. "I must speak with you on a matter of the utmost importance."

Lord Bridgewater raised a gray brow at Daniel's intensity. "What is this, Ashworth? You seem quite solemn."

Daniel gave a short laugh and shook his head. "This is a joyous occasion, I assure you. At least, that is my intention."

The earl appeared thoughtful and bade Daniel to sit.

"I'm here this day, sir, to ask for your daughter's hand in

marriage."

His searched the older gentleman's face for any indication of his acceptance or denial of his offer. The bemusement on the man's face confounded him.

"Forgive me, Ashworth," the man said with a sly smile, "but I do not recall your name among the many cards and flowers."

"True," he allowed. "The competition is fierce."

"And you wish to emerge the victor?" the earl asked him. "My daughter is a prize, I will allow. But surely there must be more incentive for you to make such an offer."

"She is unlike any other woman of my acquaintance," Daniel said. "And I would be very happy with her as my wife."

"Do you love her?"

"I doubt the existence of that particular emotion, sir."

The earl leaned back in his chair, rubbing his chin. "Then tell me, son," he countered. "Tell me precisely what it is you feel for my daughter that compels you to make her your wife."

Daniel was at a loss. He knew that he couldn't tell Mary's father that she set him on fire with the lightest touch. That her lips were sweeter than anything he had ever tasted. And the feelings she aroused in him? He wanted her. That was true. She was the most desirable woman he'd ever known. He wished to protect her and keep her with him always. To give her children and to grow old with her by his side.

He folded his hands and leaned toward Mary's father. The older man's face showed his keen interest, causing Daniel to sigh audibly. "Sir, I cannot put into words what I feel for Mary. But know this. I care for her and will do my best to keep her from harm's way."

The earl chuckled. "And with my headstrong daughter that feat alone may keep you engaged for many years to come."

Daniel let out a short laugh, relief flooding through him. "Then I have your permission, Lord Bridgewater?"

"Certainly, son," Lord Bridgewater assured him. "I suspect that you feel much more than you are aware, but I will not press you on the matter."

Daniel puzzled over that, choosing to focus instead on the fact that Mary's father had given his permission and she would indeed be his wife. He rose from his seat and followed the older man as he walked out of his study, bound for the parlor. The gentleman had expressed both his surprise at Daniel's offer along with his approval. Lord Bridgewater had asked about Daniel's feelings for Mary, a fact which surprised Daniel even now for such matters were not routinely discussed with regard to a marriage contract.

As they neared the parlor, Daniel became aware of voices from within. Mary's was easy to recognize, the sound lilting and musical. But the other? Damn, it was Harley.

Lord Bridgewater preceded Daniel into the room. Daniel held back for a moment, his mind working.

"I believe there is much celebrating to do this day, daughter," Mary's father say jovially.

Daniel stepped into the room behind Mary's father, his eyes on his friend.

"Good day, sir," Harley said to Lord Bridgewater. Harley halted as his eyes fell on Daniel. Daniel returned his friend's gaze evenly. "Ashworth, what are you doing here?"

Daniel froze as Harley stared at him in confusion. He looked quickly at Mary, who gave a slight shake of her head. She was wringing her hands in obvious discomfort and he didn't know quite what to do to soothe her. To his further consternation, Lord Bridgewater chose that particular moment to give Daniel a hearty pat on the back.

"You have a great friend here in Lord Harley I believe, son," the older gentleman said. "He comes so soon to offer his congratulations."

Daniel watched Harley's face turn red with anger as the truth apparently struck him. He stepped toward his friend, his mind working to find some sort of way to placate him.

"Harley, please allow me explain."

Harley punched Daniel in the mouth.

Daniel was struck to the floor by the unexpected blow. He came up on one elbow and shook his head to clear it. He ran his tongue over his lower lip, tasting blood.

"Daniel!" Mary cried out, coming to kneel beside him.

She ran her fingers gently over his face, concern clear in her violet eyes. Daniel managed a smile for her, wincing from the pain from his cut lip.

"What on earth is going on?" Mary's father asked.

"How dare you do this to me, Ashworth!" Harley growled. "What of all of those things you said to me? She is vain. She is silly. She is troublesome."

"Now, Harley…"

"You said that about me?" Mary asked Daniel, standing and placing her hands on her hips.

Daniel shook his head at her. "Mary, I was only—"

"It was all a ruse," Harley went on. "You said all of that to win her for yourself. Now get up, you cur! I wish to hit you again!"

Daniel came to his feet and faced his friend. "I admit I wanted her for myself, Harley," he said. "But I won't allow you to disrupt her father's home with this display."

Harley looked at Mary and then at her father, his breathing harsh. He mumbled an apology and faced Daniel once more.

"This is not over, Ashworth," he ground out. "My second will be in contact with you."

With that, Harley bowed to Mary and took his leave. A duel was the last thing Daniel would ever consider, given how he'd lost his brother. He let out a loud sigh. He turned to find both Mary and her father staring at him expectantly.

"I don't know what to say, sir," he said to Mary's father. "I'd hoped to speak to Harley this afternoon, but the gentleman apparently had another notion."

"Am I to believe that you aren't the first gentleman to make an offer to my daughter?"

Daniel opened his mouth to respond, but Mary was faster.

"Lord Harley told me of his intentions only yesterday, Father," Mary said, her eyes still on Daniel. She then looked at her father. "I hadn't given him my answer."

Mary's father appeared thoughtful.

"I will set this to rights, sir," Daniel said to him. "You have my word."

Lord Bridgewater stared at him for a long moment, finally nodding his gray head. He gave Mary a look of supreme exasperation and left the parlor. Daniel let out a breath and turned to his betrothed, finding her dainty brow wrinkled in supreme irritation.

"Mary," he said, reaching for her hand. "I assure you I only made those assertions to Harley in order to dissuade him."

Mary snorted in response and pulled easily out of his grasp. Suddenly she cocked her head to one side in puzzlement. "What precisely did Lord Harley mean when he mentioned his second, Daniel?" Suddenly her eyes opened wide. "Oh! He spoke of a duel, didn't he? You mustn't meet him, Daniel. You mustn't!"

Daniel barely had time to open his arms before she flung herself against him. "Mary, I would never do any such thing."

"Promise me, Daniel," she said, grabbing onto the lapels of his jacket. "Promise me that you won't meet him, or so help me I'll find a pistol and shoot you myself!"

He cupped her face with his hands, staring deeply into her

eyes. "I won't, love. You have my word on it."

Mary stared up at him, her uncertainty clear in her violet eyes. She finally nodded her belief, moving in his arms to rest her cheek against his chest. She murmured something against his waistcoat, her voice more faint than a whisper. Daniel had no true notion of what she said, but he could almost believe that the tone of her voice spoke of a vow or a prayer. Could she truly care so much for him?

He set that thought aside and stroked her hair, holding her close. "I will set this to rights, Mary," he said. "There will be no duel."

Chapter 9

Mary's mind was fairly spinning from all that had transpired in the few hours that had passed between yesterday afternoon and this morning. First Lord Harley's unexpected proposal, followed closely by Daniel's arrival and his totally surprising, completely exhilarating offer for her. She was quite certain that Daniel would be able to convince Lord Harley to cease his animosity. He was able to convince her to become his wife, wasn't he?

She recalled his kisses with a delicate shudder, closing her eyes as she imagined his beautiful mouth pressed to hers.

"Oh, Mary!" her mother cried, hurrying into the room. "Your father has just told me of your betrothal and I can scarcely believe it."

Mary started, unable to keep from smiling at her mother's obvious delight.

"Yes, Mother. I find it a bit surprising myself."

"Nonsense, child," Lady Bridgewater said with a wave of her hand. "How could the gentleman not wish you to be his wife? I had thought that Lord Harley would be the victor, but then again I've been wrong about the romantic intentions of both of your sisters. Why should I be anything else regarding yours?"

Mary nodded and opened her mouth to make a response.

"Oh, and to think that the first gentleman wishes to fight for you!" the older woman went on with enthusiasm. "It is quite a testament to your appeal to have two such eligible men fighting for the honor of having your hand, I daresay."

"Don't give that another thought, Mother," Mary chided. "Daniel has given me his word that no duel will take place and I believe him."

Mary's mother waved her hand again. "Oh, I suppose that is for the best, but what a notion to consider even for the briefest moment."

Mary rolled her eyes heavenward. Thankfully her mother soon began to speak of the nuptials. Mary allowed her mother to lead her to the front sitting room, instructing her on the compilation of a guest list. They would marry from Bridgewater Park in Somersetshire, for the estate was the perfect setting for such a celebration. Daniel would have to procure a special license, since his estate and holdings were situated in Newcastle. The fall would be a must fitting time for the wedding to take place, her mother went on. The Season would conclude in but a week's time so they had much to do in order to settle the date for the nuptials.

Mary set the image of her very dashing fiancé from her mind and sat herself at the small desk in the sitting room and picked up pen and paper, dutifully following her mother's instructions.

Jane helped Mary dress with the utmost care for the coming evening's round of parties. No doubt news of their engagement had begun to spread among the *ton*, if her mother's hastily-written announcements had reached the other matrons. But that wasn't why Mary paid more careful attention to her dress than usual. She was to be on Daniel's arm that evening, and it wouldn't do to be surpassed by her very handsome fiancé.

She sat before her vanity, clad in her best chemise and petticoat as Jane arranged her hair in an artful pile of curls. In her mind's eye she envisioned Daniel as he would look that evening. So tall and strong. So charming and handsome.

"Will Daniel berate me as he has at every other opportunity?"

"Certainly not, my lady."

"He wishes for me to be his wife, Jane. Doesn't that intimate that he now finds me very much to his liking?"

"Yes, my lady."

The maid finished with Mary's hair and went into the

dressing room to fetch her mistress' gown. Mary looked critically at her reflection one more time and found herself most acceptable. She rose and shook out her lacy skirts and stepped into the incredible gown of ivory satin which she'd selected that afternoon. It was sophisticated in cut and for once in this long Season Mary felt as though wearing such a daring dress was most fitting.

She was to be a married woman soon, she reasoned, and no longer did she feel like a silly young girl just out. She stood before the cheval mirror and stared at the expanse of skin visible above the low bodice of the gown.

"Perhaps I should change into one of my other dresses after all."

"Why, my lady?"

"It shows more of my bosom than I recall from its final fitting. What will Lord Ashworth say?"

Jane said nothing to that, but just shook her head.

"There is nothing else for it, I suppose." She looked at the clock on the bedstand. "Oh, I'm late again!"

She pulled on her long satin gloves and hurried downstairs. She found Betsy and Michael awaiting her in the foyer, Michael gazing at her with a look of mild exasperation as his wife clicked her tongue.

"Again, you leave us waiting," Betsy said without anger.

"I'm sorry, sister," Mary said, her breath coming fast. "I had much to consider this evening."

"Yes," Michael said. "We've heard of your betrothal. Most surprising, if not totally unexpected."

Betsy nodded vigorously. "Lord Ashworth is most eligible, Mary. And frightfully handsome, I daresay."

Michael arched a black brow at his wife in mock censure. Betsy laughed gaily and took his arm.

"Don't scowl so, husband," she said. "You know that I much prefer large, dark gentlemen to fair ones."

Michael shook his head at her, a smile teasing his lips.

"Now," Betsy said, turning to her little sister. "Pray tell us what delayed you on this particular evening?"

Mary sighed and told her sister the tale of the provocative gown.

***

Daniel found Harley at White's. He sat alone at a table playing a game of Patience, the cards spread in front of him as he drank deeply from the bottle of brandy at his side.

"Harley," Daniel said, his voice low.

Harley looked up from his game, staring vacantly at Daniel for a moment. That vacancy was gone in the next moment, replaced by visible anger.

He came to his feet. "Ashworth, you bastard."

Daniel looked quickly about the room and found the other gentlemen in attendance gazing at them in curiosity. He took a breath and approached Harley's table. "Do sit, friend."

Harley grasped his meaning and sat, his face set in a frown. "How dare you address me so. After what you did to me this very day? Your impudence astounds me."

Daniel sat across from him, folding his hands on top of the table. "What precisely did I do to you?"

"Don't be obtuse," Harley bit out. "You took the woman I chose as my bride, you scoundrel."

Daniel shook his head. "She's mine, Harley. And the fact that you asked for her first won't change that."

Harley seethed but to Daniel's relief he had obviously decided it wise not to make a scene there at the club.

"This isn't over, Ashworth." He leaned toward him. "You will meet me."

"I will not."

Harley pulled back, blinking his surprise. "How can you

deny me?"

Daniel shook his head. "I won't be party to such an abomination," he said. "I've given Mary my word and I intend to keep it."

Harley grunted and ran his hand over his face. "I shouldn't have made the challenge. I realize now that it would only serve to remind you of your brother."

Daniel nodded, his throat tight. "You're a good friend."

Harley signaled for a waiter and asked for another glass. He poured Daniel a brandy and himself another.

"So you've won her," Harley said, taking a long sip.

Daniel lifted his glass and leaned back in his chair. "Do you love her?"

"Ah, I don't know. Do you love her, Ashworth?"

Daniel shrugged his shoulders. "I can't put into words what precisely it is that I feel for her. But I can tell you this, friend. I think of her as far more than a beautiful woman to dress my arm and warm my bed."

Harley nodded. "She cares for you."

"However do you arrive at that opinion?"

Harley chuckled. "I saw her after I hit you, you sod. She rushed to your side, all tenderness and concern."

Daniel pondered that as he left to meet his intended's family at the Earl of Bridgewater's townhouse.

"I had thought that this dress was suitable," Mary said as Daniel stepped into the entry of Lord Bridgewater's townhouse.

"That dress is more than suitable," he said.

Mary whirled toward him in surprise. "Daniel!"

Daniel smiled and stepped toward her. "I thought to escort you to the bashes this evening, bride."

"Good evening, Ashworth," Balsam said, shaking Daniel's hand. "Congratulations are in order."

"Oh yes," Lady Balsam said. "Congratulations."

Daniel bowed. "Thank you, Lady Balsam."

"Please, call me Betsy."

Daniel nodded his consent, turning to face his intended. "Are you ready to go, love? I brought my carriage."

Mary blinked up at him. "Just you and I?"

Daniel took her hand. "Surely you're not afraid to be alone with me, your intended?" he teased.

She gave a slight shake of her head, waving her hand dismissively. "Of course not."

Daniel cocked his head to the side and considered her for a moment. She was breathtaking in the ivory gown. Very suitable, indeed. A secret smile curved her lips and he felt a flash of heat.

Taking her elbow he escorted her from the townhouse and into his waiting carriage. He sat across from her as the carriage began to move, ease in his demeanor. Mary ran her hands over her skirt, keeping her eyes downcast.

"You seem a bit out-of-sorts," he said.

Mary smiled shakily. "I cannot help but be reminded of the last time I was a passenger in your carriage, Daniel."

Daniel chuckled. "Ah, your rescue from the public house. I was a bit churlish, wasn't I?" he asked, using her words from that evening.

Mary laughed lightly, nodding. This ride was far more comfortable than that one had been. Had it only been a few weeks since that night? Amazing.

When they arrived at the bash it was in full swing. The space was much more crowded than the Winston ball of a few weeks earlier and Daniel had to shoulder his way through the throng of party-goers to greet their hostess. Mary's hand was firmly grasped in his as he pulled her along behind him. The hostess was an elderly matron who ran a practiced eye over Mary, finally giving the young couple a firm nod of approval. The fact that the matron's daughters were well settled and not in the market for a handsome young husband surely did not hinder matters.

Daniel accepted the matron's approval with good grace and led Mary into the ballroom. They soon found themselves surrounded by gentlemen, all of them eager to offer their congratulations to Daniel and to openly ogle his bride-to-be.

"My God, Ashworth," one of the men joked. "You are one lucky... Oh, excuse me, Lady Mary."

Mary hid her smile and gave the man a nod.

"We were most surprised when Harley told us of your betrothal to this rogue, Lady Mary," another man said.

"Lord Harley told you of it?" she asked in surprise.

"Yes," another laughingly put in. "And he only seemed the slightest bit jealous, unlike most of us."

Daniel managed a laugh at that, irritated with his friends' close scrutiny of her person. Her dress, of which he had so readily approved in her parents' home, was now the object of ravenous contemplation. And more than one pair of eyes fastened to the expanse of creamy flesh visible above the dress's bodice.

"Daniel," she said softly, taking his arm.

Daniel turned to her and she gave him a slight nod.

"You will excuse us, gentlemen." He placed Mary's hand on his arm. "My lady desires a dance."

Daniel led her onto the crowded dance floor and placed his hand on her waist. Wrapped in each other's arms they began to sway together to the music, capturing the easy movements of their first dance weeks earlier. Mary sighed and leaned back to gaze up at him.

"I do so love to dance with you, Daniel."

He held her a bit closer than was proper, letting his legs touch hers as they moved through the dance. His eyes caressed her form.

"My God, love," he whispered, pressing her to him. "This dress is..." He had no words.

"A shining example of high fashion?" she offered, her head tipped to one side.

He growled playfully at her and she laughed lightly.

"Never mind," he said, shaking his head. "But I believe you will be dancing with none other than myself this evening."

Mary shrugged her slight shoulders, inclining her head toward the other end of the ballroom where Daniel's friends stood watching most intently.

"I believe your friends may have other notions."

Her easy words irked him. "Pray tell me, bride," he said, his voice low. "Do you think to dance with one gentleman after another even though we're now betrothed?"

Mary's eyes widened in surprise at his outburst. "I was merely making conversation."

"Forgive me. I meant nothing by such words."

Mary nodded and followed him through the remainder of the dance, her expression set. Daniel said no more of the other gentlemen wishing to take her in their arms, keeping his conversation restricted to the subjects of the gathering and the music and the supper awaiting them. Mary answered him in a fashion, nodding in the appropriate places. She kept her eyes downcast as they moved effortlessly to the music.

When he placed his fingers beneath her chin and gently tiled her face up to his, she studied him. He supposed she was searching for a sign of his anger. She smiled, however. It was a small expression, but genuine nonetheless.

Daniel returned it as they continued through the dance.

Chapter 10

Daniel left her seated safely with her sisters and headed to the refreshment table. He found Wilton and Balsam standing there, and greeted his future brothers-in-law.

"Good evening, Wilton. Balsam."

"Ashworth," Michael said with a smile. "How are you faring?"

Daniel rolled his eyes heavenward. "I'm relieved to be in your company at this moment, gentlemen."

Wilton laughed heartily.

"Pray, tell me what has you so amused?" Daniel asked.

"I remember well the circumstances surrounding Maggie's introduction as my own when we were first in town, Ashworth. I wanted to pound every man who came within ten feet of her."

"Yes," Michael said. "It's not always easy to love a Bridgewater woman."

"Love?" Daniel repeated.

Wilton and Balsam exchanged a puzzled look, further confounding Daniel.

"I'm sorry, Ashworth," Balsam said. "I'd assumed that when you spoke to the earl he posed the question to you."

Daniel's brow furrowed as he thought about his puzzling

conversation with Mary's father.

"Bridgewater did ask about my feelings for her," he said. "But, why would such a gentleman care for such matters as love?"

"The earl is a bit unconventional in that respect," Wilton said.

"Yes," Balsam added. "And I thank God for that fact."

"What can you mean by that, Balsam?" Daniel asked.

"My financial situation," Balsam began in a low voice, "wasn't quite what I might have wished at the time I fell in love with my beautiful Betsy."

"Hmm," Daniel mused aloud. "I'd wondered why Bridgewater didn't question me more thoroughly on that matter myself."

"He cares more for other matters, Ashworth," Wilton said. "But surely he wished to know of your attachment to his youngest daughter?"

Daniel grew quiet, unwilling to speak of love as if it were a valid fact, like his ledgers or properties.

"I made him no vow on the subject," was all he would say.

The other two gentlemen drew back in surprise. Suddenly Wilton laughed and slapped Daniel on the back.

"Trust us on this. The earl believes that there is something to it if he so readily gave you Mary's lovely hand."

Daniel snorted and took two glasses of punch from the table, leaving his future brothers-in-law to follow in his wake. He could almost feel their eyes on him as he crossed the ballroom. He took long strides toward the place where Mary awaited him, pushing aside the maddening subject those two gentlemen spoke of with such ease.

He found Mary surrounded by several young ladies clad in gowns of different hues but swiftly dismissed them from his notice when she turned her face to him. How could he see another woman when his bride was sitting there wearing a beautiful smile that was surely meant only for him.

Mary's companions took note of Daniel's arrival and came swiftly to their feet, their skirts rustling.

"Good evening, Lord Ashworth," the girls said in unison, their voices high-pitched.

"Ladies," he said with a bow before turning to hand Mary a glass of punch.

He straightened and smiled at the young women, who promptly reddened and lowered their eyes. Giggling, they all dropped curtsies and left.

"Did you miss me, bride? You weren't lonely."

"They are quite taken with you, I daresay."

Daniel shook his head. "Well, they must accustom themselves to the fact that I am no longer available for their schemes. Let poor Harley and the others contend with them."

Mary nodded and threaded her arm through his.

"But what of those gentlemen, Daniel?"

Daniel refused to let his earlier anger resurface. Instead, he smiled down at her.

"They are well aware by this time that you belong to me."

When he led her out onto the terrace toward the end of the evening, he was pleased to note that the wariness was gone from her eyes. He stood behind her at the iron railing, her body close against his as on that long ago ride home from the park.

He lowered his head to her creamy shoulder, placing a lingering kiss there on the fragrant skin. "Are you enjoying your evening, love?"

"Mmm, yes," she sighed. "Are you?"

He simply shrugged.

She turned in his arms and placed her hands on his chest. "Daniel, I admit that I find this most diverting."

"Oh?"

Mary slanted him a look, her eyes sparkling. "Why, the very last time we found ourselves on a terrace such as this you were most angry with me."

Daniel nodded sagely. "I wasn't angry at you, Mary." At the skeptical click of her tongue he elaborated. "I was angry with the fat little fop who dared to touch what was mine."

Mary raised her brows. "You thought of me as yours so long ago?"

"I'm afraid that you were destined to be mine from the very moment you entered that grimy public house."

"You are teasing me."

"Not in the least, my lady." He grinned and spread his arms wide. "I surrender, love."

Mary laughed gaily. "And I surrender to you, Daniel."

He suddenly lost his grin as he imagined her spread beneath him, sweetly surrendering all that she had to him, her husband. He took her hand in his and drew her closer.

"I believe I've had enough of this assembly for one evening," he said. "Shall we go?"

***

Mary agreed, finding the notion of being alone with Daniel highly preferable to the crowded party. The heat that had come

123

into his velvet eyes made her heart beat faster and she found the sensation delicious. She'd seen no reemergence of his irritation as the evening had worn on, which led her to believe that she'd imagined its intensity on the dance floor. Why would he be angry with her? She had certainly given him no cause this time.

He'd been ever solicitous as they ate their meal in the crowded supper room, and ever gallant when she'd expressed her fatigue at the closeness of the ballroom afterwards. Smiling up at him, she followed him back into the ballroom in search of their host and hostess, eager to be free of the throng.

They soon found themselves comfortably settled in Daniel's carriage, bound for Mary's home. Daniel sat across from her as he had on their initial journey, but his eyes held the same intensity that she'd glimpsed on the terrace. Mary suddenly felt as if her skin was on fire where he let his gaze touch her.

"Mary love," he said, his voice low.

A delightful tingle coursing down her spine. "Yes?"

He shifted and came to sit beside her, a wicked grin curving his beautiful mouth. "Mary, you're mine."

His words filled her with an emotion to which she could not put a name. She raised her hand and boldly placed it on his cheek.

"And you're mine," she whispered.

He sucked in a breath. He placed a kiss in her palm, the gesture sweet and titillating at once. Suddenly he placed his hands on her waist and pulled her closer to him. He caught her gasp of surprise in his mouth, his tongue slipping in to tease hers. She touched her tongue to his, first timidly then with growing boldness. Daniel gave a moan and held her closer still. He moved his lips to her neck.

"Mary," he rasped, dropping kisses on her throat.

"Oh, Daniel," she sighed, letting her head fall back.

"Your skin is so soft." He breathed. "And you smell delicious."

Mary ran her fingers through his hair and let out a whimper, rubbing herself against him.

He eased her down onto the cushioned seat. "My God, you drive me mad."

His lips trailed over her throat to the swell of her breast, and his tongue ran lightly over her skin.

"Oh my," she gasped, her eyes on his beautiful mouth as he effortlessly set her on fire.

Daniel easily freed her breasts from their confinement in the low bodice of her gown and raised his head to stare at her.

Her breasts felt heavy, their tips straining toward what? she couldn't fathom.

"You're so beautiful," he whispered. "But then, I knew you would be."

Mary shivered as his eyes once more caressed her flesh. He bent his head again and flicked his tongue over one pink bud. She was stunned by the feelings he easily aroused within her, by the way her tender skin puckered with a pleasant tingle. He closed his mouth over her breast and she arched wildly beneath him.

"Daniel!" she cried.

Wrapping his arms around her waist, Daniel held her close as his mouth and tongue sought to devour her softness. Her skirts were soon pushed up around her waist as he tentatively touched her most private place.

"Mary," he said, bringing his lips to hers. "Ah, I want you."

Mary could scarcely think. His fingers were still stroking her, causing the most delicious bursts of pleasure. The carriage gave a lurch and he sat up to glance out the window.

"We're not at your home as yet." He ran his fingers through his hair and gazed down at her. Her legs were across his lap, her skirts a froth of petticoats around her waist. Her breasts were bare and seemed to ache for the return of his touch.

"Mary," he said again.

"Yes?" she murmured, a smile curving her lips.

She was weak with wanting. Pliable in his arms and completely at his mercy.

He reached for her skirts and covered her legs, letting out a groan of frustration. She realized her position then and quickly covered her breasts with her hands. He helped her to a sitting position and averted his eyes while she adjusted her dress.

"Oh, my."

"Forgive me," he said, his voice harsh with wanting.

Mary slanted him a look as she brushed her hands over her skirt. "Are you angry with me?"

"What?"

"Because I permitted you such liberties?"

He laughed and shook his head, taking her hand in his. "What you're seeing, love, is a man who very much desires to make his bride his own. This very night."

Mary blinked in confusion. Daniel took her hand and placed it on himself, gritting his teeth as her fingers twitched.

"You're in pain," she said.

He shook his head, groaning softly as she stroked him. "This was precisely the reaction I had at the Winston bash, Mary. When you reached beneath that table and set me on fire."

"Oh! You must be feeling what I did when your fingers were on my most private place."

Daniel nodded. She stared at the bulge in his breeches, very intrigued by the hard ridge beneath her fingertips.

"Enough," he ground out, taking her hand from him. "You will kill me."

Mary snatched her hand away. "You're very different from me, Daniel."

"It will probably be the death of me, but I'll restrain myself from showing you just how much we differ until our wedding night."

Mary nodded and came to sit beside him once more. She folded her legs beneath her and rested her head on his shoulder. Daniel placed his arm around her and dropped a kiss on her temple.

"Our wedding night," she mused aloud. "Amazing."

"Precisely how soon can we expect the nuptials to take place?"

Mary laughed lightly. "My mother insists upon the fall as

the most favorable season for weddings at Bridgewater Park."

"The fall? I'll surely die before then."

Mary nodded, her body still craving his touch.

Chapter 11

Daniel met with the Earl of Bridgewater and worked through the particulars of the marriage contract the next afternoon. The wedding would take place soon after the Season concluded on August twelfth, the exact date to be set upon shortly. Daniel consoled himself with the fact that he would have to wait no longer than a month's time to make Mary his wife, as it was now nearly the end of July. He would procure a special license, and all would be in readiness before the Season concluded.

"And what of your uncle, Ashworth?" the earl asked Daniel. "Can we expect the marquis to attend the nuptials?"

"I would hard-pressed to keep him from them, sir," he said. "It has been the man's most adamant wish for many months now."

"Will he be pleased with your choice, do you wager?"

"How could he not?" Daniel said with a grin.

The two gentlemen then discussed the issue of Mary's dowry, and Daniel was not surprised to learn that it was quite large. It would no doubt serve to expand his properties in Newcastle, going toward the upkeep and development of the many coal mines on his land. And he would use her money to build on their children's inheritance.

Children. Perhaps a strong boy to inherit the title. Or a beautiful girl to dower. He smiled to himself as the image of a girl as lovely as his wife, with her penchant for getting into trouble, flitted through his mind.

The gentlemen concluded their business and Daniel bade the earl good day. He left the study in search of his bride. He found her in the courtyard behind the townhouse, sitting on an iron bench set among several vibrantly-blooming rose bushes. Her hair was upswept, loose tendrils of spun gold framing her face. Her day dress of white sprigged with yellow flowers was most becoming. This lovely creature was to be his bride? Lord, he would have to keep her close. No doubt the many gentlemen with whom they would socialize in Newcastle would find her most fitting a conquest.

"Hello, love," he said, causing her to lift her head.

A bright smile lit her countenance. "Daniel! Have you concluded your business with Father?"

"Do you mean to ask me if have I accepted your most generous dowry?"

Mary shrugged her slight shoulders and bade him to sit beside her. The bench was in a beautiful situation, nearly hidden at one side of the lovely summer-bright garden.

"Then all is in readiness, Daniel?"

Daniel nodded and took her hand in his, threading her delicate fingers through his. "We'll have to find a use for such an exorbitant sum." He kissed her fingers. "Perhaps I can convince Balsam and Wilton to sell us several of their finest horses. What do you think of that?"

Mary's smile widened. His suggestion seemed most fitting to him in that moment. The thought of Mary perched regally on one of the fine animals, riding beside him over the grounds of his estate, filled him with an odd sense of contentment.

"Oh, that would be wonderful," Mary answered, unconsciously echoing his own thoughts. "But pray, do not purchase the filly that I rode into the park."

Daniel chuckled. "I, for one, am most grateful to that spirited animal."

Mary cocked her head to one side, a smile teasing her lips. "And why is that?"

"If that horse hadn't abandoned you in the wilds on that particular afternoon, I would have been cheated out of my first taste of these delectable lips."

Mary sighed as Daniel brought his mouth to hers. He

nibbled her lower lip, tracing his tongue over the tender flesh.

"Mmm, I do love to kiss you," he said. "You taste so sweet."

Mary wrapped her arms around his neck and returned his kiss full measure. He pressed her to him and tasted deeply of her, delighting in the little whimper she made in the back of her throat as their tongues touched. His body was taut with desire as the memory of what had transpired in his carriage the night before came rushing back to him. She seemed as eager for him now, her body pressed against him as she ran her fingers through his hair. He lifted his head and held her away from him, taking a deep calming breath.

"August cannot arrive soon enough for my sanity."

Mary nodded, her kiss-swollen lips curved in a smile. She suddenly grew pensive, her brow slightly furrowed.

"What's troubling you, Mary?"

"I don't know if I'll please you." She dropped her gaze to her lap. "I know nothing of the marriage bed," she whispered. "I'm woefully inexperienced in such matters."

He laughed softly. "I should hope so." At Mary's answering frown he smiled at her and grasped her shoulders again. "You'll please me, love. I have no doubts about the matter. If you simply do what feels good to you, sweetheart? It will please me immensely."

Mary placed her hands on his chest, toying with the buttons of his waistcoat. "But you've known so many women, Daniel."

"I've known no more women than any other gentleman of my age and station."

"Truly?" she asked, her eyes round. "Do you mean to say gentlemen like Lord Harley, as well?"

"Harley has enjoyed at least as many women as I have," he said. "Perhaps more."

Mary was thoughtful for a moment. "Even Lords Stokes and Grimsby?"

Daniel laughed out loud. "I supposed there are women who favor stuttering sticks and fat little fops."

Mary swatted his arm and laughed sweetly. Daniel drew her closer, one arm draped over her shoulders.

"We are a splendid match, love," he said. "The way you responded to me in my carriage last night?" He let out a low whistle. "Trust me on this, Mary. We are indeed a splendid match."

Mary's cheeks reddened but she did nod her agreement,

lifting her face to place her lips on his. The sound of voices stilled her. She and Daniel exchanged a glance as the source of the sounds became evident to them, coming from the open doors of the parlor at the back of the townhouse.

"They are in the garden, Michael. You must do something."

"Pray tell me, wife. What do you wish me to do?"

"Stop them! They mustn't... oh, you know my meaning."

Wise woman, Daniel thought. The thought of making Mary his in the lush garden had more than crossed his mind that afternoon. He fancied that he could imagine Balsam's silent mockery of his wife's assertions, however.

Mary covered her mouth to restrain her giggles as Daniel shook his head at her, his own lips twitching.

"Betsy, how can you believe that Ashworth would compromise her?"

"I've seen the way he looks at her, Michael. The look greatly resembles that of a certain gentleman of my own acquaintance."

Balsam' laughter was heard again.

"Stop that," his wife said. "This is no laughing matter. It won't do for my sister to be deflowered in her parents' garden!"

Mary's mouth was an O of surprise. She turned her eyes to Daniel and he found the speculation in their violet depths most interesting. The couple in the parlor drew his attention once more.

"If memory serves, you were deflowered in your parents' stables."

Mary and Daniel both laughed out loud at that, drawing the couple's attention at last. The lady's gasp was heard, along with a burst of masculine laughter from her husband. They turned as Lord and Lady Balsam strolled into the garden, the former all but dragging the latter to where Mary and Daniel sat.

"Hello, Ashworth," Balsam said. "Mary."

"Hello, Balsam," Daniel said, coming to his feet to bow to the man's wife.

"Betsy has a few concerns, Ashworth," Michael said. "Perhaps you can set her mind at ease."

"You are incorrigible," Lady Balsam scolded. "Come Mary. Mother has informed me that the seamstress is coming this afternoon and she has need to discuss the trousseau with you."

Mary came to her feet, brushing her hands over her skirts. After assuring her that he would see her before he took his leave,

Daniel kissed her lightly on her cheek and watched as the two women went into the house. When he turned back to Balsam he found the speculation on his face at bit surprising, given what he had overheard of the man's discussion with his wife.

"May I ask what has you so captivated, Balsam?"

"Is my wife correct in her assumptions, Ashworth?" he asked, all humor gone from his tone. "Did you plan to compromise our little sister, here in her parents' home?"

Daniel felt a glimmer of pique, but allowed that in the man's place he too would expect Mary's betrothed to wish to precede his wedding night. To love Mary thoroughly there among the rose bushes was an appealing thought indeed.

"I would never shame her, Balsam."

Balsam regarded him closely for a moment, finally nodding his belief. Daniel breathed a sigh of relief and asked him if he would like to join him at White's for a game or two of cards. Balsam concurred and they left in search of Mary and Betsy to advise them of their whereabouts.

The gentlemen then passed the afternoon in a most pleasant and diverting fashion, giving no further discussion to the topic of Mary's virtue and Daniel's desire to rid her of it.

***

Mary headed over to Daniel's townhouse, determination in her breast. She'd received a missive just this morning, and had abandoned her wedding preparations to see to this particular pressing matter.

Daniel's butler had admitted her, and then quickly disappeared toward the back of the house.

"You're leaving me?" Mary demanded to know, bursting into Daniel's study.

"Mary," Daniel began, rising from his chair behind the desk. "I'm leaving for Newcastle in two days, yes."

"And this is how I learn of your defection?" she asked, brandishing the note he'd sent that morning.

"I'm only going to my uncle's, love," he assured her. "And then on to Ashworth Hall. I'll be gone for no more than a week."

"A week?" she repeated. "Why would you have need to keep yourself from me for a week?"

"Mary," he said, coming around the desk to stand before her. "I'm going to Newcastle to see several matters settled before our wedding."

Placing his index finger under her chin, he lifted her face and studied her for a moment. "I've never seen you wear a pout." He rubbed his thumb over her lower lip. "I find it most fetching."

Mary snorted and turned from him, her arms crossed in front of her. "Already you tire of me."

He placed his hands on her shoulders and rubbed gently. "I'm only going to visit my uncle, love," he said again. "The Marquis of Darlington. I wish to inform him of our impending nuptials in person."

She turned to face him. "And yet you inform me of your plans in one terse little letter?"

He laughed lightly. "All right, perhaps that was not well done of me. But I meant no disrespect."

He wrapped her in his arms, resting his chin on top of her head. "There's much that must be done before I can take you to Ashworth Hall, love. The place must be made ready for the installation of its mistress, no?"

Mary shrugged dismissively. "But a week, Daniel? Surely your home isn't in such disrepair to warrant your attentions for that long?"

"Hardly." He chuckled. "But I must see to the tenants. And I must ascertain that the coal mines are in operation to my satisfaction."

Mary was unmoved, but then a dark thought occurred to

her. "You are going to see a woman," she said. "You must disentangle yourself from your mistress!"

"I have no mistress, Mary."

Mary scoffed. "Are there truly no lovely widows in that county, ready to see to your needs? No bored wives eager for a new man in their bed?"

He drew back. "Who has been filling your head with this? It's true I've never hidden myself from the prying eyes of society here in town, a fact which I now regret. But I carry myself like a gentleman at all times and I do not take liberties with my neighbors in the country. Nor with their wives."

Mary sighed and hugged herself. "I cannot bear this, Daniel," she said softly. "You've known so many women."

"Mary," he said, wrapping his arms around her once more. "I assured you when you accepted me that I would keep myself to only you, and most happily. But I assure you now that I have had fewer lovers over the years than you have had suitors in this lone Season."

Mary stared up into his eyes and knew he spoke the truth. "I suppose there have been many gentlemen courting me."

"But none have even kissed you, isn't that correct?" he asked with a smile. "Save for that fat fop, Grimsby?"

"Yes," she said. "And Lord Harley."

"Harley kissed you?"

Mary blinked up at him in surprise. "Lord Harley asked for my hand in marriage, Daniel. He kissed me that afternoon. It was not my first kiss, as you well know. You took that liberty in the park."

Daniel's dark velvet eyes glittered and she braced herself for more of his censure. To her shock and pleasure, he reached for her and brushed his fingers over her cheek in a surprisingly gentle caress.

Chapter 12

"And did you favor his kisses?" Daniel asked her with a curl to his lips. "Did you tease him as you do me now?"

"It was but one kiss."

"Did he taste you?" he asked, his voice low. "Did you welcome him as you do me now?"

She shook her head, her curls swaying about her flushed face. Daniel nodded his satisfaction and pressed his mouth to hers, hard. She opened beneath him, welcoming his tongue. She wrapped her arms around his waist, pressing herself against him. He moaned softly and ran his hands over her back, his lips trailing over her throat.

"Ah Mary," he rasped, moving his hands to her round bottom.

Mary gasped as he lifted her against him, cuddling his arousal with her hips. He lifted her and placed her on top of his desk, sending several papers fluttering to the floor. He stood between her legs, pressing against her through the skirt of her pretty blue day dress.

"My God," he ground out, pressing closer still.

He fancied that he could feel the heat of her through her skirt and petticoat. Lowering her to the desk top he began to unfasten those pearl buttons at her bodice that he'd thought so charming when she'd burst unannounced into his study. Her breasts beckoned for his touch, straining at the thin lawn of her chemise. A quick flick of his wrist untied the white satin ribbon holding the undergarment closed, freeing her to his eyes, his lips.

"Mary," he said in awe, closing his mouth over one nipple. Her back arched as he teased her with his tongue.

"Oh, Daniel!"

He reached beneath her skirts and found her hot and moist beneath her thin drawers. Straightening, he swiftly removed her drawers and placed his mouth on her. He nearly died from the taste of her. She tasted almost as sweet as her beautiful mouth. When she gasped in shock, stiffening beneath him, he raised his head. He cursed himself for a clod and kissed her mouth.

"Forgive me, love," he said on a breath. "You're not ready for such an intimacy."

Mary met his gaze, her eyes wide as she shook her head. He let out a breath and brought his mouth to her breasts once more. His fingers found her as his mouth had, first one than two as he felt her dampness grow. She was so small. So hot. He pressed deeper still until he found the proof of her virginity. Its presence filled him with an indefinable emotion, causing him to shake even as he grew painfully hard. He found the tiny nub of her desire then, working it expertly with his thumb.

"Daniel," Mary gasped, her head thrashing on the smooth desk top. "What is happening?"

He kissed her again, catching her tiny cries of growing pleasure in his mouth as he increased the pressure of his fingers. Mary stiffened again beneath him, but only for a split second. She arched wildly as her very first climax tore through her body, sobbing with the strength of it. Daniel groaned as she found her release, filled to bursting as he longed to plunge into her and breach her maidenhead. He shook with the strength of his desire as he valiantly held onto his control.

Mary calmed at last, staring up at him in shock. He withdrew his hand from her and kissed her tenderly as he closed her dress over her beautiful breasts. He helped her to a sitting position, holding her close to him.

"Ah, Mary," he said, his voice rough. "You were beautiful in your release."

She was quiet for a long moment. "I don't understand, Daniel," she said at last, her attention focused on his waistcoat.

He dropped a kiss on her wildly tousled hair. "That was your first taste of pleasure, love," he said in a low voice. "Tell me. What did you think of it?"

Mary blushed even as she smiled at him. Her brow furrowed suddenly. "I am no longer pure."

He shook his head. "I assure you, you're still pure. I left your maidenhead intact."

Mary's blush deepened. "How can you speak so easily of such matters?"

He shrugged at that. Mary cuddled against him, drawing back as she became aware of his arousal.

"You're still quite…agitated."

Daniel laughed shakily. "I didn't take you, love," he said. "But that doesn't mean that my desire for you has ebbed."

As she trailed her fingers over his waistcoat to the waistband of his breeches he marveled over the thoughtful look on her flushed face.

"Do you wish for me to give you pleasure as you did me?" she asked in a whisper.

At her words he groaned, shaking his head. He couldn't get any words to pass through his constricted throat.

"You'll need to show me," she said, her fingers tantalizingly close to the focus of her attention.

"God, no," he breathed, taking her hand in his. "No. I will

surely disgrace myself if you so much as touch me now."

Mary blinked up at him and he let out a strangled laugh at the bewilderment on her face.

"Give me a few moments to collect myself," he said, taking a deep breath. "Here, let me help you down."

Mary slid off of the desk and stood on shaking legs. She shook out her skirts and looked at him expectantly. Daniel smiled widely at her appearance, thinking that she looked tousled and well-loved, and utterly sensual. She wore her awakening to passion on her beautiful face. Her rosy lips were slightly swollen, and her violet eyes were a bit out of focus.

"Let me pour you a brandy," he said at last, thinking that a drink would no doubt serve to brace him as well.

She drank no more than a few sips from his glass. He drew her to him and kissed her lightly, tasting both the fine liquor and her own unique sweetness.

"Will you permit me now to go to Newcastle, love?" he asked her with a crooked grin.

Mary smiled and nodded, still apparently a bit befuddled.

"But for no longer than three days, Daniel."

"I will try my damnedest," he told her.

He arrived in Darlington at nightfall two days after the

incredible interlude with Mary in his study. He'd been hard-pressed to keep the memory of that afternoon at bay, and chose instead to ponder it fully on the long ride from London. Her sweet cries at the moment of her release still echoed in his mind, causing a wide grin to spread across his face even now. God, he was a lucky man to have found her. That thought sobered him. Was he being a fool as his brother had been? Would Mary prove as false a woman as Patrick's beloved Beatrice had?

No. He would keep her close, that was all there was to the matter. She would have no chance to stray from him. And if that meant that he had to keep her confined to their chambers, so be it.

He could certainly find enough to fill her time in the big bed in his rooms at Ashworth Hall. His grin firmly back in place, he emerged from the carriage and strode up the steps to his uncle's mansion, Darlington Court.

The place was immense and well-tended. Daniel was ushered in by a dour butler, the same man who had chased him all over the estate in those early years after he and Patrick had come to live with their uncle.

"Hello, Grady," Daniel said with a grin. "Is the marquis about?"

"It is late, my lord," Grady answered with a sniff. "We were not advised of your coming."

Daniel shrugged and slapped the thin old man on the back. "I assume he is installed in the back parlor, Grady?" he asked, striding through the marble entry. "No doubt a bottle of port at his elbow?"

The butler sniffed again and turned on his heel. Laughing lightly, Daniel went in search of his uncle. He did find the marquis ensconced in his magnificent study, wearing a dressing gown of deep green silk. He turned as Daniel entered the room, his dark eyes opened wide in surprise.

"Daniel my boy!" the marquis enthused, coming to his feet. "How is that you are here?"

"Hello, Uncle," Daniel smiled, shaking the man's hand.

His uncle sat himself back down in the wing chair and bade Daniel to join him in the chair opposite. Daniel did, running his eyes over the older gentleman. Save for the shock of thick white waves falling across his brow, the marquis still looked as dashing and capable as he had the day Daniel and Patrick had come to live with him.

"You look most fit, Uncle," he said, taking the offered glass of port from him.

The marquis waved his hand through the air impatiently. "You will not distract me, my boy," he said, his eyes intent. "Tell me why you are here."

Daniel sipped at his port, biding his time. At his uncle's soft growl of frustration he hid his smile.

"I'm getting married, Uncle," he said, setting his glass aside.

His uncle stared at him in utter shock. His dark eyes narrowed in Daniel's direction. "What have you done?" he asked, a white brow arched arrogantly, mirroring Daniel's much-used gesture.

"Whatever do you mean by that?"

"Have you found yourself in a predicament?"

Daniel shook his head at him. "I have not."

Daniel's uncle considered him for a moment, nodding at last. "Then please tell me about this girl that has at long last succeeded in dragging you to the altar."

Daniel drank down more of his port and smiled at his uncle. "She is a wonderful girl, Uncle," he told him. "Bright and sweet. And beautiful. My God, the girl is bloody beautiful."

The marquis leaned closer to Daniel, searching his face for what, Daniel could not wager a guess.

"What has happened to you, my boy?" he asked at last. "When last I mentioned the subject of matrimony to you, you blanched at the mere word."

"She has caught me, Uncle," he said with a grin. "And I believe that she has me precisely where I wish to be."

His uncle laughed heartily, pouring them each another glass of port. "So," he said, leaning back in his chair. "Tell me about this bloody beautiful girl that has captured you."

"She is the youngest daughter of the Earl of Bridgewater," he said. "And a sweeter girl does not exist. She is stubborn and troublesome and beautiful and she pleases me greatly."

That white eyebrow shot upward again.

"What is this?" the marquis rumbled, coming to his feet. "You've compromised the daughter of a peer? Have you taken leave of your senses, boy?"

"Easy, Uncle. I haven't shamed Mary. I would never do that to her."

The older gentleman nodded again, apparently satisfied. He settled back down. "Pray tell me then, boy," the marquis said, sipping from his glass. "What incentive drove you to propose to the girl?"

"I admit that my hand was forced," Daniel told him.

"Harley asked for her first."

"He did, did he? That rake," the marquis chuckled. "And you could not bear for your good friend to possess such a treasure?"

"She is mine, Uncle," Daniel said in earnest. "I would not let another have her, good friend or no."

"Then you care for her, do you?"

Daniel nodded in answer, his mind working. His uncle wore a most confounding look on his noble features, as if he was privy to a most interesting secret.

"What are you thinking, Uncle?"

Daniel's uncle leaned toward him. "We haven't spoken of it in many years, Daniel." His eyes grew soft. "I hadn't brought up the subject once, not even this winter when I was pressing you with such vehemence to marry."

Daniel studied his boot, feigning ignorance. "I don't know to what you are referring."

"Love, my boy," the marquis said. "Do you love this girl?"

Daniel stood and paced, walking toward the darkened windows that faced the formal gardens. He stared at the window, seeing nothing save for the brooding reflection staring back at him.

"I don't believe in love's existence, Uncle," he said at last. "I'm making Mary my wife and I'll be faithful to her. I care for her. That's all I will allow."

"Then please tell me more about this girl, Daniel," he said. "I must know more about this enchantress."

Daniel regained his good humor and turned back to the older gentleman. He then began to regale his uncle with several incredible stories regarding his beautiful bride-to-be.

"You are surely jesting, my boy!" the marquis later laughed. "A public house? Incredible."

"She does have a penchant for getting into mischief," Daniel chuckled. "I daresay that I began to fear that she would turn my hair as white as yours."

"An admirable state, I assure you," the marquis said, straightening. "The ladies find me devilishly attractive in these parts, I'll have you know."

"I presume that *you* will not find yourself in a predicament?"

His uncle laughed heartily and slapped Daniel on the back. When the hour grew late, Daniel accompanied his uncle up the grand staircase and settled himself in the chambers set aside for his personal use. He stripped and collapsed on the bed, his hands tucked behind his head. Staring up at the intricately-patterned ceiling above, he let his mind work.

His uncle's words still stung. As if Daniel would permit a nonexistent emotion like love cloud his mind. He wasn't like his brother. He would care for Mary and make her laugh and give her such pleasure that she would be weak with it. She would bear his children. But he would not weaken in his resolve. He would not let his heart get in the way of his mind. She would not betray him, either. Despite her beauty, and her affinity for getting into trouble, she would remain ever faithful. He fell asleep much later, his sleep dreamless.

As they shared their breakfast the next day, Daniel advised his uncle that he was leaving for Ashworth Hall.

"So soon, Daniel?" the marquis asked him, drinking his tea. "But you have only just arrived."

"It cannot be helped," Daniel said.

"Do you have much work awaiting you in Newcastle?"

Daniel chuckled then and set his napkin aside. "My betrothed extracted a promise from me, Uncle," he said. "I am to return to London in no less than three days. That doesn't give me much time to dawdle, now does it?"

The marquis laughed and shook his white head. The

gentleman accompanied Daniel to the drive and bade him farewell with an admonition that he would watch the post carefully for his invitation to the impending nuptials.

Chapter 13

Mary stood in her chamber, fidgeting as the seamstress adjusted the hem of her wedding gown. She'd stood on the same little stool for what felt like days as the woman fashioned one gorgeous dress after another. Mary would have a complete trousseau, along with several riding habits and thick woolen cloaks. No doubt winter in Newcastle would be quite frigid and not at all what she was used to in the more temperate county of Somersetshire, or so her mother had told her.

Her wedding dress was a stunning creation. It was a froth of lace in an amazing shade of blush pink, embellished with countless beads and ribbons. It was decided that she would wear her hair piled elegantly upon her head, with ribbons of the same blush color taking the place of a wedding veil. Mary recognized that she should be thrilled to her toes to be wearing such a dress and she was pleased in a fashion, but her mind was far from her chamber. What was Daniel about? she wondered as she changed out of the wedding gown and into her wrapper at long last. Had he been able to complete his business? Was he even now on his way to town from his estate so far to the north?

She sighed and smiled absently as the seamstress took her leave and her lady's maid waited for her to sit before the vanity.

"Your gown will surpass any other girl's this Season, child," Lady Bridgewater told her.

Mary nodded dutifully as Jane began to brush her hair. What did any other girl's dress signify when she could scarcely give her own more than a passing thought?

"Your sisters will approve of the dress, I daresay," her mother went on. "I suppose that your very dashing groom will no doubt approve of it."

That statement drew Mary's full attention at last. Her heart skipped a beat as she imagined standing before Daniel in the beautiful pink gown. She knew that he would be wearing formal black for the ceremony, his jacket spanning his broad shoulders, his breeches hugging his long powerful legs. Lord, she was a lucky woman to have found him. She giggled suddenly, recalling precisely the manner in which she had found him. That inopportune trip to the public house was the best mistake she had ever made in her entire life!

"…Mary," her mother said, drawing her attention.

"Did you say something, Mother?"

Lady Bridgewater clicked her tongue and waved her hand dismissively.

"It is of no consequence," she said, walking toward the

door. "Why don't you take a nap, child? You seem preoccupied."

Mary blinked at her mother for a moment, and then smiled. The woman left and Jane finished with dressing Mary's hair.

At last alone, Mary leaned forward and studied her reflection. She'd tried to block the delicious memories of what had happened between them in his study, as she thought herself most wanton to revel in them. But she gave them more than a passing thought as she went through her daily routines or saw to the final wedding preparations. What he'd done to her!

She'd never imagined such pleasure could exist as that she'd felt on top of his desk. But when he'd put his mouth on her most private place? She'd been scandalized and titillated at the same time. Perhaps he would attempt such an intimacy on her again. She flushed hot at the prospect. And would he like it if she were to perform such an act upon him?

It was true that she was more than a bit curious about that part of his anatomy that she had yet to see with her own eyes. When she'd touched him through his breeches in his carriage, causing him to let out the most provocative moan, her heart had pounded in response. She must speak to Betsy. Surely her sister would be able to make sense about all of these matters. Mary knew she couldn't approach her mother about such a subject. She flushed again as she imagined how such a conversation would proceed. Shuddering, she squeezed her eyes shut.

She went downstairs to the front parlor, determination strong within her. Sitting herself behind a small desk, she took out paper and pen and wrote a note to her sister requesting her assistance in a pressing matter, along with an invitation to dinner as a postscript. She saw to the note's delivery and awaited her sister's response, hoping that Betsy would see fit to answer all of her questions once she, Mary, summoned the nerve to ask them.

She sat in her parents' garden that evening, stunned to her toes. Betsy was beside her on the bench, her voice barely above a whisper as she related precisely what would occur on Mary's wedding night.

"No," Mary murmured. "That cannot be."

Betsy smiled and patted her hand in reassurance. "Trust me, sister. It's so."

The image of her groom filled Mary's mind. She gasped and looked sharply at her sister.

"But Daniel is so big," Mary said.

"What?" Betsy asked, her brow furrowed. "However would you know about such matters? What have you done?"

"Nothing. Daniel is a big man, Betsy. It would only stand to reason that all of his manly parts would be likewise."

"Enough!" Betsy said, holding up one hand. "That's all we'll say on that particular subject, Mary."

Mary nodded at last, her mind still quite muddled. Another thought sprang to her mind, one which she'd heard discussed by the older married women when they hadn't been aware of her giving them the least bit of attention.

"But what of the pain, Betsy? I've heard whispers about horrific pain."

Betsy nodded sagely. "There is a bit of pain, Mary. But it's gone quickly, never to make its reappearance."

Mary nodded, relief flooding through her.

"And the bleeding?" she whispered.

Betsy clicked her tongue. "Who has been speaking to you?"

"No one, really."

"Yes," Betsy said then. "There is some bleeding, but it's to be expected. It's not of much duration, I assure you."

Mary shuddered and hugged herself. "Pain and bleeding. It's truly a wonder that anyone would have relations at all."

Betsy grinned with nary a blush on her smooth cheeks.

"Trust your husband to teach you, Mary. You'll find that relations are quite wonderful indeed."

Mary's mind flashed with the memory of her remarkable release under Daniel's expert attentions and she smiled at last. Perhaps he would wish to show her a bit more of pleasure before they take their vows as husband and wife? And perhaps she would like to give him his measure.

***

Daniel returned to his London home within the allotted three days, exhausted from the amount of work he'd accomplished in that short time. He brought a bit of it back with him, as he couldn't tear himself from all of his duties. But the most pressing was the swift return to his betrothed, and a more delicious obligation he couldn't imagine.

The hour was late and the traffic on the thoroughfares light as his carriage made its way to his townhouse. No doubt all and sundry were entertaining themselves at one of the last few bashes of the Season. He stretched with a soft groan and took up his papers, climbing the wide steps to his front door. His butler opened the door the moment he rapped upon it.

"Hello, Trimm," Daniel said with a weary smile.

"Welcome back, my lord," the butler returned with a bow.

Daniel nodded and turned to go into his study.

"My lord," Trimm called out, causing him to turn.

"Yes?" Daniel asked with a raised brow.

"You have a visitor."

"What is this?" Daniel wondered aloud. Monica wasn't here again, was she? "Who is it, Trimm?"

"Lady Mary Bridgewater, my lord," Trimm said. "She awaits you in the parlor."

Daniel left his papers on his desk in his study and went to the back of the house. He opened the door to the parlor and stepped in, an indefinable feeling hitting him as he glimpsed the room's lone occupant.

"Mary," he said with a slow smile.

"Three days, Daniel," Mary said, her hands on her hips. "You told me that you would return in three days."

"And I have," he said, coming to stand before her.

Mary stared up at him, her head cocked to one side. Her graceful brows were arched over her lovely eyes, her rosy lips were slightly pursed. He'd never before been more pleased to see someone in his life, even with the mild irritation stamped on those beautiful features.

"I didn't see your carriage outside, love. Pray tell me, how did you come here?"

She shrugged her shoulders. "I rode."

Daniel stiffened. "Alone?" he said in disbelief. "You rode here alone at this hour?"

Mary placed her hand on his chest and he couldn't deny the effect on him. He found that the flicker of anger was quickly extinguished, replaced by a flash of hunger.

"I've missed you," he rasped, cupping the back of her head. He drew her closer.

"I've missed you, Daniel."

He placed his lips on hers. Their kiss was sweet and hot and it made him want so much more. He raised his head and let out a breath. He urged her toward one of the oversized chairs beside the fireplace and sat, pulling her down beside him.

"What have you been about these three long days, love?" he asked, trying to divert his attention from the delectable body so close to his in the chair.

Mary looked down as her fingers lightly caressed his arm. "Tedious plans have occupied my days." She sighed. "And one gown fitting after another."

Daniel laughed lightly. "But is everything in readiness?"

"For the most part." She grew quiet then, much to his

surprise.

"Mary?" he said softly, turning to face her. "Is something troubling you? I returned within three days as promised. I gave you my word."

"Your word is very important to you, isn't it?"

Daniel studied her face. What was she about?

"Yes. A gentleman's word is his bond."

Mary leaned toward him, a secret smile curving her beautiful mouth. "I couldn't stop thinking about that afternoon in your study, Daniel," she said, pressing closer.

Daniel breathed in sharply as the memory of her sweet release came back to him. "You don't know what you're doing to me, love."

"I know. You've given your word."

Recognition dawned on Daniel in that moment.

"Ah. I gave you my word that I wouldn't take you until we're married, and I mean to hold to that."

Mary sighed and leaned close to him again. "But our wedding is not so very far away."

She placed her arms around his neck and pressed close to him. Daniel could feel every curve of her body where she touched his and he bit back a moan.

"Mary, have mercy on me."

"Please, Daniel," she said, kissing his ear. "There is so much more I want you to show me."

Daniel realized the absurdity of his situation in that moment. There he was in his parlor, alone with the girl he wanted above all others. She was sweetly asking him to take her, to show her all of the pleasure that awaited them and he was stalwartly refusing? He let out a laugh and Mary drew back, her brow furrowed.

"Do I amuse you?" she asked pointedly. "I know that I am far from experienced, but I didn't realize that you found me so diverting."

He drew her closer and rubbed his hands over her back. "Believe me, Mary. I don't find you amusing at this moment. Not in the least."

Mary snorted at that.

"The Lord knows that I have denied myself precious little in my life, sweetheart," he went on. "Please allow me to be noble in this?"

Mary stared up at him, finally nodding. He kissed her again, filled with that same maddening desire that threatened to swamp him whenever her lips touched his. She leaned her head back as he brushed his lips over her throat.

"Mary," he said softly, lifting his head.

"Oh, Daniel," she said, licking her lips as she arched toward him.

He kissed the hollow of her throat, and then ran his tongue over the soft skin above her bodice. When she instinctively shifted in the chair to straddle him he nearly lost all of his resolve. He placed his hands on her bottom and held her close for an instant, cursing softly as he held her from him in the next.

"We need to get you home. Where is your carriage?"

"I rode here," she breathed.

He cursed again at the recollection. "The hour is not so late that it would be unusual for me to give you a ride home." He came to his feet. "Come. I'll see your horse returned in the morning."

Mary nodded and took his offered hand. They sat in Daniel's carriage as it made its way through the dark streets, their hands intertwined. They cuddled closer together as the wheels rolled, and Daniel was more relieved than he could say when they finally stopped.

"Good night, love," he said, handing her out of the carriage.

Mary tilted her face up to his and accepted a kiss. She entered her parents' home and he prayed for strength of body to equal his strength of will.

Chapter 14

The Season concluded and Mary and her family left town for Somersetshire. Daniel had professed a touch of relief, to her amusement. He'd claimed that the torture of keeping true to his word was nearly driving him mad.

Mary stood in the front parlor at Bridgewater Park, wringing her hands in anticipation. Daniel was due to arrive this day, and she could barely contain her excitement at the prospect of seeing his beloved face again. The past week had all but crawled by in her estimation, her time littered with now-meaningless details regarding her wedding. She wished only to have the ceremony done with. For then she could lose herself in Daniel's strong arms and he could at last show her all that he'd promised.

The distant sound of a carriage drew her attention to the large windows fronting the drive. Her heart leapt as she spied Daniel's carriage through the still-green trees that lined the long drive. Unable to stop herself, she hurried to the entryway and pulled open the door.

She managed to rein in her enthusiasm by the time she'd descended down the first few wide stone steps, clasping her hands and fairly trembling to her toes as the carriage rolled to a stop before her. Lifting her chin, she glided down the remaining steps to stand beside the carriage.

The vehicle's door was opened and she watched with interest as a tall and dashing gentleman with wavy white hair stepped out. He took a measuring glance at her, and then a very familiar smile soon spreading across his face. Daniel soon unfolded his own tall frame from within the vehicle and stood beside the older gentleman, turning his beautiful dark eyes on her at last.

"Hello, Mary," he said, his smile bright. "Please allow me to introduce to my uncle to you. This is the Marquis of Darlington."

Mary managed to tear her gaze form her betrothed to smile graciously at his uncle. She dropped a low curtsy.

"A pleasure to meet you, Lord Darlington," she said.

She straightened and the marquis took her hand in his and brought it to his lips.

"Please, my dear," he said with a smile. "Do call me Uncle. It serves your intended well." He turned again to Daniel. "You are quite right, son. She is uncommonly beautiful."

Mary looked again at Daniel, thinking fancifully that her eyes had fairly ached to see his handsome face. And his eyes.

They held an intensity that made her shiver. Daniel's beautiful mouth drew her notice then, and suddenly she could hardly wait to taste his lips with her own. The marquis chuckled. Mary flushed, certain that the gentleman could read her thoughts in that moment. She looked quickly at Daniel, smiling despite herself as she glimpsed his crooked grin.

"Is your father about, Mary?" the marquis asked her. "I haven't seen Bridgewater in nearly a year."

Mary blinked, bringing her attention to Daniel's uncle once more. "Yes, sir," she said with a nod. "You'll find him in his study."

"No doubt hiding from the many females fluttering about the house in preparation of tomorrow's festivities?" the older man teased.

"You know a gentleman's sensibilities," Mary said with a smile.

He gave her a sprightly bow and nodded to Daniel. He took himself into the house.

"Mary," Daniel said in a low voice that caused her heart to race.

She looked at him, at the heat in his velvet eyes, and threw herself into his arms. He nimbly maneuvered her behind the carriage, effectively blocking them from the view of the many windows in the mansion's façade.

"My God, you smell good," he murmured as he buried his face in her hair.

Mary pressed herself against him, reveling in the feel of his hard body against her. "I've missed you, Daniel," she breathed as he kissed her throat.

"Mmm," he said, hugging her tightly. "And I you."

She leaned back to stare up at him. "Tomorrow."

"No doubt you're thinking about the delights of tomorrow's celebration. I admit that I am thinking of the delights awaiting us afterwards."

"I am, too," she said softly.

Daniel's brows shot up in surprise. "Minx."

She gave in to the notion that had seized her as she had gazed upon him moments earlier, darting her tongue in and out of his mouth. He pulled back for an instant, growling softly in the back of his throat as he tangled his tongue with hers.

He set her from him, his breath harsh in the still midday air. She took a deep breath and ran her hands over her hair to smooth a few loose curls back into the braids coiled at the back of her head.

"Come," he said, placing her arm through his. "Let's finish this day so that tomorrow can finally make its appearance."

Mary nodded, following him into the mansion on steps as light as air.

***

The day of the wedding dawned bright, much to the delight of all concerned. Most of the guests had arrived the previous evening to take their dinner with the Earl of Bridgewater's family, taking happy advantage of the celebration to relish a few days' visit at a magnificent estate situated in a lovely county. Mary and Daniel had scarcely a moment together, however.

When they at last retired for the evening however, Daniel had taken advantage of the fact that Mary's rooms were far from the wing housing the many guest rooms. He'd pressed her tightly to him, against the wall beside her chamber door, and once more told her all that they would share within twenty-four hours' time. The interested contemplation on her face, taken with her rapid breathing so sweet in his ears, nearly proved his undoing.

And now he stood in the parlor of the great house, thoughts of such carnal intent far from his mind as he mentally ticked off the minutes until Mary would become legally his.

Only the family would attend the service, performed by a

minister long connected to the Bridgewater family. In fact, the elder gentleman had joined both of Mary's sisters to their husbands in this very room. Daniel tugged at his cravat, mindful not to disturb its intricate folds, and stepped nervously from foot to foot. He glanced at his friends Balsam and Wilton, soon to be brothers-in-law, and scowled at the smug grins pasted on their faces. What had they to be nervous about, after all?

They were certain of their wives' devotion, and were known far and wide to be most fortunate in their choices of spouse. Their wives, though beautiful, did not possess Mary's radiance, or her penchant to attract the most unwelcome attention from gentlemen both cultured and not. Had he bothered to ask either gentleman of the number of suitors they'd had to fend off to make their wives their own, perhaps he would have found a bit of solace.

His mind turned from such dark musings as his wife's sisters came into the room. They soon stood beside their husbands and turned to face the entry of the parlor. Daniel looked in the same direction, an inexplicable feeling filling him as he spied his bride on her father's arm.

Her dress was remarkable, and nearly equal to the task of dressing such a vision. Her hair shone like golden fire, the many pink ribbons tied in it not detracting from its shine. But her eyes? Her eyes were deep and bright and filled with such tenderness as he'd never glimpsed before.

"Hello, Daniel," she said softly as her father left her side.

Daniel could say nothing, his throat tight. He nodded and spared her a small smile as he turned to face the minister. Their vows were recited and Daniel only assumed that he had said them properly, as he had no recollection of them once they were pronounced husband and wife. He did hear the man's admonition to kiss his bride, and did so with tenderness.

They accepted the congratulations of her family before adjourning into the ballroom where the guests were waiting for them. They managed to share a dance before others intruded on them, eyes only on each other as all assembled gave them a wide berth.

"Lady Ashworth," Daniel said, taking her hand in his as the music began.

Mary smiled brightly up at him, placing her free hand on his shoulder. "I so love dancing with you, Daniel," she said as they turned about the room. "Even that first time."

Daniel stared at her in puzzlement for a moment. "Ah, I recall that dance. The evening so soon after we met at the public house."

Mary nodded. "I didn't want to leave your arms that night," she admitted in a whisper.

"My arms wished to be free of you," he began, "as much as you wished to leave them."

Mary blinked, letting the realization that he had been as affected as she settled upon her. They finished their first dance and regretfully parted in deference to social demands.

Mary danced with her father while Daniel turned her mother about the floor. He danced with Mary's sisters as their husbands took turns twirling with Mary. Soon guests other than the familial took their turns with the lovely bride. Daniel stood not far from the dance floor, watching her closely. Lord, she was the most beautiful creature on God's earth.

"You love her, Daniel," the marquis said at his side.

Daniel turned to find the man smiling at him. "I care for her, Uncle. She is mine."

His uncle studied him closely, causing Daniel to bristle.

"May I ask what has you so absorbed?" he asked him shortly.

"You are not your brother, Daniel," the marquis said.

"I don't understand your meaning."

"And from what I see of your bride?" the man went on. "She is nothing like Beatrice."

Daniel looked again at Mary, at the beauty that nearly made him ache.

"She is beautiful, Uncle," he said. "More beautiful than even that witch had been."

"But she has a good heart, boy," the marquis said. "She must, to be so loved by such a wonderful family."

Daniel spared a quick glance about the room, his eyes easily finding the relatives of which his uncle spoke so highly. The man was right. The Bridgewaters were a warm family, as respectable as they were affectionate. But would that make a difference in a woman's true character?

He wouldn't think about that now. It was his wedding day and he would only think of the pleasure of finally making it known to all that Mary belonged to him in every way. Let the gentlemen assembled here dance her about the room. She would be leaving with the man she belonged to, body and soul.

He simply nodded at his uncle, who returned the gesture and left him to his musings.

Chapter 15

They thought to leave the celebration soon after sharing a sumptuous wedding dinner with their guests in the supper room. Mary changed into a traveling dress, leaving her remarkable wedding gown to the able hands of Jane as the maid prepared her mistress's personal effects for the long journey into Newcastle the next day. Mary and Daniel departed Bridgewater Park directly.

Daniel had secured rooms at a very elegant inn in Bath, a couple of hours from her parents' home. This would shorten their journey into Newcastle on the morrow, as well as afford him the privacy he so craved for their first night as husband and wife. He had real doubt as to his control regarding his finally making Mary his.

He recognized that the distance and indifference that had always accompanied him when he was with a woman was nowhere to be found when Mary was near. He had but to kiss her, and he was mad with desire to peel off her many elegant clothes and take her against the nearest wall. And what would happen when he had her in his arms tonight? When she was free of all of those clothes and his for the taking?

They arrived in Bath and Daniel assisted her from the

carriage and into the inn. As they were taken to their room, Mary wore an expression of surprise on her face.

"What do you think?" he asked when they were alone.

"It's most delightful, Daniel."

"It's no public house."

She laughed and went into the dressing room. When she stepped out several long minutes later, a pretty wrapper tied about her slender waist, he took a breath to steel himself. Her glorious curls were free from their pins and ribbons, and she looked like an angel. He'd left on his breeches, and knew from the tightness in his groin he would have scandalized her otherwise.

"Mary."

He crossed to her and took her hands in his. Mary lowered her eyes to the floor as he pulled her closer. That floral scent that clung to her had a heat to it now, and his blood pounded.

She raised her eyes to his and gave him a small smile. "I'm ready," she said softly.

He'd told her just last evening that he wished to examine her completely. Was that causing the apprehension he glimpsed in her expression? He held himself in check, but he longed to fully know her body from the top of her golden head to the tips of her rosy toes. While the words whispered warmly in her ear last night had caused her to tingle in anticipation, the prospect of Daniel's ridding her of the slight protection of the thin clothes now surely filled her with nervousness.

"You're ready? I am not," he said. "I wish to savor this night, love. We've denied ourselves far too long to rush our coming together."

She nodded as he brought his lips to hers. Their kiss was tender at first as he gently rubbed her lips with his. But soon he was kissing her deeply, bending her back over his arm. She gasped as he quickly divested her of her wrapper.

He said nothing of clarity at this moment. He could barely string two thoughts together as he pressed her so tightly to him that he could scarcely tell where he ended and she began.

She was soon flat on the bed, her nightgown a memory as he covered her body with his. He had to feel all of her against him. He stood and quickly peeled off his breeches. He was full to bursting, and every touch of her body against his sent his pulse higher.

She squeezed her eyes shut as he parted her legs. He knew he could make her abandon her unease. He knew she had passion in her lovely body. When his fingers found her, she was hot and wet and he let her sweet moans and sighs wash over him as she began her ascent toward that most delicious pleasure he'd given her that one time in his study.

But when his cock replaced his fingers, it was beyond amazing.

"Daniel," she gasped. "Daniel, please wait!"

He shook his head at her, his eyes closed tight. "I cannot," he rasped, leaning up on his arms. "God help me, I cannot!"

He drove through the thin barrier of her virginity, moving fast and furiously as passion spiked. She clutched at his arms as he moved above her, and he soon shuddered in his release, cries tearing from his throat as he poured himself into her.

***

When Daniel fell to her side on the pillow, his breath still coming fast, Mary calmed herself. The pain had eased, she realized with relief, and he no longer felt so large inside of her. She was decidedly wet however, no doubt with his seed. Her sister had been most descriptive in her tutelage, and Mary was relieved now that she'd had the foresight to ask her all of the particulars of making love and what she could expect.

Betsy had said nothing of this driving need in a man, however. She glanced at him then, noting that his eyes were still closed and his beautiful mouth was curved in a most satisfied smile.

"Daniel," she whispered.

Daniel merely mumbled in response, rubbing his cheek against the pillow.

"Daniel?" she asked a bit louder, poking his shoulder with one finger.

His eyes opened and he smiled lazily at her. "Forgive me, Mary." He shifted and came to rest on one elbow. "I don't know what came over me."

Mary had no notion of what to say to such a befuddling declaration. As he pulled out of her she winced.

"I'm a clod," he said as he kissed her. "Did I hurt you very badly, love?"

She shook her head and told him that the pain had all but disappeared. He wore his relief on his face and sat up beside her. He grabbed the large branch of candles, which still burned brightly as neither of them had taken a moment to douse them, and placed it on the bedstand.

"Let me have a look at you," he said, reaching for her.

"No!"

"Please, love," he said. "I need to see how badly you're

bleeding."

She closed her eyes in mortification as he examined her. He pronounced that the bleeding had been scant and rose to walk across the room to the washstand. She said nothing as he cleaned her with a cool wet cloth.

"There," he said as her blush deepened.

He rose and returned the cloth to the washbasin. When he returned to the bed, she had regained some of her composure. He stretched out beside her and took her hand in his, anxious to right what he perceived as a grievous wrong.

"I'm so sorry about that, Mary," he said, kissing her fingers. "I had every intention of going slowly with you. It's just that when I touched you, I went a bit mad."

Mary shrugged, her eyes downcast.

"You didn't find your pleasure." He blew out a breath. "I truly am a clod."

Mary stroked her fingers over his arm and turned onto her side to face him. "I began to," she said softly. "But then you... Well, you know what you did."

Daniel shook his head contritely. "I'll make this up to you." He deftly rolled her onto her back. "Put yourself into my capable hands. And my lips."

He kissed her then, tenderly. His mouth was like magic, trailing kisses over her throat to nibble on her breast. He closed his lips around one puckered nipple, sending sparks through her body. When he parted her legs and placed his clever mouth upon her, she writhed beneath him.

"Daniel!"

Daniel smiled as he lifted his head to gaze up at her. His eyes were hot and she trembled to see such desire. He returned to his task and held her tightly to him as he drove her toward her release. Sobbing as she gave herself up to him, her climax was so sweet and complete that she believed she would never forget the way he made her feel.

"My God," he whispered as he came up and kissed her. "You're incredible."

Mary opened her eyes and stared up at him. He kissed her again and covered her with his body.

"Are you terribly sore, love?"

Mary rubbed her toes against his legs and gave a shake of her head. "It's merely a twinge, Daniel."

"Thank God for that," he murmured as he kissed her again.

He entered her slowly, and she closed her eyes as she felt herself grasping every inch of him. As she tightened around him, so close to her second release, he increased his thrusts until she was as frantic as he was. She clutched at him, her legs squeezing him about his waist.

"Mary," he said, closing his eyes. "Ah, Mary,"

Mary grabbed him then, pulling him down to her for a deep kiss. His big body began to shake with his climax and she joined him in fulfillment, calling his name on a long sigh of release.

She came to her senses as Daniel collapsed beside her for the second time that night. She barely felt the pain she'd experienced at his entrance, and was now too tired to do more than wonder at the incredible pleasure he'd given her—not once but twice! He withdrew and she retrieved her nightgown from the floor, amazed that it was still in one piece considering the speed with which he'd divested her of it. She donned the nightgown and stood there for a long moment, gnawing on her thumbnail.

Rarely had she ever shared a bed with anyone, save for the few times when a dark dream had frightened her as a child and she'd gone to one of her sisters for comfort. Should she stay with him through the night? She'd heard that many husbands and wives maintained separate sleeping quarters, though neither of her sisters adhered to that custom. Had they been at Ashworth

Hall she would have any number of rooms to which to flee until the morning. But since Daniel had not secured any room save for this chamber and its adjoining sitting room, she had no choice but to spend the night sleeping beside him in the bed.

Hoping that he would not be distressed to find her sharing his space, she stretched out on the bed as far from him as she could manage considering how much of the bed he occupied. Turning away from him she settled into her pillow and wearily closed her eyes. Suddenly a strong arm wrapped around her waist and her eyes snapped open. Daniel pulled her toward him, curving his body to hers as he settled her close to him.

"Wife," he said, kissing her ear.

Mary said nothing, a strange feeling bubbling up inside of her at the satisfaction she heard in his voice.

She closed her eyes again, a smile curving her lips as she allowed herself to feel utterly cherished.

Chapter 16

The next day they rode into Newcastle, situated in the county of Northumberland. As they passed through the town of Newcastle, Mary noted that many of the shopkeepers and residents of the town proper came out to wave to the carriage. She caught bits and pieces of the exclamations from the townsfolk through the open window of the carriage. Some remarked on the great fortune to have the earl back in the country, while others wondered about the new countess. Congratulations rang out and Daniel was obliged to lift the window shade and wave at them, grinning ear-to-ear as he did so.

"Show us your bride, my lord!" one man shouted.

"Let us see the new countess!" said another man.

Daniel looked back at Mary, his brows raised in question. She nodded and took a moment to tuck her hair into her straw bonnet. She was grateful that she'd chosen a simple traveling dress today, topped with a favorite blue velvet spencer. Without Jane's assistance, her hair was simply dressed as well.

Daniel moved back and allowed her to lean out the window. She took a breath and waved one hand in a gesture of greeting, smiling at the curious people lining the cobblestone street.

"What beauty, Lord Ashworth." a woman said.

"You've chosen a most fitting countess," an older man said.

Mary bowed her head in thanks for their compliments and settled back against her seat, her cheeks warm. Daniel laughed lightly, pride as well as amusement evident in his wide smile.

"I believe the denizens much admire and respect you, Daniel," Mary said with a smile of her own.

Daniel nodded and waved once more out the window. He turned to face her again, stretching his long legs in the carriage.

"Ashworth Hall is situated just a few miles north of the village, Mary. The family has been very good to these people over the years. In fact, the hall employs many of them, as do the coal mines." He smiled crookedly, his eyes alight. "They feel quite a natural interest in all that concerns us, I'm afraid. They always have. Why, when Patrick—"

He stopped and reddened, his mouth closed tight.

"Patrick?" Mary asked. "Who is Patrick?"

"It doesn't concern you," he snapped.

His curtness discouraged any more inquiring on Mary's part. She spoke then of the beautiful rolling hills that led from the town and he told her that they would soon be coming onto Ashworth land.

The mansion was quite beautiful and impressive. It was situated most agreeably, and the approach to the house gave the visitor a tantalizing glimpse of pink brick through the many trees which lined the road. Set on a rise, the hall overlooked a magnificent lake and rolling grounds of deep green. Numerous pillars stood at the entry of the house, supporting a great pediment over the main entryway. Many windows dotted the front façade, indicating to Mary the guarantee of many comfortable rooms within. A substantial stone drive met the wide steps which led to the large white doors set beneath that pediment.

"Ashworth Hall is most impressive, Daniel," Mary said with a smile. "And very pretty."

"Do you find it to your satisfaction, Lady Ashworth?" he asked.

She nodded and turned to gaze once more at the house as the carriage made its approach. They alighted the carriage and began to make their way up the wide steps. Suddenly Daniel grabbed Mary and held her cradled in his arms.

"Daniel!" she squealed, grabbing onto his shoulders. "Put

me down!"

Daniel shook his head, taking long strides up the stairs and through the now-open front doors. "A wife must be carried over the threshold."

Mary shook out her skirts after he set her back onto her feet.

"Such a display," she said, smiling herself.

The servants were soon assembled and introduced to the new mistress of the manor. As it was well-past time for tea, she and Daniel went abovestairs to ready for dinner. He preceded her up the grand staircase and escorted her to his rooms.

Mary looked about the large sitting room decorated in russet and gold, and thought it most pleasant a space. Large wing chairs flanked a fireplace topped by a gilded mantle, appearing very cozy and comfortable. Beyond the room was the sleeping chamber with a very large bed set up on a platform. It was framed by intricately-carved posts, heavy and austere. A coverlet of rich brown satin dressed the bed, trimmed with thick braiding of the same gold as dressed the windows. It didn't take much for Mary to imagine her magnificent husband reclining on the bed. The recollection of everything they'd shared the night before washed over her.

"It's time to ready for dinner, Daniel," she rushed out.

Daniel shrugged his broad shoulders and removed his jacket, his grin turning decidedly wicked. Mary soon found herself stretched out on the incredible bed, the satin coverlet cool beneath her bare back.

***

Mary was speaking, but Daniel was damned if he could make any sense of what she was saying. His energy was blissfully spent, his mind muddled from the intensity of his release long minutes earlier. He was on his back, waiting for what seemed like forever for his strength and wits to return to him.

"…passing strange, Daniel," Mary finished, her words finally penetrating his pleasure-induced haze.

"What?" he asked, leaning up on one elbow. "What do you find strange, love?"

Mary placed her hand on his chest. "I can't seem to accustom myself to sleeping together in the same bed."

Daniel covered her hand with his. "You're my wife, Mary. You belong here in my bed."

"But I've never shared such a space with anyone. It'll take a bit of getting used to, won't it?"

He shrugged. "I've never spent the night with another."

Mary snorted in disbelief. "You've told me of your experience, Daniel."

"I've never spent the night with another woman," he said again. "Never more than an hour's time, truth be told."

Mary slanted him a look. "You can barely move yourself after you…. Well, you grasp my meaning."

He thought again of the incredible strength of his release and the peaceful numbness that stole into his very bones when he made her his.

"What we share…" He tried to explain what he hardly understood himself but he persevered. "What's between us is far from ordinary."

Mary shook her head in befuddlement so he smiled and touched her cheek. "When you give yourself to me, I seem to give myself too. You leave me weak, love."

She raised her eyes to his. "I am your captive, husband. You may keep me with you in this splendid bed of yours."

He pulled her to him and kissed her lightly. Wrapping his arms around her, he let out a sigh of pleasant exhaustion.

"Tomorrow I'll take you riding about the estate," he said with a yawn. "You'll much enjoy the grounds."

She nodded and settled herself comfortably against him and he closed his eyes, feeling a contentment he had never before.

***

The morning came and Daniel informed Mary at breakfast that they would have to postpone their ride over the grounds. He had much to see to that morning, from speaking to his tenants and seeing to the mines, that he feared he would be busy well into the afternoon. Mary was a bit disappointed, but that feeling soon took its leave as she considered the pleasing prospect of exploring the magnificent house on her own.

"I'll make every effort to return for luncheon, sweetheart," he told her.

He stood and crossed to where she sat, bending to kiss her. Mary watched him go and let out a little sigh. He'd called her "sweetheart." Was he finding a place in his heart for her? Would he one day tell her that he loved her?

She gave an impatient shake of her head. She had Daniel's loyalty and protection. And his passion, she added with a secret smile. Love was something she dared not think of so early in their union. It simply didn't signify.

Her insistence finally convinced her mind of the logic of

her position, and she finished her breakfast in buoyed spirits. Her mind occupied now with the prospect of exploration, she drained her tea cup and rose to set about her morning.

She found many pleasant rooms on the main floor, including a splendid morning room situated very near the magnificent gardens at the back of the house. Through glass doors she could spy the still-vibrant flowers climbing over the brick walls, and several lovely sitting areas scattered about the outside space. Another favored room she discovered was a large library placed not far from what she correctly assumed was Daniel's study. The library possessed many volumes, leather-bound tomes of the classics as well as several plays both comedic and tragic. It was obvious to her well-schooled mind that many years had been spent in the accumulation of such varied books, and she was pleased to learn that her husband's family had been as well-read as they were genteel. Surely her husband possessed a learned mind to compliment his handsome face and figure.

Coming upon a pleasant sitting room toward the front of the house, she discovered a smallish desk she immediately deemed well-suited to her correspondence. Seeing no time better than the present, she set herself down at the desk and opened the top drawer. Within she found the expected stationery bearing the Ashworth crest, along with a very nice likeness of the house and a bit of the grounds and her husband's title. Making a note to herself to see to the ordering of paper bearing her own name and new title, she began to write lengthy letters to her sisters and mother, extolling the virtues of her husband and his magnificent estate so far to the north of them. Thinking to delay the chore of penning all of the many notes of thanks for their wedding gifts, surely the list of gifts was to be found somewhere in her effects, she left the letters to be delivered and returned to the library to find a suitable volume with which to while away the time until the nooning meal.

She found to her disappointment that Daniel didn't return to take luncheon with her. Tamping down feelings of rejection which she knew were totally unfounded, she dined on slices of ham served with tiny potatoes and greens no doubt pulled from the wondrous vegetable garden she'd glimpsed past the flowers and benches of the walled garden.

After taking her lunch, she found herself quite ready for further exploration of her new home. Walking past the regal dining room in which she and Daniel had supped last evening, she discovered a ballroom sized to suit a very large group of revelers. The room was obviously attended to with as much care as the other more-utilized rooms she'd seen already, and she wondered with more than idle curiosity when they could be expected to host a ball. No doubt Daniel would wish to entertain his neighbors as well as introduce his new wife to them. Mary felt no real nervousness at the prospect. She was long-used to parties and the like from her sisters' and from her own, both those held at Bridgewater Park and attended in town.

She passed out of the ballroom, humming to herself a tune which she recalled had played while she danced with her new husband last evening. A graceful glide in her step, she stopped suddenly as she found herself in a large portrait gallery. Portraits almost too numerous to count filled the space, many bearing marked resemblance to her handsome husband.

Ashworths from generations past stared down at her from atop fine horses and from elegant chaises set about the gardens. She resumed her steps as she happily perused the characters who seemed to consider with much interest the new mistress of Ashworth Hall. One portrait in particular caught her eye, that of a man who could be none other than Daniel's father. He bore such a striking resemblance that if he'd been dressed in the fashion of the day she would think with utmost certainty that he was the same man that had left her with a regal bow at breakfast.

The lady smiling beside the gentleman could be no other than Daniel's mother, for it was obvious that even the painter had sensed the high regard the two people had for each other. Mary was suddenly aware of acute regret at never knowing the couple in the portrait. She would have so liked to have another woman in the house, thinking that the fate of being married to a man with a lesser title would have been no great disappointment if it would have provided her with the opportunity to know her in-laws more intimately than from a cold painting set high on a wall of smooth plaster.

She shook her head and turned, coming to a standstill as she glimpsed a very large portrait of an incredibly handsome young man. Was this Daniel? She ran a hungry gaze over the painting. The eyes were a bit different. Perhaps the artist hadn't the skill to catch the deep velvet of her husband's incredible brown eyes or the shining gold of his thick waves. But there was something else that spoke to her from the painting.

There was an openness about the features that spoke of a loving nature. A gentleness about the eyes that was absent from her own fine husband's countenance. The man in the portrait was younger than Daniel was now, so it was in all possibility that he had indeed sat for its execution. But somehow she didn't believe it was him.

The dress of the man portrayed was too similar to that worn now to think he wasn't of the same generation. The artist had painted both his name and the year of completion very ill, and left off the subject's identity entirely. A name came to the front of Mary's mind in the next moment. Could this be the Patrick of whom Daniel had made brief mention as they rode through Newcastle? But though he was so like Daniel in this representation, she was still unsure if it was indeed her husband. And if it was Daniel, when had he lost that openness and loving nature which she fancied she could read in the portrait?

Setting that aside for the moment, Mary walked through the gallery and looked at all of the previous Ashworths gracing the walls. Here and there she could read a feature or bearing that her husband had obviously inherited. They were quite a handsome family. She left the gallery only after pausing to stare at the young man's portrait for several more minutes.

She returned to the rooms she shared with Daniel to ready for tea. The sight that met her eyes when she strolled through the sitting room and into the sleeping chamber caused her heart to skip. Daniel stood with his back to her in the center of the room, bared to the waist. His hair was tousled and smudges and soot streaked his flesh. She sucked in a breath as she watched the muscles in his back work as he tossed his shirt onto a nearby chair. He turned at the sound, his brows raised. As Mary glimpsed his face her heart began to beat again, hard and fast. He looked so incredibly virile to her, so strong and masculine, that she nearly swooned.

His face was streaked as was his body, and his darkened skin made his eyes seem almost wild. Mary was seized with the desire to run her hands over him, to grab his face in her hands as she pressed her body to his. She cared not about the dirt that would undoubtedly soil her dress, thinking only in that moment of satisfying her sharp want of him.

"Hello, love," Daniel said, a grin splitting his face.

Mary blinked rapidly, feeling her cheeks grow quite hot. She dropped her eyes to the floor in mortification and mumbled some sort of greeting, though she was unaware precisely what.

Hurrying into her dressing room, she closed the door and leaned against it for much-needed support.

Chapter 17

Daniel stared at the closed door, bemused. Whatever ailed her? While he'd found her unexpected appearance in their chamber most pleasing, he couldn't reconcile the shock he'd glimpsed in her lovely blue eyes. He shrugged and walked over to the washstand set to the right of his own dressing room. The truth of the matter hit him the moment he stood before the mirror. He looked almost wild. It was little wonder his delicate wife would find his appearance so disturbing.

She was used to his carrying himself like the gentleman he was, clad impeccably and properly groomed at all times. Certainly her nature would be disturbed by anything less appropriate. He leaned closer to examined his face more fully. Soot darkened his visage and one particularly bold streak marred his face from his right temple nearly to the corner of his mouth. The mark gave him a decidedly sinister affectation, which he had little doubt had scared Mary witless.

Mary's maid arrived and ducked into the dressing room. He scrubbed his face clean and straightened his hair, and then rang for his valet. From this time forward he would do his best to preserve his proper appearance for his wife. Never again would he allow her to find him in any manner less than suitable. Except for when he joined her in their bed, of course. Mary seemed to have no shyness then, obviously finding both his appearance and his actions quite to her satisfaction no matter how wild either of them became.

A glance at Mary's dressing room door showed that she was still within, no doubt collecting her sensibilities as well as dressing for tea. Checking his appearance once more and finding nothing amiss, he left the chamber to await his wife's arrival in the parlor.

Mary entered the parlor soon after the tea tray was brought in, clad in a fetching tea dress of pale yellow. He smiled as he turned to her, pleased to see the shock gone from her features.

"What do you think of your husband's appearance now, love?" he asked, spreading his arms wide.

Mary blinked at him for a moment in dismay. "I don't understand."

"I'm sorry you saw me in such a state, Mary." He waited for her to sit and then did likewise. "There was much to see to today, and the mines, while well-maintained, are naturally a bit grimy."

Mary's cheeks wore a blush again, which confounded him. She waved her hand and saw to the pouring of the tea. Daniel said no more of his sullied appearance, certain that its further discussion would only serve to upset her.

"What have you been about in my absence, love?" he asked, helping himself to the light biscuits which accompanied their tea.

"I've explored the house fully, Daniel, or as much as one person can in a day." She smiled. "I must commend you on your taste. The house is furnished most pleasingly."

"I can't take much of the credit, I'm afraid," he said. "My mother had an eye for such matters, and my father naturally indulged her."

"Oh, I saw their portrait in the gallery!" Her eyes lit. "They were a very handsome couple. And young."

"Yes. They've been gone too long."

"Were you very young when they died, Daniel?"

"Thirteen."

His throat tightened, which was surely absurd. His parents had been gone for nearly half his life. He stood and walked to the windows lining the back wall.

"What of the gardens, love?" he asked, hoping to turn her attention from the discussion of his family.

She didn't answer for a long moment. "I hadn't the time to

explore them fully."

He turned to find her brow knit. "Then we'll take a stroll after tea."

They passed the afternoon in a very pleasant fashion, Daniel escorting his bride through the splendid gardens while the sun continued its descent. To his relief, Mary made no more mention of the gallery or of the portraits within. When he'd mentioned Patrick's name in the carriage he could have bitten his tongue. He never wished to speak of his brother or his untimely and wholly senseless death. He surely wouldn't discuss it with her. He had little doubt that she would find the telling most distressing.

But he had another reason for keeping the knowledge from her. His own guilt in the horrid matter. If only he'd voiced his objections to his brother's hateful fiancée, the duel would never have occurred.

***

Long after dinner that night, Mary readied for bed. She was still befuddled by Daniel's terseness when she'd mentioned his parents, wishing that he could feel free to discuss any matter with her, his wife. Perhaps she wished for too much intimacy far too soon. They hadn't been married as long as her sisters had.

That was certain. Nor did she and Daniel share the kind of love that Betsy and Maggie did with their husbands. While she was quite in danger of falling in love with her confounding husband, she was doubtful of any such regard on his part. He wanted her and he was fond of her. And she told herself as she tied her wrapper about her waist that such a situation was not to be pitied.

She emerged from the dressing room to find her husband sitting in the chair beside the bed, bared once more to the waist. He bent down to remove his boots as she watched, desire stirring in her breast as his arms and shoulders worked. She must have made a sound, she wasn't quite certain, for he looked up at her in the next moment. The effect of him upon her senses took her utterly by surprise. His hair hung down, nearly obscuring his eyes. A branch of candles set on the opposite side of the bed cast an intriguing pattern across his face. A shadow fell on him, mirroring the dark slash that had marred his visage that afternoon. She was consumed with wanting, sharp and deep.

She came to stand before him. "Daniel."

He stared into her eyes, his brows raised in surprise. In a flash those eyes were smoldering with answering desire. She wouldn't play the ninny as she had that afternoon, running into her dressing room out of fear for the passion she felt for her own husband. He was hers as she was his, and she meant to indulge all of the fantasies she'd imagined. She removed her wrapper and climbed onto his lap.

"Mary, what are you about?" he managed to say before she pressed her mouth to his.

She darted her tongue in and out of his mouth, loving the unique taste of him. He welcomed her assault, soon matching her urgency with his own. She ran her lips over his cheek, running her tongue lightly over his ear.

"I want you, Daniel," she whispered boldly, her mouth on his neck. "I want to please you."

He said nothing, rubbing his hands over her back as she dropped kisses on his chest. But she could tell by the thumping heartbeat beneath her lips that he was as affected as she. She ran her hands greedily over his hard stomach, boldly flicking her tongue in his navel. She came to her knees between his outstretched legs and placed her hands on the waistband of his breeches.

"I want to please you, Daniel," she said again, working one button free. "Tell me what to do."

Daniel sharply drew in a breath. "My God, Mary." He

cupped her face in his hands. "You please me."

She smiled at him and returned to her task. Freeing him, she held him for a long moment, amazed at the object of her perusal. Strange feelings swirled within her. At once she felt frightened and thrilled and exceedingly powerful. She placed her mouth on him, timidly at first.

Daniel groaned softly and Mary glanced up at him. His eyes were closed as he leaned his head back. She grew more bold, taking him fully in her mouth. He moaned and moved a bit beneath her, telling her that he liked what she was doing. She ran her mouth along the length of him, flicking her tongue out and nipping him lightly with her teeth.

"Mary," he groaned, his movements getting stronger. "Ah, Mary."

She lifted her head and stared at him. The muscles in his throat worked madly. He was huge in her hands now, hot and heavy, and she knew instinctively that he was nearly at the edge. She lowered her head and touched her tongue lightly to the tip. He came then, throwing his head back and arching toward her as he shuddered. His climax was so sharp that she felt it herself, down to her very bones. She leaned back on her heels and waited for him to regain his senses. When he took a deep calming breath and lifted his head to face her, the contrition in his eyes surprised her.

"I'm so sorry, love," he said, his breathing harsh. "My God, when you... My God."

Mary smiled at him, pleased to her toes. "I've made you lose control, husband," she said. "Surely you can't be sorry for that."

Daniel shook his head at her and grabbed her gently by her arms. He pulled her to her feet. She favored him with another smile and pulled her nightgown up over her head, tossing it carelessly on the floor. Daniel's reaction was just what she desired it to be.

He grabbed her to him and kissed her soundly, soon tumbling her onto the bed. He kissed her breasts. He brought his mouth to her and she bowed back on the bed. She reveled in his attentions, her own release hitting her so quickly that she nearly lost her breath. When he came inside of her she cried out with the pleasure of it, with the completeness that filled her.

She was well-ready for sleep moments afterward, totally spent from his response to her caresses and her own from his. She couldn't help but feel cherished as he stroked her hair and whispered words of praise, fancying that she felt the whispers of another emotion in the deep rasp of his beloved voice.

Chapter 18

The next morning Daniel woke before his wife, and rose to enter his dressing room. He went through his morning routine without much hurry and donned his riding clothes. When he stood once more by the bed he shared with his wife, he thought about the tenderness he felt for her. Was he falling in love with her, as all and sundry seemed to insist?

He ran his eyes slowly over Mary's form, outlined by the fine bedclothes. She had discarded her nightgown without reserve last evening, and had slept beside him as naked as he. With her hair a tumble and her cheeks rosy from sleep, he could think of many more matters other than those of the heart.

"Mary," he said, reaching out to touch her shoulder.

Mary stretched languorously and peered at him from beneath one thick golden curl.

"Daniel." She yawned behind one hand and sat up in bed, regarding him closely. "You're up and dressed already?"

She glanced at the clock on the bedstand and blushed a pretty pink to see that the day was more than a few hours old. He leaned down to kiss her full lips.

"Do dress and join me for breakfast, Mary. Your riding habit would suit."

"My riding habit?" she repeated, her brow furrowed.

"Yes," he said, turning from the bed. "I believe I would much like to see you in that pretty purple one you wore in the park," he added over his shoulder, leaving her to her morning toilette.

After breakfast, Daniel accompanied Mary to the stables. If Mary suspected his motives earlier that morning, she was more than curious about them now. Her beautiful eyes narrowed on him. She flicked her braid over her shoulder and followed closely on his heels as he strode purposefully among the stalls.

"Daniel, what are you about?" she finally asked, her curiosity apparently getting the best of her.

Daniel smiled broadly and grasped her shoulders. "There," he said, turning her about to face one of the stalls. "There you are, Mary."

She was visibly stunned to find the very horse which she had teasingly instructed him not to purchase.

"Oh, Daniel," she said, stepping closer to the horse. "You bought her."

Daniel nodded and watched as she petted the horse's muzzle.

"You naughty girl," she said, smoothing the filly's tawny

mane. "And now here you are, in Newcastle."

"I told you I have a distinct partiality for this filly," he said, chuckling.

Mary smiled and stepped aside as the groom prepared the horse for its rider. It might seem silly to him if he thought too long on it, but he went to considerable lengths to replicate the afternoon when they'd shared their first kiss.

They rode about the estate, and Daniel happily provided her the particulars of its different aspects. After riding over the grounds for some time, seeing the delight on her face as they left the lush and verdant grounds for the rough and craggy landscape, they arrived at the mine set closest to Ashworth Hall. He told her of its vigorous production and safe operation. Then he led her from the mine and toward the tenant farms.

"The farms are productive, Mary," he said as they reached the first. "And at the risk of flattering myself, my tenants have only the most minor of complaints."

"My lord!" a stout man exclaimed from the yard in front of the snug cottage. "What a pleasure it is to see you and your fine lady about this morning."

Daniel called out a warm greeting to the man and reined in his mount. Mary was introduced to the family then, consisting of a pleasant-faced wife and three rosy-cheeked children, and smiled her greeting.

The farmers paid their master all of his due respect, expressing their joy over his marvelous choice of a wife. Daniel wholeheartedly agreed with their comments, and it went similarly at the other farms. He saw that Mary happily accepted the many good wishes and they rode on to the parsonage situated within the town of Newcastle itself.

Mr. Simmons, a gentlemanly man who had been looking after the souls in their part of Newcastle for the past three years, greeted them as warmly as the tenants had. He was well into his thirties, a fact that left him open to much matchmaking among the parish. He wore a pleasant smile for the Earl of Ashworth as he bade them to enter the parsonage.

"You must share our luncheon, Lord Ashworth," he said, directing them into the dining room. "Bessie has been fairly working her fingers to the bone and the good Lord knows that I cannot possibly eat all that she prepares for me."

The aforementioned Bessie, a plump gray-haired woman who obviously looked upon Mr. Simmons as a son, clicked her tongue.

Daniel grinned as he and Mary sat at the table.

"I trust you have made your famous mutton, Bessie?" he asked. "She uses some mysterious spice that she's refused to reveal to me so often that I've ceased to ask her," he told Mary.

Bessie clicked her tongue again but there was laughter in the woman's sparkling eyes. The mutton was delicious and quite tender. After concluding their luncheon Daniel and Mary took their leave of the bachelor and his watchful housekeeper, promising to visit them again when next they were in town. As they were leaving the parsonage they were met by another couple coming down the lane.

"Ah," Daniel said in Mary's ear. "Here comes the good doctor."

"Lord Ashworth!" the female half of the couple coming toward them exclaimed. "We didn't expect you to be in town."

Daniel gave a small shake of his head and shrugged his shoulders in Mary's direction. The woman soon standing before them was past middle age, as was her husband, and her eyes held speculation as they took in the new countess. Mary smiled in the woman's direction, looking to Daniel for an introduction which he readily provided.

"Lady Ashworth, do let me introduce Dr. and Mrs. Lawson," he said with a nod. "This is the Countess of

Ashworth."

"I am pleased to meet you," Mary said.

The doctor opened his mouth to make a greeting and was immediately waylaid by his wife.

"We are so very pleased to meet you, Lady Ashworth," Mrs. Lawson said, her sharp eyes softening a bit. "We'd hoped to invite you both to dine with us this day."

"Now, dear," Dr. Lawson began, "we had no way of knowing that Lord and Lady Ashworth would be in the village."

"But I see that Mr. Simmons has taken it upon himself to do the honors," Mrs. Lawson added with a sniff.

Daniel smiled once more in the lady's direction. "I'm quite certain that we would have much enjoyed taking our luncheon with you, Mrs. Lawson," he said smoothly. "Perhaps another day?"

Daniel's words calmed the woman's pique and she nodded vigorously. She placed her arm through Mary's and directed her down the street, the men falling into step behind them.

"I am quite certain that our cook can far surpass anything that Bessie could concoct, Lady Ashworth," Mrs. Lawson said with a sharp nod.

"Then I surely look forward to your cook's efforts, I

daresay," Mary put in with a pretty smile. "For Bessie's mutton was delicious."

"Mutton!" Mrs. Lawson sniffed. "Again people speak of that woman's mutton."

"Now dear," Dr. Lawson said placatingly.

"Never mind," Mrs. Lawson said over her shoulder. "When the earl and his countess dine with us they will indeed be quite pleased. Bessie's mutton, indeed."

Mary suffered the woman's well-intentioned ramblings as Daniel spoke to the doctor of the general health and gossip of the residents. When at last they parted from the doctor and his wife, Daniel was more than pleased to have Mary's attention to himself. They mounted their horses and turned them in the direction of Ashworth Hall.

"Mrs. Lawson is quite…forceful," Mary offered after they had ridden a ways.

Daniel laughed out loud at that. "Yes," he readily agreed. "She's his second wife, and quite intent on furthering her husband's social standing."

"Does the doctor need such assistance?"

"Hardly. Dr. Lawson has been tending the Ashworths for as long as I can remember and is as competent a physician as can be found, in the country or out of it."

Mary's expression was thoughtful. "It's comforting to know that we have such a man in our environs."

Her words caused the flash of a memory in Daniel's mind in that moment. When Harley had expressed the desire to sire an heir with Mary, Daniel had decided to make Mary his own. He'd been unaware of that decision until he'd stood before her in her father's house, however. Surely the passion they now shared as husband and wife with such spirited abandon would result in a child eventually. Was she also thinking about such matters as she mentioned the competent doctor?

He studied her as she rode beside him, wondering what her feelings were for him. He'd never given thought to such provoking issues in all of his adult life. Did she wish to carry his child? Did that mean that he was more to her than merely her handsome husband? That possibility would seem to contradict his previous image of her as a vain and silly young woman of society. He knew she possessed a loving heart. He'd seen that among her family. Did that emotion extend to him? She turned to face him in the next moment, her brow furrowed slightly.

"Is something wrong, Daniel?"

Daniel blinked and found a smile. "Nothing, love. My

mind was wandering, I daresay. Perhaps I'm still a bit muddled from Mrs. Lawson's prattling."

Mary nodded and turned once more in her saddle. Daniel tamped down his confounding feelings and followed his wife's lead out of Newcastle and toward his family estate, vowing to give no more thought to love and its many tangles.

***

Over the next few weeks, Daniel was kept busy with estate matters while Mary occupied herself with any number of pursuits. She painted fire screens and practiced her needlework. She saw to her correspondence and household duties. She explored both the house and the gardens more fully, never passing by the gallery without taking the time to stare up at the handsome man in the large gilded frame. She made no mention of it to Daniel, however. He'd grown distant when she'd mentioned his parents on that first afternoon, and she was loath for that coldness to make its reappearance should she mention the mysterious young man.

One day nearly two months after their nuptials, Mary decided to take a trip into Newcastle. The notion brought to her mind the strange look that had come over her husband's face as they rode from town on that afternoon several weeks earlier.

They were having what she'd deemed a pleasant conversation about Dr. Lawson and his forceful yet likable wife when he'd grown at once speculative and troubled. What ailed the man?

She set that quandary aside and readied for her day. Only her maid would accompany her into the town, since Daniel was quite busy seeing to the estate.

The day was a bit chilly, as October was nearly at its end. But the sun shone brightly on Mary and Jane as they alighted Daniel's carriage and strolled down the thoroughfare toward the shops. The appearance of Dr. and Mrs. Lawson caused her to come to a stop after browsing through the goods in only two of those shops.

"Hello, Lady Ashworth!" Mrs. Lawson enthused. "What brings you into town this day? Will you join us for luncheon?"

Mary smiled at the woman's exuberance, taken with her husband's indulgent smile. "Hello, Dr. Lawson," she said with a nod. "Mrs. Lawson, I thank you for the invitation. But I'm merely here to do some shopping."

The woman looked fairly crest-fallen. A thought hit Mary in the next moment. "Would you and Dr. Lawson wish to join us for dinner at Ashworth Hall this evening?"

"Oh my, yes!" Mrs. Lawson said, her gray curls bouncing

as she nodded her head excitedly. "Did you hear that, dear?" she continued in a loud voice, glancing about the thoroughfare to ascertain that they had the attention of the other folks present. "We are to dine with the earl and his wife."

"That would be lovely, Lady Ashworth," Dr. Lawson said in a much more subdued tone.

After settling upon a time, the couple left Mary to her tasks. Mary found her cloak more than sufficient cover for her day dress of blue muslin, and as she stopped in front of the milliner's she removed her hood and tilted her face up to the sun for a brief moment. Out of the corner of her eye she spied a woman regarding her in very close fashion. Mary turned to face her and the woman looked away. *How odd.* Giving no more thought to the stranger, she turned to follow Jane into the shop.

"Hello, Lady Ashworth," a man said to her right.

Mary turned to find Mr. Simmons coming toward her from across the street, a smile on his face, and smiled in response.

"Good day, Mr. Simmons. How are you?"

"Quite well," the man answered. "Doing a bit of shopping this day?"

Mary nodded again. "Thank you again for the wonderful luncheon, Mr. Simmons. I've thought of Bessie's mutton often these past weeks."

"She still speaks to all who will listen that we were the first to dine with Lord and Lady Ashworth," he said with a grin. "And is the earl in town with you?"

Mary shook her head. "Lord Ashworth has much to occupy him on the estate, I'm afraid."

Mr. Simmons' eyes brightened. "Then may I offer my assistance with your purchases?"

"No, thank you," Mary returned, curving her lips into a small smile. "I have my maid with me and I believe I shall keep my purchases to the minimum in any case."

"As you wish," he said.

"Would you care to join Lord Ashworth and myself for dinner this evening, Mr. Simmons?" Mary asked. "Dr. and Mrs. Lawson will be dining at the hall."

He smiled widely at her words. "That would be delightful, Lady Ashworth," he said. "I daresay Bessie will be a bit put out, but I suspect she'll secretly relish having the evening off."

Mary nodded. With a jaunty tip of his hat, he left her to her shopping. Mary stepped into the store and noted that Jane was busy perusing the fine fabrics lining one wall. Trusting her maid to uncover the best of the lot, she turned her attention to the array of needles and silk threads and the like to discover a new project with which to spend her autumn evenings.

"I would take care with such matters," a woman said beside her.

Mary started and turned, finding the woman who'd been regarding her so strangely minutes earlier. She arched a brow at the woman's puzzling comment. The smile that curved the woman's face was anything but friendly and Mary found her pointed looks disconcerting. Even in the subdued lighting within the shop Mary could see that the woman had at one time been very pretty. But the harsh lines bracketing her mouth and crinkling the corners of her eyes told Mary that she looked perhaps even older than her years might prove. And for a reason she could not fathom, the woman's close scrutiny made her feel oddly unclean.

"If you will excuse me," Mary said to the woman, turning to put as much distance between herself and the stranger.

"I saw how the good vicar paid such attention to you," the woman provided. "The Ashworth men can be quite jealous."

Mary turned to face her, her stomach giving a tiny flip. "Do you know the family?"

"You are the Countess of Ashworth, I presume," the

woman said with a slight sneer, not quite answering Mary's question.

"Yes," Mary said warily, perplexed by the glint in the woman's pale blue eyes.

"That was to be my title."

Mary couldn't hide her surprise at the woman's words.

"I am Lady Beatrice Blair," she informed Mary. "I was set to marry the earl when... Well, suffice it to say that matters did not quite turn out as I might have expected. My husband is a baronet, however."

"You were set to marry Daniel?" Mary asked, unable to keep the amazement out of her voice.

The woman laughed harshly. "No. He was but a boy when I knew him, though no doubt he has grown to be as handsome as Patrick was."

"Patrick?" Mary could not help but ask, recalling Daniel's mention of the name as they drove through Newcastle months earlier. "Who is Patrick?"

Lady Beatrice stared hard at Mary. "Surely Daniel...I am sorry. I should call him Lord Ashworth now. Didn't he tell you of his own dear brother?"

Daniel's brother? Mary's throat tightened. And this woman

was to wed him?

"I was unaware."

The woman laughed again and waved her hand in the air.

"I wouldn't think that Patrick's little brother would give my name voice," she said. "He and I did not part on good terms."

Mary couldn't bear the woman's company any longer. The cruel smile twisting her features, taken with the coldness of her tone, filled Mary with disgust.

"I must find my maid."

"Do watch yourself when you're not in your husband's company, my dear," Beatrice offered with a click of her tongue. "They are a jealous lot. Patrick's jealousy led to his untimely demise, I'm sorry to say. Tragedy, that."

Mary's mind was spinning from the woman's words. First she said that she was to marry Patrick, of whom Mary had heard nothing to date. And then to intimate that he had died suddenly, due to his jealous nature?

"You are quite pretty," Beatrice said in parting. "You may be prettier than even I was."

Mary said no more to the woman. She located Jane and settled their purchases, hurrying to the carriage. She would find

Daniel and question him, she decided as the carriage rolled away from town. He would explain the woman's words to her satisfaction. He had a brother? Why did he never speak of him to her, his wife? Hadn't he grown to trust her over these past months? Didn't he wish to share more with her than the passion that flowed so thick between them?

Had she known of the hateful woman, she would have undoubtedly been more prepared for such an attack. Who was Beatrice to the Ashworths? And why did her words of warning, certainly given with no warm regard, fill her with both anger and dread?

Chapter 19

Mary swept her cloak from her shoulders as she entered the hall. She located her husband in the parlor, settled in a chair beside the modest fire burning in the hearth.

"Hello, love," Daniel said, coming to his feet. "I trust you spent a pleasant day in town?"

Mary stared hard at him, wondering precisely what secrets he held behind those beautiful brown eyes. He kissed her and she felt her resolve weakening. She shook her head to quell her confusing thoughts and stepped back.

"I met someone in town, Daniel," she began, watching his face closely for a reaction. "Lady Beatrice Blair."

Daniel's eyes grew round. As Mary watched, his face twisted into a sneer.

"Beatrice, that lying whore!" He slammed his fist on the mantle. "How dare she come back to Newcastle?"

Mary watched as he began to pace in agitation, his anger pouring over her. Never before had she seen him so furious, even when she herself had vexed him on several occasions. She reached out to him and grabbed his arm. When he turned to her she nearly recoiled from the coldness hardening his beautiful eyes. Summoning all of the indignation she'd accumulated on the trip from town, she straightened her shoulders and stood her ground.

"She told me of Patrick."

Daniel's expression faltered and Mary glimpsed a hurt so deep that she nearly felt it herself. "Patrick," he groaned, settling back into the chair. "How dare that witch utter his name?"

"Why didn't you tell me of him, Daniel?"

Daniel came to his feet again, resuming his pacing. "It was none of your concern, Mary."

"None of my concern?" she repeated in amazement. "How can you say such words? He was your brother."

"Yes," Daniel said sharply. "He was my brother, and all the family I had left to me after our parents died, save for my uncle."

Mary used the silence that followed to puzzle over his statement. Beatrice's words echoed in her mind and she spoke them aloud.

"Lady Beatrice said that Patrick's jealousy led to his death."

Daniel spun to face her, his eyes round. "Patrick's jealousy?" he raged. "His death was all Beatrice's doing. She killed him as sure as if she shot him herself!"

She was stunned. "Patrick was shot?"

"Yes." He ran a hand over his face. "In a duel to defend that bitch's honor."

Mary said nothing to that, and no response was needed to pull the story from Daniel.

"The lovely Beatrice was betrothed to my brother, Mary," he said, taking a breath. "She played him false with nearly every man of her acquaintance, only my brother was too besotted to notice. When he at last caught her in the act he assumed that the gentleman in question had compromised her." He choked out a laugh. "Compromised her? The woman who delighted in enticing men into her bed? Ah, I don't blame Blair for Patrick's death despite his firing the fatal shot. It was my fault for not telling Patrick about her perfidy sooner. Patrick forced Blair into the duel, that was certain. And now the poor sod is saddled with her as a wife. Justice, I suppose."

Daniel turned from her then, staring into the fire. Mary could nearly feel the swirl of emotions warring within him. She reached out toward him again, touching his arm lightly.

"Daniel," she said gently. "It's foolish to blame yourself for Patrick's death."

"Foolish? Patrick was the fool to ever trust a such a vain

and deceitful woman, Mary," he said. "I will never make that mistake."

Mary saw red, immediately recalling all that he'd said of her to Lord Harley before they wed.

"Do you think that I am like Beatrice?" she asked in a near-whisper. "Do you still believe I'm vain?"

Daniel's mouth thinned to a hard line. "I didn't say that," he said shortly. "But I know that I'll never be such a fool. I'll never make the mistake of loving any woman."

His words cut her to the quick, her anger replaced swiftly by deep hurt. Her heart clenched as she realized that he truly believed his own assertions. She couldn't stay in the room with him another moment. Mumbling something about readying for tea, she fled the parlor.

Upstairs in their chamber, Mary fell upon the bed. Soft sobs racked her frame as she hugged her middle. Daniel would never come to love her. He would never come to trust her with his heart. She would have his passion and protection, but nothing else. She knew then that she could never expect him to feel for her the way she'd come to feel for him these past months.

"I love him," she murmured.

It was the first time she'd acknowledged that to herself.

And now it was certain that he distrusted all women, his own wife included. However could she build a life with such a man? How could she expect him to welcome into his heart any children they might have when that heart was so full of distrust?

***

In the parlor downstairs, Daniel regained his composure. He wasn't at all certain of what he'd said to send Mary fleeing from his sight. No, his mind had been filled with the raw hatred he felt at the mention of Beatrice's name. And for Mary to force him to discuss Patrick's death with her? He wouldn't let her know of how he'd failed his brother. He wouldn't speak to her of Patrick again.

When the hour for tea had come and gone, he rose from his self-imposed confinement in the arm chair and climbed the grand staircase. He entered the chamber he shared with his wife, surprised to find her sleeping on the coverlet. Her hair was in a tangle, her day dress crumpled. Tears streaked her cheeks. Guilt slashed at him.

He shouldn't have been so cross with her. But she shouldn't have mentioned that bitch's name in his presence. Lord only knew what other lies Beatrice had spun. He would put an end to it. That was certain. And he and Mary could resume the life that they'd begun to share.

Mary stirred on the bed, drawing his eyes to her face.

"Daniel," she whispered tearfully, still lost in sleep.

Daniel's heart clenched at the mournful sound. He sat beside her on the bed, his hand reaching out as if of its own accord to smooth the tangled curls from her face.

"Mary," he said, stroking her cheek.

Mary's eyes fluttered open, their depths a bit cloudy. "Daniel," she said again, relief clear in her voice. She suddenly shook her head and sat up in the bed.

As he watched the soft look was gone from her eyes as sure as if she had shuttered them.

"Excuse me," she said stiffly, pulling away from him.

Daniel watched as she stood and glanced at the clock.

"It is well past tea," he offered in an attempt at jest.

Mary took a breath and nodded, her face set. "We must ready for dinner, then. I didn't have the opportunity to tell you earlier, but Dr. Lawson and his wife are joining us for dinner. Along with Mr. Simmons."

Daniel cursed softly. When she'd looked up at him from their bed, some indefinable emotion making her eyes a deep violet, he'd sorely wished to put aside their horrid exchange. But now with her all but rigid in her stance, he knew that prospect was out of his reach for the moment. He nodded and watched as she walked swiftly into her dressing room and closed the door. Sighing irritably, he saw to his own dress and awaited her in the sitting room.

Dinner was abysmal in Daniel's opinion. Mr. Simmons fawned over Mary, his eyes running far too freely over her silk-clad form. And Mary seemed to be encouraging the fool's attentions, bestowing her lovely smile on the man more than once. Mrs. Lawson's voice prattled in his ear as he struggled to keep his focus on the conversation, causing his head to pound. He was relieved when the gentlemen left the ladies after the meal, as happy to be away from Mrs. Lawson as to pry Simmons away from Mary.

"How have you been, Simmons?" Daniel asked the man as they shared a brandy with the doctor. "Any new members of the congregation to capture your notice?"

Mr. Simmons laughed lightly. "You sound a bit like the matrons in town, Lord Ashworth. Do you also wish to see me married and settled?"

Daniel shrugged and drank deeply of his brandy. "It is a desirable state."

"I admit that I do feel envious of your situation," Simmons said. "One cannot expect you to view matrimony as anything but desirable."

Daniel blinked at the man's words. Before he could give voice to his growing irritation, Dr. Lawson joined the conversation.

"Lady Ashworth is a charming woman," the older man said. "And it is wonderful to see you settled at long last."

Daniel smiled. "You sound a bit like my uncle," he told the doctor.

"I've known you nearly as long as he has," the man said. "Your entire family, for that matter."

Daniel thought immediately of Patrick. Lawson had been summoned to the scene of his death on that long-ago morning, able only to confirm what Daniel had already guessed. They hadn't spoken of that event in the years since and Daniel would not broach the subject now.

"Why don't we rejoin the ladies?" he said, setting down his glass.

"I cannot think of a more pleasant prospect," Simmons offered as he preceded Daniel from the study.

Long after their guests departed, Daniel entered their

rooms to find Mary without her maid and nearly ready for bed.

She unpinned her hair and turned to enter her dressing room.

"That was a horrid display this evening, wife," he said, his voice low.

She gaped at him. "May I ask to what you are referring?" she asked, her hands planted on her hips.

Daniel cursed and plowed his fingers through his hair.

"You damn well know my meaning," he said. "Relishing in that man's attentions."

"What man?"

"Encouraging his bowing and scraping. It was disgusting."

Mary threw her hands into the air. "No. Are you speaking of Mr. Simmons? I was unaware of his bowing and scraping. Should I have been flattered?"

"Don't jest with me," Daniel said in a warning tone. "The manner in which you carried yourself?"

"I carried myself as the Countess of Ashworth," Mary said, her chin raised. "I treated all of our guests properly."

"Like hell," he growled. "You welcomed that besotted fool's attentions, Mary. Don't deny it."

Mary snorted. "You cannot mean what you are saying.

Why, I gave as much consideration to Dr. Lawson as I did to Mr. Simmons. Do you believe that I would welcome that gentleman's attentions as well? He's a bit older than my own father you know, and I suppose that should be a consideration when one is contemplating an assignation."

Daniel knew he was being unreasonable but couldn't seem to stop himself. When she turned from him he caught her arm with one hand. She looked up at him, her eyes flashing.

"Let me go," she said, her voice soft.

Daniel shook his head at her, pulling her close to him. "You won't make a fool of me in my own home," he commanded. "You won't play me false."

"I would never!" Tears shimmered in her eyes and she pulled out of his grasp. "Never mind," she said, turning her face from his. "It's obvious that you won't believe a word I say."

Daniel would not be denied. He held her again and she couldn't look away from him. "You won't play me false, Mary," he said, his voice cracking. "You won't."

He crushed his mouth to hers, his tongue mating wildly with hers. When he lifted his head he didn't feel that anger. That jealousy. If he had to put a name to what he felt at the moment? It was cold fear.

"I will never take a lover, Daniel," she said, reaching up to touch his cheek. "Never."

He closed his eyes and nodded slowly, his mouth working silently. *Thank God.*

They were soon entangled on the bed. He breathed her name as he lavished his attentions on her breasts, drawing deep moans of pleasure from her. When his fingers found her, she was ready for him.

"Daniel!" she gasped. "Please, Daniel."

Daniel stood and quickly shed his clothes. He parted her legs and came inside of her, using deep, hard stokes that spoke of his own urgency.

"Mary," he rasped, his mouth on hers. "Ah, Mary."

Mary reached her peak as he drove into her one last time, clutching tightly to his shoulders as he held himself above her. He was soon heavy on her as his head found the pillow, sweet contentment filling him. She rose to finish her preparations for bed. When she returned, clad in a soft nightgown, he regarded her closely.

"You left our bed," he said sleepily.

She simply climbed in the bed beside him and yawned. "Good night," she said, turning away from him.

Daniel turned toward her and threw his arm over her waist, covering both of her hands in one of his.

"You're mine, Mary," he said, kissing her ear.

Mary twined her fingers in his, clasping tightly. "Always, Daniel."

Chapter 20

Several days had passed since the uncomfortable dinner party. Daniel didn't speak of it to Mary again, loath to revisit the horrid argument that had followed so swiftly on the heels of their guests' departure. But he did ponder all that had happened at the conclusion of that argument as he sat at the desk in his study. His wife's passion had matched his, her words as sweet in his ears as her body was beneath his. He longed to believe those words.

She'd made him a promise that evening, one that he sorely wished he could trust. But she was a woman. A beautiful woman who would continue to have men falling at her feet for many years to come. Would she one day set aside her marriage vows and succumb to such eager suitors?

"Like hell she will."

He found Mary in the front sitting room, her head bent over the top of the small writing desk. She paused in her writing, resting her dainty chin in one hand. Daniel studied her flawless profile for that unguarded moment. Lord, she was lovely. And she was his. Always, she'd said in their bed. Always. Suddenly she turned toward him, her eyes wide in surprise.

"Daniel," she said, a smile curving her lips. "I didn't hear you come in."

Daniel shrugged his shoulders and walked over to her. He glanced down at the sheet of paper beneath her pen.

"What is this?" he asked.

Mary set down the pen, waving her hand dismissively. "A list of items I forgot to purchase when I was last in Newcastle."

"You're going into town?" he asked, managing to keep his voice even.

To his relief she shook her head, a look of resignation on her face.

"I was planning to send Jane."

"I'll get you whatever you need," he said, picking up the list.

He puzzled over the words for a moment, reading nothing into the list of colors and fabrics and threads.

She snatched it from him, laughing lightly. "If you are indeed going to fill this order," she said, picking up her pen once more, "then I believe I must be far more descriptive."

When Daniel had the amended list in his hands, he bent to drop a kiss on her lips. "I shall not be gone long," he said, straightening. "Despite this very long list of yours. I have to place some orders at the blacksmith's and I wish to drop in on Dr. Lawson." He stopped to consider her once more. "Do you wish to join me?"

He saw the hesitation and knew precisely what she was thinking. No doubt they would run into Simmons. And apparently she had no desire to provoke the man's attentions so soon after her argument with her husband.

"No," she told him at last. "I have some correspondence which I've been neglecting, as well as several projects awaiting my hand."

Daniel nodded and left her, taking the memory of her parting smile with him on the short ride into town.

Upon leaving the residence of Dr. and Mrs. Lawson, after dutifully eating a very large piece of their cook's very dry cake, he saw to his business at the blacksmith's. That bit of work concluded, he withdrew Mary's list from his pocket and raised his head to consider which shop would provide him with such fripperies.

"The Earl of Ashworth," a female voice said behind him. "In town without his wife?"

Daniel turned to find Beatrice standing before him. He breathed in sharply as anger clenched his stomach.

"Do not speak to me, Beatrice," he growled. "I don't believe you would much like all that I would say in return."

To his amazement the woman smiled. The expression had the effect of deepening the lines at the corners of her eyes and mouth. "You've grown to be the very image of Patrick. Although your voice has a hard edge to it that his never possessed."

Daniel could feel his pulse drumming in his ears. "How dare you speak his name, you—"

"Careful, my lord," she cut in, her eyes narrowing. "It wouldn't do at all for the benefactor of Newcastle to be overheard speaking in a less than illustrious manner."

Before Daniel could give voice to all of the vicious comments swirling in his head, the lady's husband joined them. Daniel took a moment to take in the man's appearance. As Beatrice's own face showed, Blair too looked far older than his years.

"It's good to see you, Lord Ashworth," the man said in a soft voice.

"Blair," Daniel said with a nod. "Why are you in Newcastle?" he asked him pointedly.

Blair's ruddy face grew redder. "Family business," he said. "My father passed away and I had need to see to his holdings."

Daniel threw a glance at Beatrice, not surprised to see the

elation in her eyes. No doubt the old man had left quite a bit to his son in his death.

"I'm sorry, Blair," Daniel said.

Blair looked up at him for a long moment, contrition once more clear in his eyes. "Come, Beatrice."

He turned away from Daniel and walked toward the modest carriage sitting beside the road. Beatrice clicked her tongue at her husband's retreating back and faced Daniel once more.

"I saw your wife in town," she told him, a glint in her eye. "She is quite beautiful. No doubt she attracts a bit of attention?"

Daniel wouldn't acknowledge the woman's hateful words despite their unnerving accuracy.

"I would keep her close," the woman said in parting. "One can never tell what is in a woman's heart."

"My wife is nothing like you," he said with conviction. "Her beauty exceeds yours, as does her heart. She isn't a deceitful whore like you."

"I would be careful if I were you, my lord," she sneered. "Anyone who overhears you would think you were as jealous a man as your brother was."

Daniel's blood pounded in his ears. "Do not speak of

Patrick, Beatrice. So help me God, if you so much as speak his name again I will throttle you here and now."

Beatrice scowled at that, saying no more as she turned to join her waiting husband in their carriage. She suddenly stopped, smiling wickedly as she faced Daniel again.

"Why, if it isn't the handsome vicar," she said, nodding her head in the man's direction. "I saw him in deep conversation with your lovely young wife just the other day."

Daniel saw Simmons coming toward them and cursed his bloody bad luck. "Simmons," he said, nodding curtly as the man stopped before him.

"Hello, Lord Ashworth," the vicar returned with a smile.

As Daniel watched, the man's smile faded as his eyes settled on Beatrice.

"Lady Blair," Simmons said stiffly.

Beatrice eyed both men closely, delight on her face. "I'm surprised to find you in town, Mr. Simmons," she said with a tilt of her head. "With Lord Ashworth here, I would imagine your services might be wanted elsewhere."

Daniel found his hands clenched in fists and deliberately relaxed them. God, he wanted to strangle her. To his credit, Simmons reddened only slightly at the woman's blatant insinuation.

"Beatrice," Daniel began, his voice steady, "you will cease this or I'll make certain that you won't be welcome anywhere in Newcastle again. You will be known for the harlot you are."

"Don't think to threaten me, my lord," she sneered. "I don't believe you would relish the consequences."

She turned from both men and sauntered toward her husband's waiting carriage.

"One can never tell what is in a woman's heart, Lord Ashworth," she said over her shoulder. "You should remember that with regards to your own beautiful wife."

Bloody hell. Just seeing that bitch was enough to send the anger and hurt coursing through him afresh. What did she know of Mary's heart? What did he himself know if it?

"That woman has been in Newcastle for less than a fortnight," Simmons said beside him, his voice low. "And from what I have heard she has conducted herself in a manner which could only be viewed as unseemly."

"She is a cold-hearted deceitful woman, Simmons," Daniel said firmly. He took a measuring glance at the young vicar. "I trust that you didn't fall prey to her dubious charms."

Simmons laughed without humor. "Hardly," he told

Daniel. "I daresay my tastes run in an entirely different direction."

Daniel refused to read more into the man's words, unwilling to prick his own ire at the man's attentions toward Mary. He bade the man farewell and wished him a good day, taking himself into the nearest shop to see to Mary's list of fripperies.

***

Mary paced the parlor, her thoughts churning. Her needlework and other such projects held no lure for her, much to her chagrin. Time and again she began a letter to her sister Betsy, only to find her mind wandering. Daniel filled her thoughts: his growing reserve, the distrust she sensed not far beneath the surface whenever they happened to speak to one another. However could she write of such matters to her sister? Surely Betsy wouldn't understand how a new wife could already be so disheartened in her marriage. And Mary was loath for her sister to come to the realization that she didn't possess a true love match. Love was so important.

She'd believed that she would find that and she had, in a fashion. She loved Daniel more than she cared to think on this pensive afternoon. But there was no such regard on her husband's side. Of that, she was certain. After several aborted missives to Betsy, she surrendered to her melancholy and roamed about the house for much of the morning.

She had taken herself into the gallery directly after luncheon, puzzling over the portrait she now knew belonged to Patrick. The young man in the picture bore a striking resemblance to Daniel, both in countenance and build. But Patrick's eyes were soft and expressive. His face was guileless and happy. Nowhere was there anger, nor the hard look of distrust that so often clouded her husband's beautiful dark eyes.

Would Daniel ever favor her with such a tender look? Never, her mind whispered. Patrick's horrible death had put an end to such possibilities.

Mary paused now to gaze out the parlor windows that overlooked the gardens. Sighing, she thought of that long-ago afternoon when she and Daniel had sat in her father's gardens at Bridgewater Park. She'd expressed her fears of inadequacy in the marriage bed that day, which Daniel easily assuaged with his sweet words and kisses. He hadn't been wrong about the pleasure they would give each other. And while she'd held no illusions that Daniel truly loved her as they'd planned their nuptials then, she had held a kernel of hope that their relationship would grow into a true romance as her sisters' marriages obviously were. Now she no longer held such hope.

The sound of footsteps coming from the hall outside the parlor startled her out of her reverie. No doubt Daniel returned from Newcastle. She fixed a smile on her face and turned to greet her husband, intent on putting the subjects of love and trust out of her mind. She rang for tea and resigned herself to spending the afternoon in pleasantness if not in true harmony.

Matters improved little as autumn gave way to winter. Daniel grew more pensive. More aloof. In fact she seldom saw anything in his eyes but distrust, save for when he turned his attentions to the seduction of his wife. When he gazed at her with passion on his mind she fancied that she could see clear into his soul. Nowhere did she see the doubts for the brief moments it took for him to arouse her nearly to the point of desperation there in their bed. Gone was the distrust that was never far from her sight as they passed each other throughout the daylight hours. He trusted her body, she realized once he snored on the pillow beside her, his body comfortingly heavy upon her. Would he ever trust her heart?

So it was as the Christmas holiday approached. Mary received a missive from Betsy within a fortnight of the holiday, informing her that she and her family would be spending the time at Bridgewater Park, along with Maggie and Philip and their children. In her letter Betsy asked if Mary and Daniel would be able to attend as well. Mary approached Daniel on the subject, only to be summarily rebuffed.

"I never leave Newcastle in the winter months," he told her from his chair behind his desk. "Several of the mines are still in production. I feel that I should be on hand should anything arise demanding attention."

"But surely you have a foreman to see to such matters?" she asked without much hope.

"What of the tenant farms, wife? They are dormant by this time of year," he went on with another excuse, "but I could not in good conscience leave the estate for what would be a long journey far to the south."

Mary merely nodded at the weak explanation. She couldn't keep a sigh from escaping.

"If you wish to," he began, "you may go without me."

Mary blinked rapidly as his words settled on her. He was actually suggesting that they spend the holidays apart? Their first Christmas as husband and wife and they wouldn't be together to share it?

"Well, I hadn't given that alternative much thought."

When no protestations came from him she waved her hand dismissively. "I'll write Betsy directly and tell her that I'll see her at Bridgewater Park.

A few days later Daniel saw Mary safely settled into his carriage for the long ride south to Somersetshire. A kiss was all they shared that morning. No words of affection passed between them. Mary couldn't resist watching out the back window as she was carried far from the only place she truly wished to be.

"Happy Christmas," she murmured.

Chapter 21

Mary settled comfortably into her visit at Bridgewater Park. She passed the Christmas holiday in a pleasant fashion, struggling to keep her focus on the festivities at hand instead of on a certain gentleman ensconced far to the north. She missed him sorely, time and distance helping her put out of her mind the coldness and distrust between them. She thought only of his rare smiles, smiles that had come with much more frequency before he had begun to doubt her sincerity. And when he made love to her in their bed? She thought of his expert kisses and caresses with wanting.

A gift had arrived for Mary on Christmas Eve, a lovely fur-lined cloak of the very latest fashion. She was disappointed if not surprised that accompanying the garment was a brief note expressing her husband's wish for her to make good use of it. No mention was made of any emotion stronger than warm regard, she recognized even as she read it again days later. For what seemed the hundredth time she pored over the missive. And her heart nearly broke as she placed the note into the pocket of her day dress, hoping to tuck it out of her mind as easily as she placed it out of her sight.

She went downstairs to the parlor, seeking to lose herself

in a most satisfying if challenging task. She was to teach her niece Cecilia several of the more complicated stitches of needlework, schooling the thirteen-year-old girl as Betsy has schooled her in her turn and Maggie had schooled Betsy. Her niece, a spirited girl, bore more than a passing resemblance to Mary. She had more than a touch of the famous Bridgewater stubbornness as well, Mary thought to herself as the girl balked at learning one stitch in particular.

"Oh Aunt Mary, it is hopeless!" Cecilia cried, throwing down her linen square. "Why on earth must I learn to make such fripperies?"

Mary sighed and wisely held her tongue. She picked up the piece of cloth and turned a practiced eye to the small satin roses with slightly-lopsided petals. A glance at her sister caused her to raise a brow. Betsy sat on a nearby settee, her eyes dancing with laughter.

"Is there something you wish to say, sister?" Mary asked Betsy as she handed the linen to Cecilia.

Betsy nodded vigorously. "I believe this exchange reminds me of one of several years past, Mary."

"Never mind," Mary answered on a laugh. "You will gain much satisfaction in bringing such 'fripperies' as you call them into your home when you marry, Cecilia," she told her niece. "As a gentlewoman, it is but one of the many pursuits you must accomplish before you marry."

Cecilia sighed dramatically, fingering the long golden curls at the side of her coiffure in a gesture owing more than a passing nod to her aunt.

"I suppose," she allowed. "But it is so dreadfully boring."

"Would you rather be abovestairs in the nursery, Cecilia?" Maggie asked her daughter. "I'm certain that Missy would love to spend the time with you, not to mention your little brother."

Missy was Betsy and Michael's four-year-old daughter and she was very attached to her cousin. From her own experience Mary knew that while Cecilia enjoyed the looks of worship Missy bestowed in her direction, the thirteen-year-old much preferred passing the time in the company of her mother and aunts.

"Oh no, Mother!" Cecilia said. "Let Missy spend a bit of time with Alexander. The good Lord knows that he can well look after her."

"And lead her into mischief, no doubt," Betsy put in.

Mary smiled at that image. Maggie's son Alexander was an adorable little boy, with a ready grin and sparkling eyes. He was also free-spirited and unguarded, bestowing his smiles and hugs on all of the people charmed to be counted in his circle. Her niece's mention of the boy brought the man in Mary's life to mind. Never would she see such a free and easy smile on her husband's face as she did on the child's. She sighed, drawing the closer attention of Cecilia.

"Are you thinking of your husband, Aunt Mary?" she asked.

Mary blinked at the girl in amazement. She began to shake her head, stilled by Cecilia's dramatic sigh.

"I had so wished that Lord Ashworth would accompanied you," she said. "He is so very handsome."

Mary couldn't deny that, despite the fact that the mere mention of his name caused her yearning to increase.

"Cecilia," Maggie chided her daughter. "What would you know of such matters?"

"I am an excellent judge of such matters, Mother," she answered. "My newest uncle is most handsome. Nearly as handsome as my father, I daresay."

Mary thought that no man could compare to her husband, but wisely kept silent on that particular matter.

"And what of your other uncle, Cecilia?" Betsy laughed.

"Does he meet with your approval as well?"

"Don't encourage her, Betsy," Maggie said. "Return to your work, Cecilia, or you will join the others in the nursery."

"Yes, Mother," she sighed. "I've heard that more than one handsome man asked for your hand, Aunt Mary."

Mary shot a look of disapproval in Maggie's direction.

"Lay the blame at your mother's feet, Mary," Maggie smiled. "I only witnessed a few of your conquests. Lord Grimsby. Lord Harley."

"Now, Maggie," Mary began in weak protest.

"How many were there?" Cecilia asked, her green eyes opened wide.

"More than you can count, I daresay," Betsy offered with a saucy grin.

"Oh, I do so wish I was old enough to attend the parties next Season," Cecilia cried, leaving her needlework on her chair to take a twirl about the room. "I only hope I can draw as much attention as Aunt Mary did. To have gentlemen falling at my feet, begging for my good favor."

Mary came to her feet in an instant, her heart pounding. "Do not ever make such a wish, Cecilia. You don't know what you're saying."

Cecilia turned to stare at her in shock. That look was mirrored by Maggie and Betsy. Her cheeks flaming, she lowered her eyes to the floor.

"Excuse me," she murmured, hurrying from the room.

Mary found solitude in the front sitting room. She sat at a small writing desk and folded her arms on the top, lowering her head and letting the tears of hurt and frustration come. The door opened then, only to be closed almost silently by a careful hand. Mary stiffened slightly at the sound, fearing a confrontation she could not endure in her present state.

"Do you wish to talk about this, Mary?" Betsy asked softly.

Mary took a calming breath and dashed her hands over her face to wipe the tears from her cheeks. She turned and took in the look of worry on her sister's face. How she longed to unburden herself! To tell Betsy everything as she could when she was a young girl. But she wasn't that young girl any longer. She was a married woman who must deal with her present situation in her own way.

"You wouldn't understand, Betsy," she said at last.

Betsy shrugged and walked to where Mary still sat at the little desk. She placed her hand on Mary's shoulder.

"What is it, Mary?" she asked. "Does this have to do with your husband and why he remains in Newcastle?"

Mary shook her head sadly. "You could never understand," Mary told her sister. "My marriage isn't like yours. Like Maggie's."

Betsy wore her confusion on her face. "Whatever do you mean?"

Mary stood and walked to the window, gazing absently at the wide stone drive in front of the mansion. A sigh escaped her as her shoulders sagged.

"I don't have a love match," she said in a small voice.

Betsy was quiet for a moment. Mary turned, curious to see the reaction when it came, the disbelief that would inevitably cloud her sister's blue eyes. How could her sister understand Mary's situation when she was loved so fiercely by her husband? Mary didn't have to wait very long for Betsy's disbelief to express itself.

"That is nonsense, Mary," Betsy said. "I have seen you with your husband. You love him."

At Betsy's utterance all of the feelings Mary had been suppressing for weeks came pouring out in a rush.

"Yes, I love him!" she cried. "I love him to a degree I

hadn't believed possible." She'd never said the words aloud and their futility struck her. She hugged her middle and let out a small sob. "But he doesn't love me."

Betsy gasped and drew Mary into her arms. Mary rested her head on her sister's shoulder for a moment, taking solace in a love she knew would never desert her.

"How can that be?" Betsy asked as she stroked Mary's hair. "He must love you." She gasped and held Mary away from her. "Is there another woman?"

Mary found the outrage on her sister's face comforting if misplaced. She laughed without humor and stepped away from Betsy's comfort.

"Yes," she answered. "But not in the manner to which you suspect," she said, once more wiping tears from her cheeks.

"I don't understand."

"Daniel lost his brother years ago, Betsy," Mary said. "Due directly to a deceitful and duplicitous woman. Patrick died fighting a duel to defend that woman's honor. Daniel believes that I will betray him as that woman did his brother."

Her sister shook her head sharply. "But you would never betray him, Mary. We Bridgewater women may be a stubborn lot but our hearts are ever-loyal."

Mary shrugged and sat down again. "Daniel will never see my heart as anything but fickle. He doesn't trust me."

"He will come to," Betsy said with a nod.

"No," Mary said with a shake of her head. "He doesn't trust me because he doesn't love me. How can I live with a man who doesn't trust me, Betsy? Who doesn't love me?"

Betsy placed her hand on her sister's shoulder once more. "You told me that you love him, sister. How can you live without him?"

Betsy left her and Mary sat there alone. She let Betsy's words settle on her mind. She couldn't live without Daniel. She would surely die. She cried out in frustration. Mary withdrew the short note which had accompanied her beautiful new winter cloak and slowly read the words, searching in vain for some emotion, some indication that he missed her as sorely as she did him.

Once more she found nothing save for a kindness which one would extend to a fond acquaintance or a favorite relative. She crumpled the offending missive and tossed it without regret into the waste basket. Coming to her feet, she shook out her skirts.

She took a breath and returned to the parlor to pass the

afternoon with those of whose attachment she was secure, choosing to worry over Daniel's indifference in the solitude of her chamber later that evening.

***

Daniel sat in the dining room at Ashworth Hall, taking yet another meal in solitude. He hadn't anticipated how deeply Mary's absence would affect him. He missed her smiles and her laughter, not that either had been much in evidence these past weeks. He ached for her in their bed, where he could release the iron control in which he held his heart. He longed to hear her whispered gasps of pleasure, certain that he heard evidence of so much more than the physical in her sweet response.

The Christmas holiday had passed like any other day for him. He had seen to the delivery of Mary's gift, a cloak of blue satin that nearly matched her lovely eyes. He had written a note to accompany the present, longing to tell her how much he missed her and wanted her home with him. But he wouldn't leave himself vulnerable and open to betrayal. Mary was safe in Somersetshire. Her family would make certain that no gentleman would come to court her in her husband's absence. He was assured of nothing of the sort there in Newcastle.

He rose from the table and took himself into the parlor to

brood in front of the fireplace. Brooding occupied much of his time of late, he mused as he drank deeply of the brandy left out for him by his attentive staff. And brandy occupied much of his evenings, he thought as he stared into the amber liquid in his glass. He drained the glass and let his mind work.

He'd received a call from Mr. Simmons, and learned from him that Beatrice and her cuckold of a husband had taken themselves from Newcastle at long last. The mere thought of that woman's absence filled Daniel with relief. He'd truly feared his anger would best him were he to see her again, and he didn't favor the notion of living out his days in New Gate Prison due to his dispatching that duplicitous bitch's soul to Hell.

Daniel had thanked the man for his information, choosing to ignore the fact that he asked after Mary with such concern. Did he, a man who had never been married, believe that he was in any position to question Mary's absence? He could guess the reason for Simmons' solicitation. Surely the man wished to gaze upon Mary in rapture. To await her every charming word and graceful gesture in eager anticipation.

The recollection of Mary gazing at him, Daniel, with that soft look in her violet eyes caused his heart to clench. Lord, he missed her. He poured himself another brandy and drank it down as quickly as he had the first.

He hadn't told Simmons that the devil Beatrice herself had paid a visit at Ashworth Hall just three days prior to her quitting Newcastle. The sight of her there, in the home where she'd betrayed his beloved brother, was nearly enough to put him over the edge. After a heated exchange, during which to his great astonishment she sought to use her feminine wiles on his person, he summarily ejected her from the premises. Only half a bottle of brandy followed by a scalding hot bath had rid his mind of the memory of her utterly repugnant offer. As if he would dally with her, the woman who had cost him what he'd held most dear.

The marquis paid a visit just two days before the end of the year, and Daniel greeted his uncle with much pleasure as he bade him to join him in the parlor. The comfort he felt at his uncle's visit was short-lived as the gentleman proceeded to tell Daniel precisely how foolish he believed him to be.

"How can you send your wife from you, Daniel?" the man asked him, indignation clear on his face. "Are you daft?"

Daniel said nothing of Mary to his uncle, permitting the man vent his spleen without censure. What did his uncle know of their marriage? When the older gentleman calmed he then responded in a manner he wished would put an end to the discussion.

"Mary wished to see her family."

His uncle narrowed his eyes in Daniel's direction, causing Daniel to raise his guard. "You believe her safe among her family, don't you? If she's there, she cannot betray you, is that it?"

"What do you know of it, Uncle?" Daniel returned, his anger surging forth. "My marriage is no concern of yours."

He stalked away from the man to stare into the blazing fire behind the grate.

"You are a fool to permit Patrick's great misfortune to color your judgment," the marquis insisted. "Mary is not Beatrice."

"I will not discuss this with you."

He took himself into his study and away from his uncle's accusing eyes. The next day his uncle left Ashworth Hall for Darlington, and Daniel allowed that he felt profound relief at the man's absence.

After his uncle's short and unpleasant visit, Daniel threw himself whole-heartedly into his work on the estate. Mary hadn't written to advise him of the date of her return, but he believed she wouldn't be in Somersetshire much longer. And if his close attention to his business affairs would help him pass the time until her return, he mused, where was the harm?

In fact, on this particular evening he sat in his study long after concluding yet another lonely dinner. As the clock struck the passing of the third hour of the new year, Daniel pushed aside his ledgers. He leaned back in his chair and rubbed his hands over his face. He sought his bed at a later hour each night. He wouldn't consider the true reason for his reluctance. He wanted Mary in their chamber with him and longed to send a messenger to bring her home where she belonged.

A piece of paper drew his notice then, placed upon the smooth top of the desk. He picked it up and puzzled over the handwriting. It somewhat resembled that of his foreman, as the name signed to the note would suggest, although several of the letters seemed a bit spidery as if written by a more delicate hand. The small note spoke of a situation requiring Daniel's attention at one of the coal mines. It appeared that there had been mischief afoot at the mine, Daniel read, and that the foreman had no notion of who might have perpetrated it.

Daniel scratched his chin thoughtfully as he finished reading the short note. Who the devil would trouble themselves to approach that particular mine? It was one set farthest afield, and it had been closed since the onset of the cold weather at the end of November. But, according to the foreman, someone or other had taken to sabotage.

Daniel turned the note over and puzzled again at the handwriting. Suddenly not the least bit fatigued, he decided that he would ride out to the mine and see to the matter directly. He glanced quickly at the clock on his desk and knew that the sun would no doubt be up by the time he reached the mine, or at least soon after. He went up to his chamber not to sleep but to ready for a cold ride over rough terrain.

As the sky was just beginning to brighten Daniel arrived at the mine, cold but undaunted. His practiced eye soon noted that the mine was not sealed as securely as it had been months earlier. Several boards were pried away from the entrance and strewn on the snow-covered ground. He also saw that several tracks were evident in the snow around the entrance. Curiosity driving the awareness of his chilled hands and feet from his mind, he dismounted and kicked aside a bit of snow to reveal a patch of winter grass for the horse's meager meal.

"I'll reward you when we return to the hall."

The horse snorted in response. Daniel smiled and advanced on the mine. He called out a warning, thinking to roust out the vandals if they were about. When no answer came he carefully entered, carrying his lantern with him. Its meager light did little to dispel the gloom as he walked deeper into the crevice.

He knew that the floor of the mine dropped off sharply, so he stepped with the utmost care. Suddenly he heard a sound behind him, a soft footfall accompanied by a rustling. He began to turn toward the sound and was struck hard on the back of his head. He lost his footing and felt himself falling, his arms reaching vainly for some purchase. The blinding pain in his skull was soon eclipsed as he tumbled down the steep and rocky shaft.

Then everything went black.

Chapter 22

Mary sat bolt upright in her bed at Bridgewater Park, a scream tearing from her throat. Her heart pounded as she looked frantically about the guest chamber, recognition slowly dawning on her. Daniel! her mind screamed. Something was very wrong.

"Mary!" Betsy cried as she entered the room.

Michael followed closely on his wife's heels, worry etched on his face. "What is it?" he asked, his hands in fists. "What's wrong?"

Mary took a breath in an attempt to calm herself. So cold, her mind screamed. Daniel was cold and in pain, she knew without question.

"It's Daniel," she said. "Something happened. Something terrible."

Mary would have found the puzzlement on their faces quite humorous were she in a different frame of mind. She got out of bed and ran into the dressing room, her hair and nightgown trailing out behind her.

"I must return to Ashworth Hall," she said breathlessly, rooting through her belongings to find something fit to wear on her journey. "I must find out what happened."

"You can't do this, Mary," Betsy implored, fear clear in

her voice. "Michael, do talk her out of this foolishness."

"Mary, Betsy's right," Michael said, placing his hand on her arm to still her. "It's barely morning and you can't go anywhere is such a state."

Mary shook her head frantically, tearing out of his grasp. "Something has happened, Michael," she said again. "Don't ask me how I know. I just know."

Betsy and Michael exchanged a look which Mary refused to acknowledge. Let them think her daft, she thought as she rang for her maid. Daniel needed her and she wouldn't delay for one moment even to please her family. To Mary's chagrin her mother and father entered the chamber, adding their protestations.

"What is this nonsense?" her mother asked. "Husband, tell Mary that she must not take herself across the country on so foolish an errand."

"Now Mary," her father began, running his fingers through his hair to bring some sort of order to the mass of gray curls. "We have to talk about this."

Mary shook her head again and took her father's hand in hers. "I must go to Newcastle, Father. I don't know what has happened to Daniel. But I must go and go directly."

To her great relief the gentleman nodded sagely. "I'll send you off then, child. But do permit cook to prepare something for you before you take yourself so far away?"

Mary relented with a small smile. Her maid joined her then and the others left Mary to her swift preparations. She refused Michael's offer to accompany her, telling him that his place was with Betsy as much as hers was with Daniel. Before long she was settled in the carriage, leaving her befuddled but loving family to worry over her in her absence.

Mary found herself in Newcastle that very evening. She was bone-tired and nearly sick with worry. She'd dozed at some point during the journey, and had awoken with a start nearly as frightening as the one which had struck her that morning. Daniel was in pain, deep pain and bitterly cold. What on earth could have happened?

She briefly wondered about the wisdom of returning to Newcastle when her presence was not requested by her husband, but put aside any pride that would prevent it. Daniel needed her. Of that she was certain. And the absence of such a request would not deter her.

The Ashworth servants were startled to find their mistress in the entryway and hurried about to ready the house for her.

Mary waved away their concerns over her certain hunger and need for tea and inquired directly after their master.

"Lord Ashworth is not in the house, my lady," the butler said, his eyes showing concern.

"Where is he?" Mary asked pointedly.

The servants exchanged worried glances. The butler cleared his throat and faced his mistress once more. "He was working in his study quite late last evening, as has recently become his custom," the man answered. "His chamber was found empty this morning, his bed undisturbed."

Mary thought furiously for a moment. She'd awoken in the predawn hours. Perhaps whatever misfortune had befallen him had occurred at that ungodly hour.

"Had anyone been to visit Lord Ashworth last evening?" she asked the servant. "Did anyone call on him?"

"No, my lady," came the swift answer. "No one."

Mary paced about the entry, suddenly regretting her refusal of Michael's accompaniment. She had no notion of how she would find her husband, and even though she was reluctant to acknowledge the fact, she was ill-suited to the search. Suddenly, she knew of a person who would come to her and Daniel's aid without question.

"Send a messenger to Darlington Court," she instructed the butler. She quickly penned a note to the gentleman in question, trying her best to convey an urgency without inducing the man to undue worry. "Make haste," she told the footman summoned to see to the task.

Mary removed her cloak and walked into the parlor, coming to a stop in front of the fireplace. She barely felt the warmth coming from the substantial fire behind the grate, hugging her middle to ward off the chill she felt deep in her bones.

"What has happened to Daniel?" she whispered. "And however will I help him?

"Mary, dear," Daniel's uncle said, striding into the room. "Whatever has happened?"

At the man's appearance, Mary felt relief course through her. "Something has happened to Daniel, Uncle," she said. "Something dreadful."

"What is this?" he asked, his faced etched with worry. "Where is he?"

"I don't know."

Lord Darlington blinked in response. "I'm afraid that I do not understand you, my dear. How is it that you're here?"

"I left my father's house this morning."

"You traveled here from Somersetshire?"

"I had no choice in the matter." She crossed to the gentleman. She placed her hand on his arm, gripping it tightly. "Something dreadful had happened to Daniel. We must find him."

To her relief, the man seemed to finally grasp the urgency of the situation.

"All right, all right," the marquis soothed, patting her hand. He led her to the chair beside the fireplace. "Tea for Lady Ashworth," he told a waiting servant. "There now, Mary. Do sit a moment, dear. Tell me everything."

Mary did as he bade, a shaky laugh bubbling out of her. "You will no doubt think me mad," she said with a shake of her head. "I was awakened before dawn in my bed at my father's house. A terrible fear gripped me, and the unmistakable notion that Daniel was hurt badly."

Daniel's uncle was thoughtful for a moment. He gave a firm nod of his white head, his dark eyes twinkling. "You love him, don't you?"

Mary was taken aback for a moment. She slowly nodded. "I do love him. More than I can say."

"Then I believe you when you say that you knew he was hurt," the man continued. "Your heart is tied to his."

Mary nodded again. "But what are we to do? However will we find him?"

"Let us go to his study, Mary," Lord Darlington said, pulling her to her feet. "No doubt we'll find something of import there."

Mary and the marquis entered the study, amazed at the number of ledgers and papers set neatly upon the desk. She had no question in her mind as to the manner in which Daniel had spent his time in her absence. She watched as his uncle quickly searched the desk for any possible clue.

"Hello, what is this?" he said, holding a small paper aloft. "It seems that there is some sort of trouble at one of the mines. Knowing my nephew, he's gone to investigate the matter."

"Then we must go to him!" Mary said, hope filling her breast.

"Easy, Mary," the marquis said. "Daniel would have my head if I were to permit you to accompany me. I'll take a few of Daniel's men with me and we'll set out directly for the mine."

"Bring him home, Uncle," she implored. "Bring him home to me."

"Yes, dear. I shall."

***

Daniel slowly came awake from a dreamless sleep, and with that awakening came the awareness of pain unlike that he'd ever encountered. His head pounded with dizzying effect, his body felt battered and torn. He opened his eyes, although he perceived no more light then when his lids had covered them. A shiver wracked his body. Were it not for the numbing cold, he would surely believe he was in Hell. Where the devil was he?

He held his head in his hands, feeling a stickiness on his fingers that could only be blood. It fairly covered his face. He came up on one elbow, groaning with the effort. As he shifted his legs, raw pain surged through him anew. A scream tore from him as he twisted his right leg. He clutched at it, curses flowing from his chapped lips as he squeezed back tears.

After a while, he couldn't determine the length of time that had passed, the pain in his leg subsided enough for him to regain some of his wits. He was in the mine. Flashes of memory came to him: the cryptic note he'd found in his study, the long cold ride nearly to the boundary of his holdings, the vandalized mine shaft. No more came to him save that. He had absolutely no recollection of what had happened after he'd entered the mine.

Pain soon sent any more musings from him as his big frame shook from the cold. He clutched his greatcoat about his shoulders and closed his eyes against the pain.

"So cold," he moaned.

Sleep beckoned to him, offering solace from the icy cold and hot pain that assailed him. He resisted for long minutes, finally welcoming the respite.

Voices called out to Daniel, breaking through the sleep that had enveloped him for longer than he could remember. It sounded like his father, his mind faintly registered. But how could that be? He opened his eyes and looked about. Bobbing points of light reached him, growing ever nearer as the voices grew louder. A face was soon above his, smiling and worried both. It wasn't his father. No. It was his uncle.

"Daniel, my boy," the man said, his voice thick. "Thank God we found you."

"Uncle," Daniel rasped.

He cried out as he was lifted from the rocky floor, his leg on fire.

"Take care," his uncle instructed the other men. "We don't know the extent of the earl's injuries."

The pain proved too much for Daniel despite the men's

271

care, and as they set him into one of the work wagons he fell in and out of blessed sleep. The marquis covered him carefully with several woolen blankets and climbed into the wagon to sit beside him.

"Hang on, my boy," he said. "Your dear wife would prefer to have you returned to her in one piece."

Chapter 23

They returned to the hall as quickly as they were able, and Mary greeted them in the entryway, clutching her hands nervously. His appearance stole her breath.

The gash on the side of Daniel's face didn't trouble her as much as the apparent condition of his right leg. The fabric stretched taut over the swollen limb was darkened with sticky blood. And whether an injury to Daniel's head was the reason for his sleep or not, that was left to be determined by the doctor.

"My God, Daniel!" she cried, flying at the men carrying her husband between them on a blanket.

"Easy, my dear," Lord Darlington gently admonished, placing his hands on her shoulders to still her. "Let the men carry him to his chamber."

Mary nodded mutely and watched as they bore Daniel's big battered body up the grand staircase. She had only a glimpse of her husband and was shaken to the core. Taking a deep breath to gather her strength, she hurried up the stairs to their chamber.

The marquis waved the men from the room as Mary entered. His dark eyes held a look of worry which she read before he could school the expression.

"Daniel," she breathed, coming toward the bed.

"I've sent for Dr. Lawson," Darlington told her.

Mary nodded and drew a chair close to the bedside. Daniel's appearance there in the regal chambers was all the more shocking.

"He is so pale," she said, placing her hand on his cheek. "How can he sleep with such injuries?"

"He was lucid when we reached the mine, Mary," Darlington told her. "But he fell asleep when we loaded him into the wagon."

"He's covered with dirt and grime."

Eager to take some form of action she rang for her maid, instructing her to bring warm water and towels to the bedroom. Before Jane could return, Mary began to roll up her sleeves.

"Surely you do not wish to see to the task yourself?" Daniel's uncle asked incredulously.

"He needs to be bathed, Uncle," she said with a shrug. "I won't stand idly by while others attend my husband."

Ignoring the man's look of surprise, Mary saw to the removal of Daniel's ruined clothes. Scratches marred his big body. She refused to acknowledge the full extent of his injuries.

Daniel groaned and shifted in the bed. She jumped back as a groan of pain escaped his lips. "So cold," he murmured with a shiver.

Mary puzzled over that as his skin felt quite hot to her. She looked up at Daniel's uncle, wondering idly if her face mirrored the anxiousness evident to her on his.

"Dr. Lawson will be here soon, dear," he said with a nod. "Pray, do not trouble yourself over his condition until the man has seen to him?"

She gave a slow nod and bent to her task when Jane returned with the things she'd requested. She silently prayed as she moved the washing cloth over her husband's body. She bathed his upper body, choosing to leave the lower to the doctor's attentions not from female modesty but from outright fear. She didn't dare ascertain the condition of his right leg at the present moment. The many candles which illuminated the chamber allowed her to see in harsh relief the amount of grime, and what she feared too much to think was blood, that covered the limb.

She sent Jane for a bowl of clean water and wiped her hands on the skirt of her dress as she regarded the patient closely. Daniel was still uneasy, his head moving restlessly on the pillow. Running her fingers lovingly over his face, she murmured sweet nothings and soothing sounds.

"Lady Ashworth," Dr. Lawson said briskly as he strode into the room. "Pray, let me see to the earl."

To Mary's relief the doctor exhibited none of the timidity she'd come to expect these many months, due no doubt to the absence of the man's wife. He seemed most competent as he examined Daniel, saying nothing as his brow wrinkled in concentration.

"How long was he in the mine, Lord Darlington?" he asked Daniel's uncle.

"We're not at all certain, Lawson. Apparently he worked quite late in his study before setting out for the mine."

The doctor nodded and turned to Mary. "If you will quit the chamber, Lady Ashworth?"

"No," Mary said. "I won't leave him."

The marquis swiftly came to her side, placing his arm around her shoulders. "I'm certain that Lawson merely wishes to examine Daniel's leg wound, Mary. Then, no doubt, he will allow you in here once more."

The doctor nodded at that. Mary looked from one man to the other, finally settling her gaze on Daniel where he still lay unconscious on the bed. Reluctantly, she nodded her acquiescence and left the chamber. Once in the sitting room, she allowed the tears which had been threatening pour from beneath her lowered lashes. She hugged herself as she leaned against the wall and cried without sound or restraint.

"Mary, dear," Daniel's uncle said after what seemed a lifetime. "You may enter."

Mary turned away as she wiped the tears from her cheeks. She hurried through the opened door and joined Dr. Lawson at Daniel's bedside. Worriedly, she ran her eyes over her husband's body. Clean white bandages swathed his leg, which was no longer so frightening-looking but just as swollen. His body was now mostly covered with a sheet, no doubt in deference to her modesty. The doctor held a thick bandage to the right side of Daniel's face, no mean feat as the patient still thrashed his head about.

Lawson looked up at Mary and gave her a nod. "His leg is in a precarious condition, my lady," he said. "I don't believe that I will have need to take it, however."

"You mustn't!"

"There, there," the doctor soothed. "Remarkably the bone was not broken. I've seen to the wound, but it is quite severe. The bandage will need to be changed periodically and the leg bathed."

"I will see to it," Mary said shortly.

The doctor's brows raised a bit at that but he didn't argue with her. "I don't believe that the bump on the back of his head is the reason for his sleeping."

"But then, what?"

"Fever has set in," the doctor informed her. "And he won't allow me to keep this bandage on him."

Mary took the doctor's place at the head of the bed. She took the bandage in her hand began to lift it.

"Now," the doctor began, reaching for her. "It looks far worse than it is."

Mary shook her head and lifted the gauze. She sucked in her breath as she saw the huge gash marring his face from above his temple to below his cheekbone. The wound had ragged edges, and was deep though no more blood came from it at present. She lightly touched the gauze to it as she leaned her face to Daniel's.

"We must keep this covered, Daniel," she said softly. "Do settle yourself."

To both her amazement and the doctor's, Daniel stilled. His eyes opened then, their gaze muddied and a bit unfocused. "Mary," he murmured. "God, Mary."

She'd never been more pleased to hear her name on his lips.

"I'm here, Daniel," she said. "What can I do for you?"

He moved his lips and she believed that he asked for water.

She straightened and turned to the doctor. "Can he have something to drink, Dr. Lawson?"

"Yes, of course," was the answer. "Do let me put some laudanum in the water. It will help him sleep and keep that leg still."

The doctor handed her the glass of diluted medicine. Mary carefully held Daniel's head as she brought the glass to his lips. He swallowed greedily and closed his eyes once more.

"He should sleep soon," the doctor said. "Do give him the same dose every four hours or so, my lady. It will dull the pain in his leg."

After advising her that he would return in the morning to check on his patient, Dr. Lawson took his leave. Mary sat beside the bed once more, choosing to ignore the whispered conversation between Lord Darlington and the doctor in the sitting room. She heard the door shut and waited for the marquis to return to the bedroom. She heard the man give a sigh as he reentered the chamber.

"He is doubtful of Daniel's keeping the leg," Mary said flatly, keeping her back toward him.

"He is unsure, my child," the gentleman returned. "But Daniel's health being what it was, and will be again, Lawson has every hope that nothing so drastic should have to be undertaken."

Mary silently prayed that it would be so. The prospect of having as her husband a man who lacked a limb was not what worried her. She feared that Daniel wouldn't adjust to such a change to his physical condition. And that was if he were to survive the operation to take the limb. She opened her eyes to find the marquis trying in vain to stifle a yawn.

"Why don't you retire for the remainder of the evening, Uncle?" she offered. "No doubt the chamber regularly set aside for your use has been prepared."

"Yes," he nodded. "I trust you will take to the bed in the next chamber?"

"No," she said firmly. "I'll stay here with Daniel."

She braced herself for an argument. To her surprise the marquis simply nodded his understanding, a tired smile on his lips.

"My nephew is a lucky man," he said softly. "Send for me

should the need arise, my dear."

Mary assured him that he would not only send for him but for the servants and Dr. Lawson should Daniel require anything that she was unable to provide herself. She bade the man good night and advised the tired footman standing outside the chamber to take his own bed.

She went into the dressing room and changed into a nightgown and wrapper. Returning to the bed she saw with some relief that Daniel was sleeping soundly. But he was sprawled in the big bed and Mary didn't wish to cause him any discomfort by stretching out beside him. She longed to do just that. To wrap her arms around him and hold him close. Dragging one of the upholstered chairs set before the fireplace to the side of the bed seemed a plausible compromise.

She straightened and placed her palm against Daniel's forehead. Evidence of the fever greeted her touch. She dropped a kiss on his cheek and settled herself as comfortably as possible in the chair.

"Good night, Daniel," she said as she closed her eyes. "Sleep well."

A sound awoke Mary, one which was vaguely familiar to her ears. She sat bolt upright in the chair, her eyes flying to her husband. He thrashed about on the bed, a fierce frown on his face.

"Beatrice, you miserable whore," he muttered, curling his lip in distaste. "Where is Patrick?"

"Shh, Daniel," Mary soothed, placing her hands on his shoulders with gentle insistence.

Daniel shook his head violently on the pillow. "Patrick, stop!" he cried. "No!"

Daniel began to cry, deep sobs that tore at Mary's heart. "Hang on, Patrick," he sobbed. "Don't leave me. Pray, don't leave me here alone."

Never had Mary heard such anguish in her husband's voice, such raw hurt. The veil was gone from his countenance and Mary could see that he felt emotions far deeper than he ever allowed to her.

"I'm all alone," he murmured as the tears dried on his face. "All alone."

The desperation in his voice touched her to her very soul.

"I'm here, Daniel," Mary said, her own tears choking her voice. "It's Mary."

Daniel's brows shot upward, though his eyes remained closed tight. "Mary," he whispered. "Ah God, where is Mary?"

She grabbed his hand in hers tightly. "Shh, husband," she said, kissing his hand. "I'm here."

His mouth turned down into a frown as he shook his head. "I sent her from me."

"No, Daniel," she said, clutching at his hand. "I'm here."

"If only Mary loved me," he rasped. "God, if only."

Mary's throat tightened. Tossing aside her fear of making such a disclosure, she placed her hands on his face to still him as she gave him the words he seemed to crave.

"I love you, Daniel," she said. "I love you so much."

"No," he murmured.

"I love you," she said again.

Daniel's eyes opened then, their velvet depths dark and clouded. Could he see her? Could he hear her?

"Mary," he said, his voice harsh. "My beauty."

She smiled at him. She lost that smile when, with a strength she found astonishing, he grabbed her to him. She managed to somehow keep herself off of his injured leg as she found herself draped along the length of him.

"Mary," Daniel said again, his eyes closed tight as his fingers tangled in her hair.

He crushed her to him, sealing his mouth to hers. Their

kiss was deep and Mary shook with its intensity. Daniel's mouth was hot on her throat. He captured her breasts as he tore at her wrapper and nightgown. Mary gasped at the desire he swiftly provoked within her.

The evidence of his arousal surprised her as his hands grabbed onto her hips and held her against him. She couldn't have kept herself from him if she'd wished to. His urgency spoke to her very soul. She pushed aside the thin sheet keeping him from her.

"I need you, Mary," he rasped, straining toward her. "God, I need your love."

"Daniel," she whispered as she took him inside of her. "I love you, Daniel."

He drove up into her, wild in his movements. Mary clutched at his shoulders as her body answered his rhythm, taking him deeper into herself as she rode him. Daniel spilled his seed then, arching off of the bed as her own climax tore through her. Mary held on tightly as he settled, her breath coming fast. She was amazed at what had transpired in so few moments. His body was still burning hot beneath hers and she quickly removed herself from him. She covered him with the sheet and straightened her own attire.

"Oh my," she breathed, running her fingers through her tangled curls.

She took a deep breath and regarded Daniel once more. He appeared to be sleeping more comfortably. His brow was smooth and his lips curved in a slight smile. Daniel wished for her love?

"Amazing," she breathed.

Settling into the chair once more, she hugged herself and fell into an exhausted slumber.

Chapter 24

"How did you fare last evening, Mary?" the marquis asked the next morning as they awaited the doctor's arrival.

Mary's mind went unerringly back to the passion she and Daniel had shared in the still and dark early morning hours. He'd asked for her love. Was it the fever talking? Or did he truly wish to make their marriage into a love match?

Daniel did look better. He was sweating profusely, however. His golden hair was damp and curling at his brow.

"I believe his fever has broken," his uncle said.

"I pray that's so," Mary murmured.

The doctor arrived within the hour, sending thoughts of love and passion from her mind. She was wholly concerned with Daniel's physical condition and willed herself to spare no time on thoughts of his emotional state at the moment.

The medical man confirmed the marquis' supposition. He asked Mary to look away as he saw to the removal of the bandages swathing Daniel's leg and she did so.

"The wound appears to be healing," he noted. "And the leg is far less swollen than last evening."

Mary breathed a sigh of relief at that good news, whispering a quick prayer of thanks as Lawson carefully changed the bandages and straightened.

"He appears to have spent an uneventful night," the man
went on. "I trust he gave you no trouble, Lady Ashworth?"

A flush crawled up her cheeks and gave a quick shake of
her head. How could she tell either gentlemen what had
transpired between them in the wee hours of the morning? And
as Daniel's condition certainly seemed none the worse for his
nocturnal passions, what possible information could such a
revelation serve?

"He cried out periodically but he slept soundly for most of
the night," was all she could manage to say for the moment.

"I can't say that the condition of his leg will be unaffected
by the injury," Dr. Lawson said. "Though I no longer fear that
the more drastic operation will have to be undertaken."

"Oh, that is good news," Mary breathed, pressing her hand
against her chest.

"And what of his head wound, Lawson?" the marquis
asked.

The doctor gently probed the back of Daniel's head for
several moments, finally nodding with satisfaction. "The bump
has reduced in size significantly."

He then carefully examined the gash on the side of

Daniel's face as Mary and the marquis looked on. It remained quite red and angry.

"What of the cut, Dr. Lawson?" she asked. "Should we attempt to wrap it?"

Lawson gave her a firm nod. He cleansed it, applied some ointment and wrapped it with fresh gauze.

"Do see that the bandage stays in place, my lady," he instructed. "I do believe the mark may remain."

"What does that matter?" Mary asked with a wave of her hand. "I want Daniel to get better, Doctor. That is my main concern."

Daniel let out a moan then, soft to her ears but not imperceptible.

"Daniel," she said, sitting once more beside him. "Daniel, are you all right?"

***

Daniel opened his eyes, squinting as the sunlight in the chamber set his head to throbbing. A face stared down at him, one so sweet that for a moment he believed it was an angel. No. Not an angel. His Mary.

"Mary," he said, his throat parched. "Mary, is that you?"

Mary placed her hand in his. "Yes, Daniel. Your uncle and

Dr. Lawson are here, as well."

He moved his eyes about the room, his gaze lighting on each man for a moment. He licked his chapped lips. "Water?"

Mary quickly poured him a glass and held it for him. He struggled into a sitting position.

"No, Daniel," she said. "You must be careful."

He blinked at her in confusion, his sluggish body finally surrendering to her wishes. He took a long sip of the water and sighed.

"My God, I feel like hell." He placed his hand on his head, only to puzzle over the bandage on his face. "What is this?"

"Easy, my lord," Dr. Lawson said. "That bandage must remain in place."

Daniel probed the bandage, wincing at the pain the action caused. He dropped his hand and sighed again.

"What the devil happened to me?" he asked.

Daniel watched as Mary and his uncle exchanged a look of worry. The marquis then approached the bed and Daniel looked up at him expectantly.

"You had quite an adventure, my boy," Daniel's uncle said with a smile. "Worried your wife half to death in the process, however."

Daniel searched his mind for some recollection. "There was a note. Something about one of the mines."

"Yes," his uncle said. "Mary and I found it in your study. That's how we knew where to look for you."

A shiver passed through him as he faintly recalled the events of last evening.

"Do you remember what happened, Daniel?" Mary asked softly.

Daniel studied Mary for a long moment before answering her question. When had she come home? And he'd never seen her in such a state, he thought as he took in her dress and hair, let alone seen such a frown of worry marring her smooth forehead.

"I remember riding out to the mine," he told her. "I don't recall what happened then. Why are you here?"

Mary pulled back at that. Daniel watched as she lowered her lashes in what he could only presume was evasion.

"I had to come," was all she said, further confounding him.

"Mary came home and sent for me directly, my boy," the marquis offered. "I shudder to think what might have happened to you had she not."

But how could that be? He had no notion that she was to return to Ashworth Hall. What had compelled her to shorten the visit to her family?

"But I don't…ah!" he cried out as he once more attempted to sit up in the bed.

"Easy," his uncle said.

"Daniel!" Mary cried out at the same time.

Daniel looked down the length of his body, amazed by the appearance of a swollen bandage-wrapped limb taking the place of his right leg. He tried once more to move the leg, the action causing it to feel strange and heavy.

"What's the matter with my leg, Lawson?"

"You injured it quite seriously," the doctor said. "Apparently you twisted it in your fall, and cut it up quite badly. It will take a long while to mend."

Daniel fisted his hands in frustration. A quick look at Mary showed that she appeared exhausted as well as worried.

"How long have I been in bed?" he asked her.

"They brought you back here late last night."

A blush covered her cheeks and he puzzled over that. She cleared her throat and stood, running her hands over the skirt of her simple muslin dress in a clear show of nervousness.

"I'm a horrid mess," she murmured. "If you gentlemen will excuse me?"

The doctor and Lord Darlington nodded as she all but ran into her dressing room. Daniel heard the door shut and turned his attention to his uncle.

"What is ailing Mary?" he asked him.

"She does seem a bit out of sorts," his uncle said. "No doubt she is quite fatigued."

Daniel turned to the doctor. "How long will I be incapacitated, Lawson?"

"That's difficult to say, my lord. You must rest. That I cannot overly stress."

Suddenly a wave of fatigue washed over Daniel and he found no trouble following the doctor's orders. He settled back down into the bed and closed his eyes. His leg felt like it was on fire and his head fairly throbbed but he was alive and no longer consumed by the numbing cold that had gripped him last night. Or was that the night before?

"We'll leave you to rest, my boy," his uncle said.

Footsteps faded away as he shifted in the bed. He cursed at the pain the slight movement caused his leg. A rustle of skirts drew his attention, along with the brush of soft lips on his cheek.

"Sleep Daniel," Mary's voice softly instructed.

He did, his sleep blessedly dreamless.

When he awoke, the afternoon light faintly lit the chamber. A quick glance at the clock on the mantle told him that more hours had passed than he would have otherwise presumed. He still felt bone-weary, although he was pleased to note that the throbbing in his head had subsided.

A flash of color caught his eye and he turned to see Mary entering the sleeping chamber, a smile on her face.

"Oh, you're awake," she said.

Daniel took a moment to note her appearance, which was markedly different from what he had perceived earlier. Her hair was neatly coiffed and her dress of mossy green silk was without wrinkles. Faint smudges darkened the skin beneath her violet eyes, but her sweet smile more than eclipsed that fault. Was that smile meant for him?

"Yes," he said. "Although I feel like bloody hell."

Her fair brows drew together as she touched her hand to his forehead. Her touch was light and he couldn't help but revel in it, brief though it was.

"You have no fever, thank the good Lord," she murmured as she removed her hand from him. "How does your head feel?"

Daniel shrugged in answer. He suddenly realized that the thin sheet on the bed barely covered him and quickly remedied that situation. The unmistakable scent of dirt and sweat assailed his nostrils.

"God, I smell rank," he observed. "I need a bath."

"Oh no," Mary said, her eyes round. "You must be careful with your leg, Daniel."

She hurriedly rang for warm water and fresh towels to be delivered directly to the chamber and turned once more to the bedside. Her eyes slowly ran over his body.

"We shall have to do the best that we can," she told him with a small smile.

That appealing blush covered her cheeks once more, causing notions that should be far from his mind to surface. Before he could give his thoughts words his uncle entered the chamber, followed closely by servants bearing several pitchers of water.

"Taking a bath, my boy?" The marquis smiled broadly. "I say that is a welcome notion, eh Mary?"

Mary laughed lightly, the sound tugging at Daniel's heart. She made a motion to roll up her sleeves, suddenly checking her movement.

"I'll wait outside," she rushed out.

Daniel watched as his uncle followed her into the sitting

room, mildly curious about Mary's strange behavior. He washed himself as well as he could manage, and had his valet fetch him a nightshirt. Running his fingers through his hair caused him some discomfort, both from the bump and the bandaged cut. By the time he was finished, he was tired but feeling somewhat better. A knock on the door separating the sitting room from the chamber drew his attention.

"Are you decent, my boy?" his uncle asked, poking his head into the chamber.

"As far as I can tell," Daniel answered.

Darlington walked into the chamber, a smile on his face. "You easily scared ten years off of my life, Daniel."

Daniel smiled wearily at that. "Where is Mary?"

"She is seeing to some correspondence," the older gentleman said. "I believe she is informing her family of all that has transpired. She left her father's house very early yesterday morning and they must be quite worried about her."

Daniel puzzled over that. "How is it that she came to return to Ashworth Hall? And why in such urgency?"

"That is a mystery," the man returned with a secret smile.

Daniel was suddenly too tired to question the man further.

"Why don't you rest, my boy?" his uncle said.

Frowning in frustration, Daniel closed his eyes and rested his head on his pillow. Why did Mary come back to Newcastle? How did she know that he needed her? Before his mind could wrap itself around any plausible answer, sleep once more claimed him.

Chapter 25

Three weeks passed, and with them the danger of Daniel's losing his leg. Mary had learned of this from Dr. Lawson upon the conclusion of one of his daily visits and her relief had been great. The marquis had taken his leave of Ashworth Hall the previous week to see to his own affairs, confident in his nephew's full recovery under both his doctor's and his wife's care. This afternoon Lawson was once more with Daniel as Mary awaited the man's report in the parlor. To her dismay the doctor descended the grand staircase with a look of exasperation on his face.

"Is something wrong, Dr. Lawson?" she asked.

The doctor sighed irritably, rubbing his hand over his face. "Three days ago I left a cane for his use, my lady. Though he professes to need nothing of the sort. If I may say so, Lord Ashworth can be a most contrary gentleman."

Mary smiled knowingly at that statement, relieved that nothing more than Daniel's stubbornness plagued the doctor on this day. She assured Lawson that she would personally see to it that Daniel took all necessary care with his leg. She bade the man farewell and climbed the staircase to their rooms. Taking a breath to steel herself against her husband's foul mood, she passed through the sitting room and entered the sleeping chamber.

"What, precisely, did you say to Dr. Lawson, Daniel?" she asked as she crossed toward the bed.

Daniel scowled at her from the bed, shooting a look of derision toward the cane which leaned against the door to his dressing room. Of course. *The cane.*

"I have no need for such a ridiculous item," he grumbled.

She arched a brow at him, her mind working to find a reasonable argument for such an unreasonable statement. "Have you attempted to get about the room without it?"

Daniel snorted in answer. Mary sighed in irritation. For days now Daniel had been surly and incommunicative, a fact she'd tried to ignore. The previous week she'd ceased sleeping in the chair beside him in the chamber and taken up residence in a nearby bedroom, and apparently he felt the change with no discernible distress.

Several visits to the chamber throughout the day failed to achieve better discourse between them, and Mary was nearly at her wit's end. But this day his manner was decidedly worse toward her and she could not fathom the reason.

"Lawson is a cautious old woman," Daniel said. "I have no

need for a cane and I won't use one."

Mary stared at him, finding a change in his appearance as well as his demeanor. She suddenly took note of his smoothly-shaven cheeks and neatly combed hair. The bandage which had covered the right side of his face had been deemed unnecessary for days now and she'd grown accustomed to the sight of the wound. But now with his face clean-shaven the imperfection was pronounced, not that it caused her any distress. Surely Daniel had thoroughly examined it. Could that be the root of his foul mood this day?

When her eyes met his the distrust evident prior to Christmas revisited, accompanied by more than a touch of hostility. She blinked rapidly, hoping that she was mistaken. His next words proved that she most definitely was not.

"May I ask what draws your interest, wife?" Daniel asked shortly. "Surely I am not so altered since last you saw me?"

"You shaved this morning," she said in response. "I'm pleased to see those whiskers gone," she added with a small smile.

Daniel's eyes hardened and the futility of her situation struck her fully. Swallowing any threatening tears, she walked stiffly to the straight-backed chair beside the bed and sat.

"What are you about this day, Daniel? Perhaps we can stroll about in the gardens."

"With that cursed cane?" He snorted. "I think not."

Mary gave a slight shrug. "Then perhaps we can play a game of cards. Or see to your correspondence?"

"I don't need your assistance to attend to such matters, Mary," he grumbled. "Nor do I need you to amuse me."

"But I can bring you your papers."

"I can find my own way to my study."

Mary stood then, anger causing her pulse to race. "I'll leave you then, sir," she said. "Perhaps I'll find you improved in spirits this evening."

She turned to leave, coming to a standstill as his next words reached her at the door.

"In sprits, wife?" he muttered darkly. "Or in looks?"

Choking back angry tears, she left the chamber.

***

Daniel watched Mary's slender back stiffen at his words, and felt a bit of guilt. But he'd seen the preoccupation in her expression when she'd gazed upon his hideous mark. She'd stared at him like he was some sort of oddity, he fumed as he swung his legs to the side of the bed. He cursed fluently as his leg threatened to give way beneath him, clutching to the bedpost as thoughts of Mary temporarily fled his mind. He held his breath as he pushed off from the post, letting it out with relief when his two feet were nearly equally engaged. Walking would be a feat to be sure.

He shot another dark look at the cursed cane resting beside his dressing room door. There was nothing for it, he decided as he hobbled over to it. He took up the cane and straightened. He found to his chagrin that he could bear his weight on the mending leg quite well with the cane.

His mind swiftly returned to his wife as he entered the dressing room and crossed to the washstand. Leaning on the stand, he peered resolutely into the mirror atop. The mark appeared not to have altered in the least. He had little wonder at Mary's discomfort in his presence. How long before she sought solace with her family once more? Surely she wouldn't wish to stay with a man marked as he was, with a gash so puckered and red marring his visage.

Already she'd taken herself from their bed. She couldn't bear to be with him even with her eyes closed in slumber! As for the prospect of sharing once more the passion which had filled their former life together?

"Enough," he grumbled.

He rang for his valet and readied for dinner, steeling himself for Mary's thinly-veiled distaste at his appearance despite the care taken with his dress.

When he arrived in the parlor to find Mary engrossed in the nightscape beyond the windows, he took the opportunity to observe her undetected. She looked every inch the beautiful countess, and his body reacted swiftly with desire. He tamped down that fierce wanting.

"Good evening, wife," Daniel said, drawing her from her apparent absorption in the view of the darkened gardens outside the window.

Mary turned and froze. Her gaze was hungry on him, and he wondered just what she saw. Surely she found fault with him. He was no longer the dashing man she'd married.

"Good evening, husband," she said as she crossed to him. "How nice to be taking our meals together once more."

He felt a chill at her words. Time and again over the past weeks she'd seemed to crave an invitation to join him for his meals there in the chamber, lingering long after the covered tray was delivered to the table in the sitting room. But he'd simply waited for her to take herself downstairs to the dining room. And now that they were returning to the former custom of taking their meals together once more, would the stiffness and distance between finally dissipate?

Daniel quirked his mouth in a humorless smile and held out his left arm to her.

"Shall we go into the dining room?" he asked without much enthusiasm.

Mary placed her hand tentatively on his arm and permitted him to lead her in to dinner. The mealtime began without any of the easy banter and light conversation which had filled the room prior to her taking her holiday at Bridgewater Park. If he were honest with himself, matters were strained long before she accepted Betsy's invitation for Christmas.

"Quite a bit of correspondence awaits you attention, Daniel," she said lightly.

Daniel arched a brow at her. "I will see to it."

"I believe your friends have learned of your accident," she said, setting her glass down beside her plate. "Do you wish my assistance in answering the letters?"

Daniel shot her a cold look. "I can do quite well without your help."

Mary placed her linen napkin beside her barely-touched

plate of rare roast beef and stood. "Then I assume you can do quite well without my company as well," she said coolly. "Although I daresay you shall scarcely notice."

Before he could make any argument to the contrary, she left the dining room. Sometime later he climbed the stairs without much effort due to the help of the cursed cane, his mind working. The evening had been a disaster. Mary had stared at him when he arrived in the parlor, looking for what he would not hazard a guess. When her eyes had alighted on the cane, he couldn't help but assume that she found the item nearly as distasteful as the scar on his face.

Dinner was an ordeal, despite the sumptuous meal and fine wine. Why couldn't he speak to her with courtesy? But she shouldn't have offered her assistance in something as simple as seeing to some correspondence. She'd mentioned that he'd received letters from his friends and acquaintances in town. Was she so hungry for social contact that she thought to seek the attention of such friends for herself? Cursing his mind for its wanderings, he set aside the cane and sat in a chair beside the bed.

A sound drew his attention to Mary's dressing room door and he watched as she emerged, her eyes wide and lips parted in surprise. As he watched, she straightened and assumed composure. He sought to ignore the fact that her thin nightgown and wrapper hid little of her from neither his eyes nor his memory. He nodded curtly to her and turned his attention to the removal of his boots, cursing softly as the task proved more difficult than he had imagined.

"Let me help you," Mary said softly.

Daniel hesitated, finally giving her another nod. He leaned back in the chair as she came to kneel before him. She removed his left boot without much difficulty and set it aside. The right proved more tenacious, as his leg was a bit stiff. She straddled the leg and put her back to him, grasping the heel of the boot and pulling gingerly. Daniel ran his eyes over her form, her thin nightclothes nearly disappearing from his eyes. She was incredible.

Her glorious hair, freed from the evening's pins and brushed into shining glory, nearly reached the floor as she bent to her task. The graceful curve of her slender back, the roundness of her bottom, sent pleasurable tremors through him. He imagined grasping the hems of her wrapper and gown, slowly lifting it to bare her delectable bottom to his eyes. He could almost feel the smoothness of her skin beneath his fingertips, the growing dampness of the golden curls at the juncture of her silken thighs as his touch readied her. He wished to part those thighs. To free himself and pull her against him. To come inside of her completely.

The image in his mind was so vivid, the sounds of pleasure she would make nearly in his ears, that he let out a groan of acute frustration. Mary jerked upright and glanced over her shoulder, her brows drawn together.

"Did I hurt your leg?" she asked.

Daniel blinked to clear his mind and shook his head in answer. She studied him closely and for a moment he wondered if she could read his wicked thoughts. Not so wicked, really. She was his wife. But a wife who deserved far more than the man he was now.

"No," he said, his voice hoarse.

She returned to her task and his right foot was soon free of the boot. She carefully set his foot down on the carpet and stood. He winced as she touched his thigh briefly for support, her fingers dangerously close to his arousal, and she pulled her hand from him.

"I'm sorry," she said, kneeling before him once more. "Let me ease you."

Her words, meant in all innocence, caused desire to flood through him. When she began to massage his thigh, it became almost too much to bear.

"Enough!" he said, his voice rough with wanting. "Leave me, Mary."

She raised her face to him, her eyes huge. "But your leg?"

"I don't need you to play the role of nursemaid."

Mary stood, blinking rapidly as Daniel steeled himself against the hurt he saw in her beautiful violet eyes. She ran from the room, her soft sobs following her. He removed the rest of his clothes and climbed into the big lonely bed. She was far better off than had she stayed and been subjected to lovemaking by a man who was now far beneath her.

She deserved much better than the wreck of a man he had become.

Chapter 26

The early morning hours brought a new discomfort to Daniel's senses, although the state in which he'd found himself after Mary's tantalizing ministrations the previous evening had caused him to lose more than a few hours of sleep. As he descended the stairs, bound for the breakfast room, the sight which greeted his eyes did little to lighten his mood. Mary was standing in the foyer speaking to a gentleman. She wore a pretty blue day dress and a bright smile.

Daniel narrowed his eyes on the man's broad back as he drew closer to the pair. The visitor then nodded at Mary, turning his face a bit. Damn it to Hell. It was Harley.

Daniel caught Mary's eye at last and drew back at the expression on her face. She brightened, her eyes sparkling as they found his. Surely that warm smile wasn't meant for him.

"Daniel," she enthused, coming to stand beside him. "Look who has arrived."

Daniel forced a benevolence he didn't feel and switched the cane to his left hand to offer his right to his good friend in greeting.

"Ashworth, you old devil," Harley smiled as he shook Daniel's hand. "Word of your accident reached London and I couldn't stay away."

"Harley," Daniel said with a nod. "How thoughtful of you."

Mary lowered her lashes—in embarrassment or guilt, Daniel would not surmise—and Harley's smile widened. The gentleman faced Daniel once more, his eyes twinkling.

"I daresay your wife's care has wrought a remarkable recovery," he said. "The talk in town was that you were fairly incapacitated."

Daniel smiled grimly. "I'll survive."

The three of them stood in silence for a long moment. Daniel watched as Mary's fingers brushed delicately over her skirts in a show of her nervousness. She seemed to sense his scrutiny and dropped her hands to her sides.

"I've invited Lord Harley to breakfast, of course," Mary stated. "And to stay here at the hall."

Daniel managed to keep his irritation in check, though he knew not how. He merely nodded his assent and took up his cane as the three of them proceeded into the breakfast room. Had Mary sent for the man who had very nearly won her hand in marriage? Was that the correspondence to which she was seeing when she'd left him alone in their chamber during the early weeks of his recovery?

He sat down at the table, finding himself quite willing to delay taking his meal for the moment.

"You look quite dashing with that cane, Ashworth," Harley said as he served himself from the sideboard. "Quite dashing, indeed."

Daniel smirked at his friend, managing a grunt of thanks for Mary as she set a plate of ham and eggs before him. He said nothing as his wife and her guest exchanged banalities. As talk of the dwindled society evident in London was delivered, he studied the two of them. Mary seemed quite animated as she listened to Harley's stories of the most recent developments in town. Her eyes were bright as she sat beside the dark-haired gentleman, her expression far different from that which she bestowed on her own husband save for that brief moment at the bottom of the stairs.

He was startled to realize that his very beautiful wife was now more suited to the man who had first asked for her hand than she was to the wreck to whom she was now tied.

How much time would pass before that thought occurred to her?

Daniel stood in his study that evening, drinking deeply

from his supply of fine brandy. He hadn't imagined that a dinner could be any worse than the previous evening's, but he'd discovered that he had been woefully mistaken on that count.

Mary had looked her usual incredible self, although she wouldn't meet his eyes across the table's polished surface. Harley had been jovial as always. Mary's manner toward her husband had been decidedly different from that toward her guest, however. An expression of apprehension had darkened her beautiful eyes whenever she favored him with the briefest glance.

She'd removed herself from the dining room when dessert had been served, and much like the conclusion of this morning's breakfast she'd uttered a hasty wish of good evening to their visitor and not a word for her husband.

He drained his glass and forced his attention to his unwanted guest.

"When are you taking your leave, Harley?" he asked bluntly.

Harley blinked before he barked out a short laugh. "Ah, it's like that, is it? Really, Ashworth. Do you find my company so distasteful after so many months without it?"

Daniel looked into the guileless face of his long-time

friend and couldn't rouse anger at him. What was Harley that Daniel had not fancied himself before his wedding? Daniel had sailed effortlessly through society, taking whatever opportunities arose to seek pleasure with a woman despite that woman's state of attachment to another man. But he would be damned if Harley took advantage of the fact that Mary was now without a fitting protector.

"You may stay as long as you like, friend," he told Harley at last. "Do remember that the opportunities here in the country to not approach the amusements of more varied society."

Daniel's comment had hit its mark. Harley lost his smile as a worried frown marred his pleasant face.

"You do me grievous injury, sir," he said, his voice holding more sadness than anger. "And I'm not the only person who suffers from such a misunderstanding on your part."

Daniel didn't miss the man's meaning. He drained his glass and set it forcefully upon the desk. "You know nothing of the matter, Harley. And you would do well to keep your fine-looking self out of it."

Harley's eyes widened in what Daniel could well guess was sudden cognizance. "Ashworth, you don't believe that your wife would ever find you distasteful?"

Daniel held up his hand to silence him.

"Mary looks upon your visit as a respite from her daily care and worry over her husband's state, friend," he said, choosing to ignore the desperation he could hear in his own voice. "I don't believe that she should continue here at the hall."

Harley's blue eyes showed his dismay at Daniel's statement. "How can you utter such words? Your wife loves you, Ashworth. She is utterly devoted to you."

Daniel shook his head firmly, a sadness settling around his heart. No woman would devote herself solely to one man, despite any appearance to the contrary. His grievous injury only served to speed their inevitable separation.

"Perhaps she was devoted," was all he would allow regarding that prospect. "At present there is nothing to keep her here in Newcastle."

"What are you saying?" Harley asked. "You need her."

"I need no one," Daniel snapped, pleased to feel a sting of anger to dull the hurt he was inflicting upon himself. "And she certainly doesn't need to saddle herself with the pitiful man I have become."

Harley stared at Daniel, shaking his head ever so slightly. "You don't know what you're saying. Your accident must have rattled your brains."

Daniel mulled over that statement for a moment.

"My mind has never been more clear. Mary belongs far from here. Pray, see her back to her family in Somersetshire."

"What?"

"Do not misunderstand me, Harley," Daniel added, his voice firm. "Mary is my wife and my wife she shall remain. Don't think to take advantage of this situation."

Harley winced as Daniel's words penetrated. "I would never."

"Good night, Harley." Daniel raked his fingers through his hair. "I'm finished with this discussion."

Harley stood there, hands spread in a show of frustrated confusion. He finally took a measuring sigh and nodded. "Good night, Ashworth," he said, setting his own glass beside Daniel's.

He left the study without another word, leaving Daniel to ponder his actions in solitude.

***

Mary had managed to avoid being in the gentlemen's company for the remainder of the day and it was with much trepidation that she had dressed for dinner that evening. She'd hoped that a day spent in close proximity with his very good friend would brighten Daniel's spirits but she didn't wager on such a turn of events. At the very least she would have been pleased to see the jealousy gone from his eyes whenever she and Lord Harley exchanged the most frivolous conversational tidbits. It was not to be so, and she'd chosen to excuse herself from the dining room as she had from the breakfast room that morning.

Only Lord Harley had offered any objection to her taking her leave at so early an hour, she recalled with dejection. Daniel merely offered more dark and speculative glances from where he had sat at the head of the table. Closeting herself in the small library upstairs, she'd passed the evening in melancholy solitude. The hour grown late at last, she entered her dressing room to ready for bed, eager to take herself to the small bedchamber that had become her sanctuary.

When she emerged she was startled to find Daniel in the bedroom, the familiar brooding look fixed on his handsome face. His eyes held a glimmer of something to which she couldn't put a name, their velvet-brown depths mesmerizing. She stared at his face as if memorizing every plane and angle. The strong chin. The beautiful brows which topped his eyes. The dashing mark on his cheek. She was seized with the notion that this was to be the last time she ever laid her eyes on him.

"Good night, Daniel," she murmured, walking past him.

His hand shot out and gripped her arm. He quickly released her and cleared his throat.

"This will be your last night in that chamber, Mary," he said.

Mary felt hope fill her breast. Did he at last miss her in his bed? Did he want her in his arms? His next words dashed her hopes to the fine carpet beneath her feet.

"You will leave with Harley on the morrow," he said.

Anger suddenly surged through her. "How dare you accuse me of such disloyalty?"

The reluctant smile that curved his firm mouth caused her to start. She stared at him, certain that she was mired deeply in a dream as the smile was swiftly replaced by an angry scowl.

"I accuse you of nothing, wife. Harley is to take you to Bridgewater Park and that is the end of it."

Mary shook her head, her curls swaying as she sought to make sense of the situation. She stepped toward him, boldly placing her hand on his rigid arm.

"I have no desire to leave Ashworth Hall, Daniel," she told him. "Why do you believe I would?"

He pulled away from her, plowing his fingers through his

hair until it stood on end. "You've taken yourself from my chamber, Mary. Why wouldn't you take yourself from my home?"

"I didn't realize you gave my absence much notice."

Daniel's eyes widened and she once more felt burgeoning hope. Did he truly want her again?

"I'm a man," he said, turning from her.

She stifled a sob at his dismissal of the incredible passion and tenderness they'd once shared as husband and wife.

"Daniel, no."

"You can't bear to touch me, Mary." He turned to face her once more. "Admit it. You find my appearance abhorrent."

Mary's heart fell to her stomach. "That is not true," she whispered as she backed away from him.

"Then tell me why we haven't been intimate since before you went to your family at Christmas."

He had no memory of the fevered passion they'd shared the night he was returned to her from the mine, then. How could he not remember professing his need for her? His need for her love? She would tell him none of it. She swallowed the tears that choked her and turned from him.

"But know this, Mary," he said, his voice low. "You are

my wife and you will remain so despite the distance separating us."

He truly believed she was simply waiting for any opportunity to betray him?

"As you wish it, Daniel," she said stiffly. "I'll tell Jane to ready my things."

The air in the chamber seemed chilled to her as he said nothing in response.

The next morning Mary dressed with dutiful care if not much enthusiasm, donning a traveling dress of burgundy. After gaining Jane's assurance that all was in ready for her departure for Somersetshire, she paused just outside her dressing room and glanced about the master's chamber. She would never again share the space with her husband. She would never lay upon the large bed, blissfully spent in her husband's strong arms as he snored beside her. Stifling a sob, she left the chamber.

Lord Harley looked most uncomfortable as she sat across from him at the breakfast table. She glanced without interest at the meager repast set in front of her. Her appetite was nonexistent. She'd spent the night crying, deep wrenching sobs that had left her eyes swollen and her throat raw. How could Daniel wish her away from him? She pushed aside her untouched plate of eggs.

"Are you ready, Lady Ashworth?" Harley asked her, his voice low.

She lifted her head and studied the handsome man for a moment, easily reading the uncertainty in his blue eyes. What did he think of her husband's self-imposed isolation? What did he think of their marriage?

Shame threatened to swamp her once more and she squared her shoulders and smiled bravely at him. "Yes, Lord Harley," she answered as she rose from her chair.

She took his offered arm and left the breakfast room.

Chapter 27

Daniel watched as his wife stood poised beside Harley's carriage, the cloak he'd given her for Christmas draped elegantly over her slight shoulders. It had taken all of his strength last evening to keep himself from the bedroom next to the master's chamber, the longing in his heart as strong as that in his body. She'd made no true protestation to his statement of her abhorrence. Her eyes had widened but he hadn't the strength to decipher that expression. She'd acceded to his suggestion to take herself far from Newcastle. He glimpsed her red-rimmed eyes from beneath the hood of her cloak. Had he been wise to force this separation?

She averted her gaze as she refused Harley's offered arm, giving a slight shake of her golden head as she settled herself against the cushioned seat. Harley hesitated, his face showing his discomfiture as he turned to Daniel.

"Ashworth, are you certain in this?"

Daniel held himself stiff and waved his hand dismissively. "See her safely settled with her family, Harley."

Harley nodded and stepped into the carriage, settling himself on the seat across from Mary. Daniel closed the door and clutched at the frame for one long moment, gazing at the top of

Mary's bowed head visible through the small window. Without another word he slapped the side of the vehicle and stepped aside.

He watched the carriage as it rolled down the long drive. As it carried his wife farther away from him. He fancied that her white face was visible in the back window just before the vehicle disappeared from view. Cursing himself for a fool, he took himself into his big lonely house.

His life soon fell into a reliable pattern. He saw to his estate business during the days and saw to depleting his ample store of liquor during the nights. His staff steered clear of him. His friends in Newcastle did likewise. When Dr. Lawson had paid a call on him to see to his leg he'd shown surprise at learning of Mary's absence. Thankfully for Daniel, the medical man hadn't pressed him for an explanation that Daniel was unwilling to give. Several invitations arrived from the families in the town, invitations which he summarily refused. Thus the last few weeks of winter passed.

With spring's arrival he found it necessary to return to London. The Season would soon commence, and he wished to see to his business before becoming mired in all of the invitations and parties which would soon draw his attention.

Surely no one knew the full extent of his injuries. Once word of his disfigurement was common knowledge he would be plagued with such invitations no more.

He hadn't heard a word of Mary, save for Harley's brief note advising him of her safe arrival in Somersetshire. His friend had voiced his disapproval once more in his missive, causing Daniel to crumple the offending letter and toss it to the floor. What did Harley know of his marriage? Mary was far better off in the country with her family than tied to a man who no doubt turned her stomach in revulsion.

As a result of all of these dark musings, he felt as though he was in a kind of half-life. How long could he expect Mary to remain his wife in name only? He wasn't worthy of her, yet he didn't want another to possess her. Did he foolishly believe that his infirmity, his horrid appearance, would somehow lessen over time?

When he arrived at his townhouse, Trimm greeted him with barely-disguised confusion. He didn't ask after Lady Ashworth, Daniel was pleased to note. Daniel informed the servant to see his belongings settled in his chamber and took himself into his study to ready for the early meeting he'd arranged with his solicitors on the morrow.

***

On Mary's mostly-silent trip from Newcastle she'd felt ill, the lack of hunger that had plagued her at breakfast persisting long past luncheon. The rocking of the carriage had affected her as well, which she had thought most odd as she had never experienced any discomfort previously under such conditions.

She'd mentioned none of this to her traveling companion, however. Harley had been most solicitous she recalled, and he'd refrained from making any mention of her husband as he spoke fleetingly of the countryside and the like. When he'd left Bridgewater Park for London, for even prior to the Season life was far more exciting there than in the country, she'd barely taken note of the gentleman's absence.

In the weeks since? Her spirits and her health hadn't much improved. Surely she was simply heartsick. Betsy and Michael would soon arrive to take her to London in their carriage. Mary's sister had written quite regularly and, after expressing her surprise at Mary's present address, had tried unsuccessfully to glean the truth of the situation from her. Betsy was tenacious as well as well-meaning, and wouldn't cease her questioning until she learned the whole ugly truth. No doubt the ride to London would be most uncomfortable despite the company and fine state of the carriage.

Mary rose from the bed, letting out a heavy sigh. It was the hour of luncheon and she couldn't rouse the least bit of hunger at the prospect. What was Daniel about at this very moment? Did he miss her half as much as she missed him? His angry words had shocked her on their last night together, and they echoed in her ears still. He thought her so vain as to find him repulsive? How could he believe that such an inconsequential mark on his face would lessen her devotion to him? That the minor incapacitation of his leg would turn her away from him?

"But he doesn't know I love him," she whispered.

Her mind's wanderings caused her stomach to give an odd lurch. Mary banished that thought from her mind and took herself down to lunch, though the meal held little attraction for her.

Betsy and Michael arrived two days later, the former wearing a look of curious concern in her blue eyes as they ran carefully over Mary's face when she met them in the foyer.

"Hello, sister," Betsy said, taking Mary's chilled hands in her own. "Are you quite all right?"

Mary gently pulled her fingers from hers, a weak smile on her lips. "I'm a bit tired, Betsy. How did you leave little Missy?"

Michael laughed at that. "She was quite put-out to be excluded from our journey."

Mary felt a true smile curve her lips for the first time in weeks. Betsy and Michael's little girl was well on her way to carrying on the Bridgewater trait of stubbornness. A thought suddenly flickered in her mind, lost the very moment she attempted to grab a firmer hold of it.

"Mary?" Betsy asked.

Mary blinked and faced her sister once more. "Yes? Is something troubling you, Betsy?"

Betsy's brow furrowed in obvious confusion. "I was going to ask you that precise question."

Mary felt a laugh tickling in her chest. Lord, she was going daft. She found the look of bemusement on both of their faces so comical that she had to bite her lip to keep the laughter from bubbling forth.

"I'm fine, sister," she said. "I've been preparing for tomorrow's journey and I daresay my mind is still a bit preoccupied."

She easily read the disbelief in Betsy's eyes and sighed again. Betsy and Michael exchanged a worried look and Mary braced herself for further inquisitions. Thankfully, her mother hurried into the entryway then, wearing a big smile for her daughter and son-in-law and no doubt eager to innumerate the calls they must make immediately upon their arrival in London.

"You must give Lord Addington our kindest regards, daughter," Lady Bridgewater said as she ushered the three of them into the parlor for tea. "It has been ages since your father and I have paid a call on him. And Lady Stuart, her legs have been paining her and I…"

Mary let her mother's prattling wash over her, thankful that the woman had no such instructions for her youngest daughter. Would Daniel be in town?

She helped herself to the fluffy biscuits on the tea tray, suddenly ravenous. She found this most interesting, since a scant hour before she had found her stomach once more in upheaval. Surely Daniel would know that she would stay with Betsy and Michael. Should she write him? What, precisely, would his response be?

In her mind's eye she saw him storming the entrance of Michael's townhouse, adamant that she join him at his home. A wry smile curved her lips as she lifted her teacup and took a sip. Not bloody likely. She wouldn't tell him that she was coming to town, she decided as she stuffed another sweet biscuit into her mouth. Perhaps she would storm the entrance of *his* townhouse. The laugh she'd stifled earlier bubbled forth, muffled by the crumbling cookie in her mouth. Her eyes round, she held her hand to her mouth once more and looked about to find the assembled members of her family staring at her, their mouths agape.

"What ails you, Mary?" her mother was first to ask.

Mary swallowed with a loud gulp and brushed a few wayward crumbs off of her skirts. She was suddenly seized with the inexplicable urge to cry, her tears burning hot in her eyes.

"Excuse me," she sobbed, rising to make a quick exit from the parlor.

She hurried up the grand staircase to her chamber. When she entered the room she closed the door tight and slumped against it, her body weak with melancholy. Burying her face in her hands, she sobbed brokenly for several long minutes. What the devil was wrong with her?

As suddenly as the tears had assailed her, they ceased. She raised her head cautiously, sniffling. Dashing the tears from her cheeks, she took a deep calming breath.

"I am surely going daft," she said, her voice sounding hoarse to her own ears.

Her bed beckoned then and she willingly answered its call, not bothering to turn back the coverlet or even taking the time to remove more than her shoes.

"Oh, Daniel," she sighed, wrapping her arms around her middle.

She turned onto her side and curled herself into a ball. Squeezing her eyes shut, her wet lashes resting comfortingly against her cheeks, she fell into a sleep filled with the strangest dream.

In her mind she was floating on her back in the cool, clear water of the wide stream which ran through the estate in Newcastle, her gossamer-thin underclothes drifting about her. Ashworth Hall was visible in the distance. She felt free and light, the sun on her face in pleasing contrast to the slight sting of the water which surrounded her. Voices suddenly became evident to her ears and she lazily turned her attention to them. Children's singing, her sleeping mind faintly registered. Lisping voices raised in song—a nursery rhyme, she easily grasped, whose meaning she knew not. But the sounds filled her with happiness and she smiled even in her slumber.

"Mary!" Daniel's voice called teasingly. "Mary, love!"

Her sleeping form turned on the coverlet as in her mind she

faced the shore. Daniel stood there on the sloping bank, laughing lightly and beckoning to her. The look of love and happiness on his face caused her heart to give a leap.

"Daniel!" she cried happily in her dream, whispering the name in the reality of her chamber.

"Mary!" a female voice called to her.

Mary frowned, slowly recognizing the tone of that voice. She stirred, reluctant to leave the peace and contentment of her dream world. But leave it she did, her eyes fluttering open to see her mother's face above hers. Worry etched the woman's still-handsome face as she gently shook Mary's shoulder.

"Mother," Mary said with a yawn. She raised herself onto her elbows and sighed, regretfully letting the last vestiges of the pleasant dream drift away from her consciousness.

"I'm worried about you, child," her mother said, sitting beside her on the bed. "Are you quite all right? You gave me quite a scare when you left the parlor in such a hurry."

"Have I been gone long?" Mary asked haltingly, her mind still a bit muddled from her unexpected nap.

Lady Bridgewater gave her a small smile. "It is nearly dinner time."

Mary nodded and began to rise from the bed. Her mother's

hand on her shoulder stilled her. Mary looked up in question.

"You love him, don't you?"

"Yes," Mary said simply.

She watched as her mother obviously processed the information. Mary had always sensed that her parents shared a marriage more of respect and companionship than of love, but neither of them seemed to look upon the situation with anything other than complacency. Luckily for Mary's young and tender heart, she'd always had her sisters' marriages to give her true examples of love and passion. It was what she wanted—what she'd always wanted, if she were honest with herself.

"I love him with all of my heart, Mother," she said.

Lady Bridgewater shrugged her shoulders and let out a sigh. "Then you ought to do something about this."

Mary blinked up at the woman. "What can I do?"

"I know not," her mother answered with another sigh. "I know nothing of such matters. But I believe you can avail yourself upon your sister Betsy's opinion."

Mary's eyes grew round. However could she mention the deplorable condition of her marriage to her sister? What would she think? To her relief, her mother said nothing more on the subject. She merely patted Mary on the shoulder once more and stood.

"I trust we'll see you in the parlor soon, dear?" she asked with a soft smile.

Mary nodded again and watched as the woman left the chamber. She rose and took a measuring sigh, longing to give in to the notion of cuddling once more into the covers and losing herself in her confusing—but oh so comforting—dream.

Chapter 28

Daniel woke with his head on his desk, his mind muddled from the strange and oddly pleasant dream that had filled it. He rubbed his hands over his face and let out a breath. Since returning to town he'd occupied himself alternately with his work and his drink, which he told himself well-suited him. Keeping late hours in his study, accompanied by only his ledgers and bottles of brandy, kept him from taking to his big lonely bed until he was ready to collapse from exhaustion.

As a result, he went through his days in a state of mild fatigue, pleased to focus his wavering attention on work with nothing else intruding upon him. But never before this afternoon had he actually fallen asleep in his study. He closed his eyes again and pondered the images that had assailed his sleeping mind.

Mary. They'd been at Ashworth Hall, and she was floating like a sea nymph in the stream. The sun glinted off of her silken hair, and outlined every luscious curve of her body in the wet underclothes. Songs filled the clean-scented air, songs with words he couldn't fathom but whose melody was as sweet as he had ever heard. He called to Mary in the dream, and the smile she turned on him filled him with hope and love.

"My God," he rasped as he shook his head.

He'd finally done it. He'd finally rattled his brain completely!

Daniel shook his head again and rose from the chair, willing the dream to let loose of its grasp on him. But he couldn't banish the sweet feelings the images had evoked. Lord, how he missed her. Her smile. Her passion.

"Ah, Mary."

A knock sounded at the study door, thankfully drawing his attention from his maddening thoughts.

"My lord?" Trimm said from the other side of the door.

"Yes," he called gruffly. "What is it?"

"You have a visitor, my lord," Trimm answered, his voice strained and a little high-pitched.

Daniel stood and straightened his sleep-rumpled clothes. He had an image to protect, he thought with a smirk. No one had yet seen him or his injury, save for Harley. Now was as good a time as any to begin the inevitable spread of the news of his disfigurement through the *ton*. He stepped to the window and stared unseeing out at the courtyard.

"Send them in," he told Trimm.

A rustle of skirts soon drew his attention, filling his heart with the hope that had assailed him upon waking from his befuddling dream. That hope was dashed as he spied his visitor.

"Monica?"

"Oh, Ashworth!" she gushed. "How wonderful to see you." She froze, her mouth agape. "Oh, your face! How awful!"

A smile actually teased his lips at the woman's words of shock. "Thank you, Lady Small," he returned with a mock-bow. "And it is wonderful to see you, too."

Monica took in gasping breaths, holding her hand to her chest. She appeared odd to him, her eyes darting about the room nervously as if looking for escape.

"Ashworth," she began, looking away from him. "I had heard of your return to town. And that you were alone."

"Alone?" Daniel asked.

"Your wife is not with you, is she?"

Daniel felt a welcome flash of anger. "No. Mary is not here."

"I don't blame her," Monica said.

"Why are you here, Monica?" he asked, taking a few steps toward her.

He saw her dark eyes fall on his cane, her lips curled as she watched his slight limp.

"Your leg, Ashworth," she said in apparent disgust. "What the devil is wrong with your leg?"

"I injured it, Monica," he said flatly. He smiled thinly. "The scar hidden beneath my breeches far over-shadows the one on my face, I assure you."

A look of nausea crossed his former bed-partner's face, assuring him that she no longer found the thought his breeches and what was beneath them the least bit appetizing.

"I must go," she said, turning toward the door.

"No, Monica," he said, grasping her arm. "Tell me why you're here. And why you're so pleased to find my wife far from here."

IIc watched as her discomfort was swiftly replaced with anger so hot that he was stunned. He dropped his hand from her.

"Don't touch me!" she shrieked at him.

Daniel's eyes widened as he took a step back from her. "Monica, do calm yourself."

"You are a monster, do you know that?" she asked, her voice raised nearly to the point of hysteria. "A hideous monster! I never want you to touch me. Never!"

Daniel held his hands outstretched, palms to the ceiling. "I assure you, I have no desire to touch you."

"You were to be mine, you bastard!" she spat. "You were to be mine, not that silly little girl's."

He said nothing as she began to pace about the study, her hands flying about. What the devil ailed the woman? He'd never seen her in such a state.

"You were mine," she muttered. "It was all settled. I came to tell you that day, you miserable cur. I came to tell you and before I could get the words out of my mouth you dismissed me. Me! And now it pains me to look at what I was so anxious to possess!"

Daniel felt a shiver of dread at the woman's words. She'd seemed quite agitated to him that day in his study. The day he'd put an end to their liaison. And her anger, though it failed to touch him, was no less evident then as now.

"Tell me what, Monica?" he asked with trepidation. "What is it you came to tell me?"

She whirled on him, her eyes wild. "I was expecting your child, you insensitive rotter!"

The words struck him like a blow. A baby? His recent dream came back to him. Children's voices, he suddenly recalled. Mary smiling at him. Could Mary be carrying his child?

He forced his attention back to the wild woman there in his

study, sensing the violence lurking below her very fashionable façade.

"Monica," he said, his hands reaching for her in an effort to still her. "I didn't know."

"Don't touch me!" she shouted again. A hysterical laugh issued from her lips, raising the hairs on the back of his neck. "I wanted you, Ashworth. I wanted you to sweep me into your arms and at last say those words that you so carefully prevented yourself from ever uttering. What a fool I was. You'd already taken that girl, hadn't you? You wanted her, not me. You loved her!"

Daniel blinked at her words. Had he loved Mary? Even then?

"I had your bastard," Monica said, holding her chin high. "And thankfully, he died."

The words seeped through his mind. His son? He shuddered. Dead?

"Monica," he said, his voice thick. "I'm so sorry."

"Sorry? You're sorry? I bore your bastard. His tiny face was so like yours! I bore him and buried him the same day. He was born far too early." She stopped to take in a measuring breath.

"When I returned to town after my confinement, I learned that you had married that Bridgewater child. You worthless scoundrel!" She suddenly flew at him, her fists pounding his chest. "I hate you! Oh, I hate you!"

"Shh," he said, grasping her wrists to hold her still. "It will be all right."

She froze, and then collapsed against him, sobbing brokenly against his chest. In the next moment she raised her head, malevolence burning in her eyes once more.

"I wanted you dead, you cur," she said, her voice holding an odd sing-song quality. "I followed you to Newcastle. Did you know that?"

He dropped his hands from her in shock, watching warily as she ran her hands over her hair, her dress.

"I knew that you'd sent your silly little wife from you at Christmas time," she said in that odd lilting voice. "I went to you, Ashworth. To Ashworth Hall. Do you know what I found there?"

Daniel had no notion and merely shook his head, words failing him.

"Another woman!" Monica cried. "Another woman, her beauty nothing when compared to mine. A woman well-past her prime."

Beatrice. Monica must have seen Beatrice leaving the hall.

"You chose yet another over me!" she hissed. "I could stand it no longer. So I sent you a note."

Daniel's heart beat dully in his chest. "Monica, what did you do?"

"A little note to gain your cooperation at last," she went on as if she hadn't heard him.

He knew then. He recalled it as clearly as if it had happened just that morning. The rustling he'd heard just before the blinding pain had crashed into him in the mine. It was no doubt the sound of a woman's skirts. His dismay turned swiftly to anger.

"It was you," he growled, his hands in fists. "You tried to kill me!"

"Yes," Monica laughed harshly. "And I nearly succeeded. I admit I was relieved to learn that you still lived. But seeing you now, so horribly disfigured and maimed, perhaps your dying would have been preferable?"

Daniel grabbed Monica about the shoulders, shaking her until her head snapped back and the sickening laughter at last ceased.

She faced him, her eyes cloudy, her mouth slack. "You will live your life alone, Ashworth," she said softly, chilling him to the bone. "No woman will want you now, especially your little wife. Your only son lies buried, cold and still. As cold and still as your heart."

"Monica," he said, struggling to regain his demeanor.

Monica held up one hand.

"Do not trouble yourself about me, Lord Ashworth," she said with a nod. "I will find another gentleman to entertain me. I thank God that you no longer appeal to me, ugly as you now are. I will think no more of you. Nor of your son."

She left the study and Daniel sank back into his chair behind the desk.

"A son."

A child born not out of love but of lust and taken from the earth before Daniel had even one glimpse of him.

He buried his face in his hands and wept.

***

Mary sat in the front parlor of Betsy and Michael's townhouse, her hand gently stroking her belly as she stared absently out at the passing carriages and horses visible on the street outside the tall window. Her stomach had been most unpredictable of late. But that condition troubled her far less than the odd mood swings which had plagued her since coming to London with her sister. Repeatedly she found herself wavering between tears and laughter, and more than once she'd claimed a headache and taken to her guest chamber for some much-needed solace.

She'd been in London for several days now, and in that time she was no closer to a decision regarding her estrangement from Daniel. She longed to storm the door of his townhouse as she'd pondered days earlier, but she was quite uncertain of her reception.

"Silly girl," she murmured.

She knew full-well what her husband's response would be. He would send her from him, perhaps informing her that he was now seeking a more permanent severing of their ties to one another. Her heart clenched at the thought of his taking himself forever from her. How maudlin. A sob escaped her.

"Oh, what is wrong with me?" she sighed aloud.

"At last you ask a question I can answer, sister," Betsy said as she walked into the room.

Mary started, finding the smile on her sister's face most disconcerting. As she watched, Betsy closed the doors leading to

the hall off of the small parlor and faced her once more.

"Betsy," Mary began, "what are you about?"

"What is troubling you, little sister, is quite simple," she said with a widening grin. "You are expecting your husband's child."

Mary sat there, dumbstruck. "But how?"

Betsy's light laughter broke through her confusion. "I believe we had this discussion prior to your wedding."

Mary looked up at her sister, into those blue eyes so like her own, and laughed out loud. Suddenly it all made sense to her. The mood swings, the waning appetite.

"A baby," she said softly, her hand once more tracing over her belly. "I didn't know."

"Sometimes we ignore what we don't wish to face, Mary," Betsy said gently.

"Yes." Mary sighed. "A baby. A blessing."

Betsy approached and placed her hand comfortingly on her shoulder. "What will you do?"

Mary knew precisely what her sister meant by her question. What would she do about Daniel?

"I don't know."

"You will," Betsy said with a nod. "That Bridgewater

stubbornness has never failed a one of us yet."

Mary laughed again and nodded, wiping away the tears that had begun to slide down her cheeks.

"I'm a dreadful mess," she said, giving her sister a watery smile.

"That's most fitting," Betsy nodded. "No matter what you decide, Mary, your life will no longer be the same. Trust me on this."

Mary took her sister's words to heart and grasped her hand in hers. "Thank you, Betsy. I'll find a way to bring us back together."

Betsy kissed Mary's brow and left her to her thoughts. Mary smiled and hugged her middle.

"A baby!"

No doubt conceived on that very night when the fever had robbed Daniel of his reserve and he'd asked her for her love.

A true smile curved her lips as a plan began to form in her mind.

Chapter 29

The days following Monica's revelations passed in a fog of liquor and despair for Daniel. Monica's words stung him, her disclosures more than he believed he could bear. He'd had a son, he thought with crushing guilt. A child whose existence he'd never known. Whose face he would never see.

Monica's hateful words regarding his hideous appearance merely served to confirm all that Daniel had expected since sending Mary from him. Surely Mary felt as Monica did. But Mary possesses a kind heart. She was nothing like Monica. Daniel rubbed his hands over his face and rang for Trimm to see his dinner brought there to the study, his sanctuary and prison.

"You have a visitor, my lord," Trimm replied.

Daniel barked out a harsh laugh. "So the social whirlwind begins at last. Do send them in, Trimm."

Daniel lifted the brandy bottle to refill his glass, only to find a few drops within.

"Well hell," he muttered, struggling to his feet.

"You are a bloody fool," came a stern voice from the doorway of the study.

Daniel raised his eyes, wincing at the scowl darkening the gentleman's visage.

"Hello, Uncle," he said with a mock-salute. "Whatever brings you here?"

The older gentleman clicked his tongue and closed the study door. "You're drunk."

"Not precisely," Daniel quipped, taking an unopened bottle from the cabinet across from his desk. "But I mean to remedy that, rest assured."

A string of curses spilled from the marquis' lips, surprising Daniel enough to still him. As often as he'd had cause to reprimand Daniel while he was growing up, the marquis had never used profanity. A glance at the man's eyes told him he was angrier than Daniel had ever seen him.

"What ails you, Uncle?" Daniel asked, keeping his tone light. "Such language doesn't suit you."

"And wallowing in self-pity does not suit you," Daniel's uncle returned.

Daniel shrugged and set the bottle aside, settling into his chair once more. "I would offer you a drink, but I don't wish to know what words would greet that offer."

"Hush," the marquis chided. "You are a bloody fool."

"So you've said," Daniel said, a prickle of anger in his belly. "I trust you have more to tell me?"

"Do you know where your wife is?"

Daniel feigned an indifference he didn't feel, gazing in interest at the fine carpet beneath his desk. "With her family, I assume."

"Yes," his uncle said. "Here in town."

Daniel's head shot up at those words. "Have you seen her?" He winced, hearing the desperation in his voice.

"Ah." The marquis smiled. "You miss her."

Daniel shrugged and studied the empty glass on the desk. "She is my wife."

The marquis slammed his fists on the desk hard enough to make it shudder. "Damn it to Hell!" he shouted. "Have you gone completely daft then? Do you not see what's right in front of you?"

Daniel came to his feet, welcoming the anger surging through him. "Pray, state your meaning, Uncle. State it and go."

The marquis took a breath and Daniel saw compassion replace the anger in his dark eyes. "You need her, son."

"No," Daniel said, turning from the truth in the man's statement and demeanor. "Mary doesn't belong with me."

"It was Mary who sensed what had happened to you, you fool!" the older gentleman told him. "She was far from

Newcastle and yet she knew something had happened to you."

Daniel's heart began to pound at that incredible prospect. "Nonsense."

"It's true, Daniel," the marquis said. "And that isn't all she did. She sent for me and ordered me to bring you back to her. She nursed you, boy. Don't you remember?"

Daniel let his mind work on what his uncle was saying to him. Mary had nursed him? But how could that be?

"She bathed you," his uncle went on. "She saw to your injuries."

"She bathed me?" Daniel asked in amazement.

The marquis wore a look of supreme irritation. "She rolled up her fine sleeves and saw to your needs. She took your care wholly to heart, Daniel. She is not the woman you think she is," his uncle said, turning to go. "And you, I fear, are not the man I thought you were."

Without another word, the man left Daniel to ponder his words. Had he been wrong about her from the beginning?

He ran his fingers through his hair, bringing the unruly mass into some semblance of control. He let his fingers trace the raised scar on the side of his face, his mind working.

"Mary took care of me?"

She'd seen the extent of his injuries and not run screaming from the chamber? He stood and grasped the unopened bottle of brandy from the desk. He set it back into the cabinet and gave a firm nod. Dinner. A decent meal would restore what the liquor had not. And no doubt he would need all of his strength, of mind and of body, to fully contemplate his next course of action.

Later that night, Daniel turned restlessly in his bed. *Mary.* She'd cared for him. Did she love him? Did he love her? He cursed softly and stared up at the patterned ceiling above his bed as his mind worked in fevered circles.

Monica's reaction to his disfigurement no longer plagued him. He'd never seen such distaste on his wife's exquisite face. If Mary had seemed apprehensive in his presence, surely that had as much to do with his foul demeanor as his scarred visage. He'd been a beast to her these last weeks. Hell, he'd been impossible since before the Christmas holiday.

"Mary," he murmured.

He squeezed his eyes shut and cursed again. A sound pricked his ears, soft and compelling in the dark chamber. Dainty footfalls, his mind registered. The opening and closing of the chamber door. His muddled mind was surely playing tricks on him.

"Daniel," Mary whispered in the dark.

His heart pounded as he looked hesitantly in the direction. He blinked at the vision poised near the door, certain that he was mistaken.

"It cannot be," he rasped, closing his eyes once more.

A soft laugh reached him, wrapping around him like a cozy blanket.

"Daniel," Mary said again, stepping closer.

His eye snapped open. He sat up in his bed, staring round-eyed at his estranged wife. Swallowing audibly, she removed her cloak and placed it over a nearby chair.

"We must talk, Daniel," she said.

"Pray, tell me wife," he began, his voice low. "What, precisely, do you propose that we discuss?"

She shrugged and began to unfasten the tiny buttons on the front of the bodice of her dress. The heat was evident in her eyes. Heat coupled with a nervousness he couldn't ignore.

"This has gone on far too long, husband," she whispered. "One of us must set this matter to rights."

Daniel nodded. He watched avidly as she stepped out of her dress. Her petticoat soon followed the garment to the floor to puddle around her ankles. She stepped toward him, wearing nothing but her chemise—and her tender heart.

"Mary," Daniel said as she reached the side of the big bed. "I cannot believe you are here."

Mary gave him a shaky smile and stretched out beside him on the bed. He said nothing as he drew her into his arms and kissed her deeply. Mary ran her fingers through his hair and tangled her tongue with his. He moaned and lifted his mouth from hers, giving a slight shake of his head.

"Ah, Mary," he said raggedly, dropping a kiss on her brow. "Does this mean that you love me?"

Mary placed her hand against his cheek. "I love you."

Daniel sharply drew in a breath, his body tensing beside hers. He laughed softly as her eyes took their careful study of his body. He was aroused and hard against her soft supple body.

She blushed and gave him a smile. "You want me, Daniel."

Daniel nodded slowly. "And you want me, don't you love?"

"Yes. But I didn't think you can tell as much from looking at me."

Daniel nodded again. "But I can," he told her. "I know your body so well. I've seen it in my dreams these past weeks."

She bit her lower lip. "But how can you tell?"

"Here," he said, cupping her breast.

She caught her breath as his fingers brushed over the puckered flesh of her nipple.

"Yes," he said, circling her nipple with his thumb. "This is one way."

He brought his mouth to her breast and gently suckled her. Mary rolled onto her back, clutching his head to her as she brought him with her.

"Daniel," she gasped, arching beneath him.

He laughed softly. As his fingers trailed down her body, her legs fell open.

"And here," he murmured against her breast. "Ah, you're wet."

He caressed her, slowly at first. When he brought his mouth to her she seemed to lose control.

"Oh, Daniel!" she cried, her head thrashing on the pillow.

His tongue stroked her slowly, deeply. His fingers started a rhythm to drive her mad. He lifted his head and dropped a kiss on her belly.

"Give me the words again, Mary," he insisted softly.

"Oh," she gasped, so close to her release.

"Tell me you love me."

"I love you, Daniel!" she cried.

He drove his tongue into her sweet flesh and sent her unerringly over the edge into ecstasy. He watched in amazement, as awed by her release as by the evident truth of her words. She loved him. My God, he was a lucky man.

He kissed her lips and held her until her breathing slowed. Her eyes opened then, a bit clouded. But it was there in their violet depths. She loved him.

"Ah, Mary," he said, kissing her again.

He spread her thighs and came inside of her. Nothing had ever felt so right to him. She held him with more than her arms and her body. She held him with her heart.

Groaning in surrender, he increased his thrusts and rode them both toward climax.

"Ah, Mary," he moaned, his control all but a memory. "I love you!"

He poured himself into her, his seed and his heart.

"Ah God, I love you," he said, falling on the pillow beside her head.

***

When Mary's wits returned, she had no notion of the length of time that had passed. She opened his eyes to find

Daniel regarding her with that emotion he'd just proclaimed.

"And what are you thinking, Lady Ashworth?" he asked, wrapping his arms around her.

She shrugged, a smile curving her lips. "I can scarcely think, husband," she said. "Did you truly say those words?"

Daniel grinned sheepishly. "I was an utter fool not to recognize it before, love."

"I won't argue with your logic," she teased.

He laughed and drew her closer. "But my appearance," he began, his voice stilted. "You haven't come near me since before Christmas."

She couldn't help but smile. "You don't remember, do you?" she asked softly. "On the night you were returned to me from the mine?"

As she watched his mind worked. Was he remembering that long-ago night?

"No," he said. "Surely that was a dream."

"You asked for me to love you that night, Daniel," she said. "And I did."

She touched the scar on his face. He flinched for only a moment. "This mark does nothing to diminish you in my eyes." She dropped a gentle kiss on the scar. "If anything, it only adds to your appeal."

"That's nonsense."

She shook her head, her tousled curls swaying from the motion. "No," she said, drawing her fingers down to his leg.

He watched as she lightly touched the scar on his thigh. "Does that mark disgust you?"

Mary merely shook her head again. His breath caught as she rained kisses on his thigh. She grasped his arousal in her hands and kissed the tip. He seemed to lose himself. Grabbing her about her waist, he lifted her atop him. She began to ride him, as urgent as he. He arched off of the bed as his climax hit, holding her tightly to him. Mary joined him in fulfillment, soon collapsing against his chest.

"My God," he rasped.

"Mmm," Mary offered in answer.

Daniel drew her to his side once more, dropping a kiss on her brow. "My accident in the mine, Mary," he began. "It was no accident."

Her heart pounded. "The hell you say!" She sat up beside him, her hands clenched into fists. "Tell me the name of the blackguard who did this to you, Daniel. He could have killed you!"

"*She* could have killed me," he said.

"What?" Mary asked, blinking rapidly. "It was a woman?"

Daniel sat up beside her in the bed, dragging his fingers through his hair. "Ah, God," he said, closing his eyes for a moment. "I've brought all of this on myself and nearly lost you because of it."

Mary watched him closely, worry beating in her breast. "Tell me, Daniel."

"It was Monica," he told her. "Lady Small."

Anger pure and righteous surged through her. "Why that miserable harlot! That harridan, that…that…!"

"Easy, love," Daniel soothed, grasping her shoulders gently but firmly. "She wasn't completely to blame for her actions. I believe she has suffered."

Mary gave an unladylike snort at that. He smiled ruefully and told her the rest of the tale. Her heart ached as he told her of the baby he would never know, guilt clear in his expression. Mary held his hand in reassurance, tears burning in her eyes.

"You see, Mary," he said at last. "I fathered a child through no want of my own. One I shall never see. I'm a worthless rotter."

"No, Daniel," Mary said fervently, cupping his face with

her hands. "You are a wonderful man. I love you, and I promise you that I would never give my heart to a man not worthy of it."

He kissed her gently, hugging her close as they rested once more on the bed.

"You love me," he said. "Me."

"And our child," Mary added softly.

Daniel froze, and then lifted his head to gaze at her. "Mary, are you…?" He couldn't seem to form the words.

She nodded slowly, a bit warily. Daniel blinked at her and then gave a whoop of joy and swept her into his arms, raining kisses on her laughing mouth.

"I love you, Mary," he said. "I will attempt to become the man you deserve."

Mary placed her hands on his face, giving him a smile as big as the love in her heart.

"Oh, Daniel. You already are."

Epilogue
October 1830

Lady Mary Ashworth, the Countess of Ashworth, was pleasantly exhausted. She leaned back against the plumped pillows set behind her on the massive bed in the chamber she now happily shared with her husband at Ashworth Hall, her mind still a bit fuzzy. Her breath caught as she thought of all that had transpired in the last few months.

At Daniel's insistence, they'd said nothing to the authorities of Lady Monica Small's involvement in his accident at the mine. The one time she and the woman had crossed paths, when Daniel and Mary had been riding in a carriage in Hyde Park near the end of the summer, the lady's eyes had lost their haughty gleam as they settled unerringly on Mary's swollen midsection. The woman's hurt had been most evident to Mary in that moment, and she no longer pressed Daniel to take legal actions toward the widow.

Daniel's leg no longer pained him, save for on excessively rainy days. The cursed cane had long since been relegated to the back of his dressing room, much to his relief although Mary had never given the item much thought. The rakish scar on his face had lightened, though that too didn't matter a whit to Mary. She loved her husband fiercely, and by his very frequent declarations of the same she was well-satisfied that his heart and hers were indeed one.

A soft, compelling sound called her attention from her mind's wanderings, causing her heart to clench most pleasurably. Her eyes fell on the cherry-wood cradle set close to the bed. In the cradle rested the future Earl of Ashworth, Mary's newly-arrived son, Patrick.

A smile curving her lips, Mary reached into the cradle and deftly plucked the bundle from its satin bedclothes. Nestling the babe in the crook of her left arm, Mary gazed in amazement at the little person who looked so much like his father.

"Hello, little lordling," she cooed, dropping a kiss on his wispy golden curls.

The baby stared up her, his velvety-brown eyes focused intently on her face. A scowl soon crossed his tiny face and he let out a fierce howl. Mary laughed gaily and kissed him once more.

"Hungry, are you?" she asked the baby, baring her breast and letting him root.

Settling back against the pillows as the baby began to

suckle, she sighed and reveled in the infinite sweetness of the moment. She let her eyes close as the baby made greedy noises at her breast, humming softly in contentment.

***

Daniel entered their rooms quietly, fearing that both Mary and the child would be sleeping. He crossed through the sitting room and entered the sleeping chamber. The sight framed there between the thick carved posts of the bed caused his heart to swell.

Mary, her lustrous hair floating about her shoulders, nearly matched those golden wisps visible above the swaddling blanket holding his son. His son, he marveled.

Coming closer to the bed, he noted the tiny pink fingers alternately clutching and releasing the white lawn nearly covering Mary's breast. The sounds of the baby's delight reached him, causing him to chuckle. Mary's head lifted at the sound, her eyes glowing as she smiled at him.

"Hello, Daniel," she said softly.

He smiled his relief. How can she be so composed? Not two hours earlier, her screams of agony had filled the chamber causing him to ache to go to her despite Dr. Lawson's outrage at such a notion. Daniel had nearly throttled the man. My God, he'd never been so frightened in his life. And now she rested there in the bed, so beautiful and serene and fresh. And he himself felt as worn-out and wilted as the limp cravat hanging at his throat.

"Mary," he said, hearing the awe in his voice.

Her face beamed as she eased the baby from her breast. The tiny child squawked in protest, finally turning his big brown eyes on his father. Daniel regarded the baby for a long moment, coming to sit beside Mary on the bed.

"Your son looks far different than he did when last you saw him," Mary said.

Daniel nodded and reached out to stroke the little round cheek. He had stormed the chamber as Mary's frightening screams grew fainter, coming to the bed just as the doctor caught the baby in his capable hands. A quick glimpse of the babe was all that Lawson had allowed, and there had been so much blood.

The baby blinked, gazing at Daniel with an expression which he imagined was part interest, part irritation. The baby turned to bury his face in Mary's bosom, obviously wishing to continue his meal. Mary shifted the baby and discretely offered him the breast, sighing as the child settled beside her.

"He has his father's singleness of purpose," she offered,

lowering her lashes.

"I cannot blame the little mite," Daniel said, delighting in the faint blush that colored her cheeks at his remark.

Troubled thoughts worked their way into his mind despite the incredible gift God had granted him on this day. Mary raised her eyes to his, giving him a nod of infinite significance.

"You're thinking of the other child," she said softly.

Daniel hesitated, finally nodding his defeat. He reached out to touch the small hand resting against Mary's breast, grasping the fingers gently.

"This is the child of my heart, Mary," he said, his voice thick. "Our child. And yet?"

He couldn't find the words to express all that he was feeling.

"Shh," Mary soothed. "I understand. But I believe our child has a bit of his brother in him," she said, causing him to lift his gaze to hers once more. "As surely as you have a bit of yours in you."

Daniel swallowed past the emotions threatening to swamp him. He leaned forward and dropped a gentle kiss on her lips.

"You are amazing, Mary."

The smile that curved her lips eased the weight that had

settled around his heart. The sparkle in her eyes gave him a warning.

"You no longer think me vain and silly, Daniel?" she teased.

He laughed and draped an arm over her shoulders. He gazed down at his son who had at last surrendered his mother's breast. The baby's rosebud mouth was agape, his lashes lowered.

They were silent as they sat there, but Daniel's mind worked. He'd been a fool. First in mistaking Mary for a silly chit, then in failing to recognize the love that was clear in front of him.

"I should have recognized it that moment," he said, his voice low so as not to disturb the now-sleeping infant.

"What moment?" she countered, slanting him a look.

He grinned at her. "The very moment a certain golden beauty sailed into a grimy public house and stole my heart."

She just smiled and shook her head.

Time and again he'd come to her rescue. Yet in the end, it was her love and determination that had saved him. Both from the accident in the mine and the coldness that had surrounded his heart.

She was his. His beauty and his love. Forever.

About the Author

JoMarie DeGioia is a bestselling author of Historical and Contemporary Romance. She's known Mickey Mouse from the "inside," has been a copyeditor for her tiny town's newspaper, and a bookseller. A hybrid author, she also writes Young Adult Fantasy/Adventure stories, New Adult Romance and Paranormal Romance. She gets lost in DIY projects around the house and works out plot ideas during long runs. She divides her time between Central Florida and New England.

Discover other books by JoMarie DeGioia

The Bridgewater Brides series, including

The Heir's Treasure

The Viscount's Vixen

The Earl's Beauty

The Gentlemen Undercover series, including

A Hero and a Gentleman

The Shopgirls of Bond Street series, including

That Determined Mister Latham

The Dashing Nobles series, including

More Than Passion

Pride and Fire

Just Perfect

More Than Charming

The Gentlemen Undercover series, including

A Hero and a Gentleman

The Cypress Corners series, including

Finding Harmony

Taming Jake

Loving Cassie

Winning Ben

Showing Jessie

Seeing Shannon (Barefoot Bay Kindle Worlds Novella)

Dreaming Eli

Giving Chase (Barefoot Bay Kindle Worlds Novella)

Kissing Bree

The Gifted YA Fantasy/Adventure Trilogy, including

Gifted

Braunachs of the Dell series, including

Luke's Gold

Patrick's Promise

Connect with me online

Twitter: https://twitter.com/JoMarieDeGioia

Facebook: https://www.facebook.com/JoMarie.DeGioia.Author

Website: www.jomariedegioia.com